UNCIVIL WAR

Twin tales from Nottinghamshire

NOEL HARROWER

Illustrations by Lin Milner-Brown

Matador
9 Priory Business Park,
Wistow Road, Kibworth Beauchamp,
Leicestershire. LE8 0RX
Tel: (+44) 116 279 2299
Fax: (+44) 116 279 2277
Email: books@troubador.co.uk
Web: www.troubador.co.uk/matador

ISBN 978 1784620 400

British Library Cataloguing in Publication Data.
A catalogue record for this book is available from the British Library.

Typeset by Troubador Publishing Ltd, Leicester, UK
Printed and bound in the UK by TJ International, Padstow, Cornwall

Matador is an imprint of Troubador Publishing Ltd

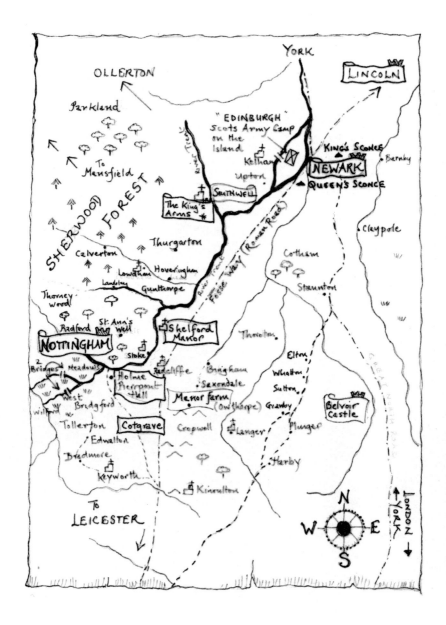

A hand drawn map sketched by Tom Marriott covering the period of the hostilities between the towns of Nottingham and Newark, 1642-1646

FORTRESS NOTTINGHAM

Nottingham Castle

This book is dedicated to Roger Grainger who first encouraged me to go on writing and telling tales, and to Maureen Buxton, who is so very fond of English history tales, and also to the countless thousands of child soldiers across the world and through all the ages.

CHAPTERS

Tom

CHAPTER 1

PERILOUS TIMES

York – May 1641

Crash! Smashing glass and the thud of falling timbers on a stone floor. Tom and his fellow servants leapt from their slumbers to face an unknown peril. It was crow black in the strange parlour and no one knew what had happened until Mr Oliver, the steward, lit a taper from his flint-stone. The big mullion window had been shattered by an oak branch; it lay across the flags, and a mob was baying for blood outside. "Hang the roundheads!" they were crying. "Drum them out of town!"

A burly youth, brandishing a club, was clambering up to the window frame, trying to push his way through whilst others were pressing behind him. Suddenly, the inner door opened and John Hutchinson and Henry Ireton rushed in, armed with rapiers, though they were barefoot and in their night shirts. The brute turned and fled from the window. The crowd retreated a few yards.

"Cowards!" shouted Hutchinson, "Bullies and cowards, all of you!" He stood framed in the window, but the crowd did not stir.

"Where's the night watch?" cried the steward, but Henry Ireton laughed. "Most like, it was the watch set them on to us. We're in York don't forget, and the king's here with his court and the town is loyal to him. We chanced our fortune when we presented our petition. Now, they want to see us pay the price."

There were shouts from down the street, but no further disturbance. A flash of a sword had done the trick. When they were quite satisfied that things had been calmed, the gentlemen retired to their bedchambers, and the servants lay down again to huddle in their cloaks on the stone-flagged floor, but Tom did not sleep again that night. The room was now open to the wind, and the sound of distant angry voices drifted in.

Tom lay pondering all that had happened in the last few months: starting work as stable lad for Squire Hutchinson and going to live at Owthorpe Manor, the long ride to York with his master and the steward, the lodging they were now staying at in this big Puritan house and finally the fury of the squire and Master Ireton, when their petition to the king was so summarily dismissed.

Tom marvelled that he had been drawn into such momentous events. It had all begun ten weeks ago, on that never to be forgotten day.

* * *

"Fetch my boots, boy! They had better be clean this time, or you'll get a clip on the ear!"

Tom ran to bring the riding boots, glad that he had polished them that morning. He knew he worked for a hard taskmaster but an honest one. When John Hutchinson wanted his boots or needed his horse to be tacked, it had to be done immediately, otherwise there would be trouble, but on the other hand his shilling was always paid on time. Today, the atmosphere was tense because his master was going to collect signatures for his petition to the king.

Tom helped the squire to pull on the long riding boots. Then John Hutchinson looked him in the eye. "You're a useful lad. You can come with me and help." Tom did not understand, but he was happy to oblige.

He considered his master a fair man who treated him well, as long as has did as he was told. So they trotted up the lane together, the squire on his big, roan horse, Steadfast, and Tom on impetuous young Hasty.

Tom plucked up courage to ask "What's this petition all about, master?"

"It's right that you should know, the king expects all landowners to pay for the building and upkeep of his ships to help him fight his Scottish wars – ship tax in Nottinghamshire, forsooth! We couldn't be further from the sea." John Hutchinson was scornful. "But that doesn't stop his men from cutting down some of our best forest trees for timber – oh no! And there's

2

another thing annoys me even more. He's interfering with our church worship, imposing Catholic practices on us and bringing back the bad old days of Queen Mary's time, when people bowed to graven images. He should hark to his parliament. My father's an M.P. for this county, as you know. Well, he saw the king arrogantly march into the House of Commons and try to arrest those members who'd spoken out against such things. This petition, like others from all over England, is one from honest folk urging our monarch to rule us only by the laws of this country, as established with parliament's consent."

Tom listened carefully to what his master said when he called on his wealthy neighbours, like Joseph Widmerpool and Squire Tunstall. He got their support, and on several occasions Tom was sent into the servant's quarters to get the men to scrawl their names. If they could not write they put a simple cross and Tom, who had been to the Nottingham school, asked them for their names and spelt it out for them, adding the words, "his mark." Most were proud to see their names in print. A few questioned whether it might get them into trouble, but the general feeling was that "if the master wants us to sign, it must be right."

They went about this task together on many days after that, and John's younger brother, George, got signatures from the town tradesmen, and their cousin, Henry Ireton, got signatures from places to the west of Nottingham.

"Be careful, John, for my sake and for that of the child to be!" Lucy Hutchinson was on edge the day before her husband was due to take his petition to the king. Tom noted that his mistress was often moody and sometimes imperious. He always found it difficult to puzzle out how she would react to things. Sometimes she could be light-hearted, but today she was tearful.

"Never fear, Lucy, I'll have good men to support me, Cousin Ireton and Oliver, our worthy steward," he was jesting with her. "Why, we can even have Tom Marriott come to take care of our horses."

This was the first Tom had heard of his being involved in the journey to York, where the king was now staying. He was astonished. Perhaps John Hutchinson had been too busy to think about the horses. Perhaps he had thought of taking old Ben, the ostler, and then changed his mind. Whatever the reason, Mr

Hutchinson was smiling at him. "You'll ride with us to York, won't you, Marriott, and help keep us out of mischief?"

Tom's heart soared. "Yes, sir, I'll mind the horses." He had never ridden further than Derby or Loughborough. To go with the master to York with a petition for the king, would be a great adventure.

Lucy was worried and turned to scold the servants sharply.

Yet, Tom remembered, he had seen her only three days ago cantering carefree over the fields, like any stable lad. There was no telling with women.

* * *

John Hutchinson drew reign at the gates of Newstead Abbey. They had ridden here from York, spending a night on the way. Now they had reached Hucknall. Home was within another three hour ride, but the master said: "I'm leaving you here, Oliver. I think I'll call on my Byron cousins and see how the wind blows. I'm spending my night at my brother's house in Nottingham. We need all the friends we can muster. Tell my lady, I'll be at Owthorpe for supper tomorrow."

Mr Oliver shook his head as the young squire disappeared down the long tree-lined drive. "He's wasting his time, is the master. Those seven Byron brothers are young devils, spoiling for a fight. They'll back the king, and look to be rewarded with lands for their services, like royal princes. The Byrons never battle over principles, but only for the takings."

* * *

Later that night, Mr Oliver summoned the servants.

"Our master's in a fair rage," he told them "The king cared not a fig for his petition! It was read by some foppish underling, along with similar petitions from all over the country – I know for sure there were petitions from Lincoln, Derby and York, and signed by eminent folks too. The king did not even ask to see them!

"I 'eard you were attacked..." chipped in the cook.

"Aye, that we were! There was a mob at the door when we left the great hall, jeering and calling us names. They followed us down the street and must 'ave noted our lodgings. When we'd all gone to our beds, there was a great banging and a mob howling back "hang all the roundheads!" – then, saints preserve us – a missile shattered the great mullion glass – t'was a mercy we weren't cut to shreds! Some of them louts started to clamber through the hole in the casement. If Master John and Henry Ireton had not arrived in their nightshirts with swords drawn in readiness, God knows what would have been the upshot."

"Was there a fight?" Ned, the scullery boy asked, eager for more action.

"Nay, lad – one sight of those naked blades and the rascally scullions scuttled back whence they came, but where was the night watch? That's what we was askin'. For all we could tell they had put them up to it!"

"Mercy on us!" cried the cook. "We don't want a mob like that here tonight, and the master still in Nottingham."

"There's no reason for them to come here, as long as we all keep cool heads, so no gossiping, mind."

* * *

Despite the warning, Tom was full of the tale at supper that night. As it was his mother's birthday, he had joined his family, who worked a farm nearby. His sister, Meg, was home too. The last time he had seen Meg was the day he had proudly announced to his assembled family that he had been chosen by John Hutchinson to help the steward collect signatures for the petition against taxes. His sister had laughed at him then. Tom was cross. He felt sure it was just because she was a maidservant to the Countess of Kingston at Pierrepont Hall that she gave herself such airs and graces.

"Madam says your Master Hutchinson is no better than a jumped up tom-fool," she'd said. "The Hutchinsons are not a county family like the Pierreponts. Do you really think the king's going to be told what he should do by commoners and country clodpolls?"

Tom had left in a huff, hearing her sarcastic words smarting in his mind…She'd made him feel small and simple-minded, and he knew better than her on these things.

Today he did not feel disposed to share all the details about the happening in York, as he would have liked to have done.

Instead he told his family the bare facts, and waited for their reaction. His mother looked down and clicked her tongue, but said nothing. His father warned, "Keep your head low, my boy. These are dangerous times."

Meg looked at the floor, not speaking for a while. Then she said, almost in a whisper: "While I was dressing Mistress Pierrepont this morning, she let slip that Lord Newark is going to Nottingham tomorrow to seize their powder and weapons on behalf of the king."

The full significance of her words did not really sink in until Tom was riding back to Owthorpe later that night. It was a lonely road, full of fearful shadows. He was afraid. He had overheard his master and Henry Ireton saying that the gunpowder and armaments held at the Shire Hall in the town, were there for the protection of the people. How could the people defend themselves if these things were taken away?

Suddenly, the road looked far more threatening: familiar trees and landmarks took on sinister shapes. Tom was disturbed by the pounding of the horse's hooves, which seemed to tell the sleeping countryside that he was a lone late traveller. He imagined he could see dark ruffians behind every bush, waiting to attack.

At last he saw the outline of Owthorpe Manor looming ahead. He quietly slipped out of the saddle and stirrups, whispered gently to the nervous horse, and entered the stable. His steps sounded loud on the flagstones as he crossed the yard to the kitchen. By the embers of a dying fire, a dog stirred from its sleep, recognised him, and then closed its eyes again. Relieved that he had not awakened anyone, he climbed the rickety ladder to his loft-bed. He could hear Ben, the old coachman, snoring in the darkness. This meant that he was saved from a rant about returning too late.

The lad groped his way towards the large straw mattress, which he shared with Ned, the scullery boy. Ned turned in his sleep as Tom dropped his stockings, breeches and shirt on the floor and crawled under the wool coverlet.

Tom did not sleep that night. The bats were restless, the owls were noisy and there was a rat gnawing somewhere down below. He lay, tossing and turning, acutely aware of all the night sounds, thinking what he might do.

The cook's words came back to him. "We don't want a mob here and the master still in Nottingham." It was true. It could well happen. John Hutchinson had been rebuked by the king, and now

Lord Newark was coming to seize the town armoury. A crowd might well be stirred up to attack the hall. The house where he had stayed in York had been attacked – why not Owthorpe? There was also talk of the mistress being pregnant again. If there was violence who knew what could happen? She might lose the child. But then if John Hutchinson was in Nottingham, the mob might get him there. With a shock, he realised that the Hutchinson town house was only a stone's throw from the Shire Hall, where the armour was kept. Lord Newark was going to seize it tomorrow. The master must be warned.

Tom thought: *Should I go and wake Mr Oliver and tell him what Meg has said? No, I don't think so. He can be sarcastic and we aren't on the best of terms. Should I wait until morning and speak with the mistress? That's no good – it'll be too late. Should I waken old Ben and explain everything to him? No – Ben's deaf and I'd have to shout. He'd be furious and not understand? The only option's to warn Master John myself.*

Tom had felt a bond with his master ever since that night last spring, when by the golden light of the big horn lantern, they had worked together in the loose-box to ease the birth of a foal. He must ride to Nottingham at first light to warn his master…It was his plain duty, even though he might be scolded for neglecting household tasks and for taking the horse again without permission. He was sure his master would not blame him – he would understand once the warning was delivered. There was a risk. The gossip might not be true, but in his mind, Tom felt it worth taking.

Tom slipped out of his bed at cockcrow, his heart pounding against his ribs.

As he hurriedly dressed, he was aware of Ned stirring.

"Tom? Why are you up so early?"

"Naught to do with you!" hissed Tom.

"You're for it when Ben wakes. He told you to be back with the horse straight after supper."

But Tom was shinning down the ladder and crossing the kitchen.

Minutes later, Hasty was saddled again and led to the drinking trough. Then Tom was away through the gate. Ben's angry face appeared at the window but it was too late for him to interfere. Tom grinned and waved him a cheeky farewell, setting the horse's head in the direction of Nottingham.

CHAPTER 2

TURMOIL IN THE TOWN

The road to Nottingham was familiar to Tom, but he had not set out on it so early before in the day. Dawn was breaking over the Vale of Belvoir and he shivered in the chill morning air as he clattered through the village of Cotgrave, and on past the lane that led to his father's farm. All the way, he was turning over in his mind what he would do when he reached the town:

I'll ride directly to the Hutchinson house on High Pavement and ask to see the master. If, by any mischance, neither he nor his brother, George are there, I'll go to the mayor's tannery and ask to speak to Alderman James 'on a matter of grave urgency'. Otherwise, Lord Newark's men might arouse all the vandals in Nottingham and encourage them to attack the houses of the known petitioners.

The Hutchinsons, Henry Ireton and John James the mayor would be the first targets. Tom did not care much about the aldermen – the brusque tanners and other tradesmen who seemed to rule the town, and had also signed the petition. He knew, however, that they could be useful allies if things turned ugly; after all, they were the ones in command of the town watch.

He reached the old stone bridge, with its twenty arches spanning the muddy River Trent. The road divided here; the bridge carried a high causeway for pedestrians, but Tom took the lower bridle-path fording swampy water-meadows, where ripples of flood water glinted between a carpet of crocuses and other wild flowers. The way was slippery so the horse had to pick its steps gently. Some market traders were crossing also with their carts and there was only passage for one at a time. Before him, Nottingham was set on two rounded hills: the near one to the right was a huddle of roofs, topped by the tower of old St. Mary's, and the far one to the left, a gaunt cliff capped by the ruinous castle. It seemed to Tom, peering through the morning haze, that it had the air of a sea-girt town and it made him feel like a knight of old bent on some perilous mission.

Soon the mud track gave way to a firm cobbled road, which curved up the steep hillside into the town. He rode up Vault Hill and under the archway spanning the road, which seemed like an entrance.

Outside St.Mary's Church, there were delays as several carts tried to pass a group of mounted horsemen. Tom edged his way through and headed for Hutchinson House on High Pavement. After leaving the horse in the safe hands of a stable-boy, he knocked boldly on the back door. He knew the manservant who opened it.

"Hello, Will...is Master John here? I must speak with him. It is a matter of great import!"

"Is it indeed?" Will was sarcastic. "Master John left this morning in some haste." The man was all for shutting the door.

"Please – I have to speak with Master George then!" Tom had his foot in the door. He had come too far to be put off by a surly manservant.

"Whatever for? You can't come bursting in here, lad, demanding to see the gentry. What's come over you?"

Tom had no time to argue his case; he darted under the man's arm and ran down the hallway, almost colliding with George Hutchinson, who was curious about the raised voices at his kitchen door.

"Master Hutchinson – I must speak with you! Lord Newark is coming into town this day and he means to seize all the ammunition and weapons!"

"What's this, boy? How do you know of this? Who sent you?" He fired questions like bullets at Tom.

As Tom blurted out his story, George Hutchinson showed concern. He patted the lad on his shoulder. "You did the right thing, Tom. John has gone to see the mayor. We'll make haste and join him. Come with me!"

Mr George led Tom outside and over the road to the home of Alderman James in Halifax Lane. They were quickly admitted to an oak-beamed upper sitting room, where Tom saw his master in earnest conversation with a plump, middle-aged woman.

"I'm sorry to interrupt," announced George, "but your boy, Tom, has ridden over from Owthorpe with serious news. His sister's in service at Pierrepont Hall, and she's heard that Lord Newark means to seize the ammunition and weapons today from Shire Hall."

"He's there already – with Sir John Digby!" John replied. "Mistress James is telling me so – she has it from the gaoler, who lives below the Hall. He slipped out to warn the mayor but, alas, he's away at his tannery in Narrow Marsh…"

"What's to be done?"said George, crossing to the window in a vain attempt to see the troublemakers.

"We'll go there now – you and I – and stop them" – John replied, as he pulled on his cloak. "But first George, go back to your house to collect your strongest men – they must tell everyone! We need a crowd outside the Shire Hall shouting that no one can take away their means of defence, not even the king himself – least of all Henry Pierrepont! Tom, you go find Alderman Drury and get his help. What are you waiting for, boy? Run!"

Tom knew the Drury family well, having lodged with his classmate Sam, when they were both pupils at Nottingham High School two years ago. He hurtled down High Pavement, passing the Shire Hall, where he noted two men and a youth minding some half a dozen tired horses, tethered ominously by the door. On he ran, past Weekday Cross, where the morning market was being set up. He dodged round several baskets of produce, setting the dogs barking, and sped into Middle Pavement. Half way down the hill he stopped at Vault Hall, on the corner of the steep lane spanning the crumbling archway.

He paused, panting at the door. It suddenly opened and Alice, Sam's younger sister appeared, dressed in her Puritan black gown and white cap. Despite this, she gave him her usual impish grin.

Alice had been helping her mother and their cook skin rabbits that morning for the evening meal but now she had taken off the white apron because it was splashed with blood, and she was being sent with a message to her father in the tannery.

"Why Tom …what ails you? You're in a fine pother!" Tom had no time to give her all the facts. He just had breath to ask: "Where's your father, Alice? He's needed urgently!"

"He's at his tannery, as usual. You'd best come along with me! You can tell me more as we go…"

They hurried through the old town gateway and down Vault Hill. The steep winding road led to the underground cave, which Alderman Drury had commandeered for his tannery. As they went, Tom blurted out an odd tale that she could hardly understand, concerning the mayor and the town weapons. All she was clear about was that Tom had an urgent message for her father.

The tannery entrance was through a narrow passage between high tenement buildings. Huge bovine skins hung on ropes, drying over their heads. The air was fetid with a stench coming from large vats further inside. Small boys and girls, their faces and arms stained and grimy, hauled tubs, containing newly-tanned hides. They were too tired by labour to even look up at the strangers darting past them. Alice had grown used to these sights, and knew her way when the tunnel branched out into several caves, penetrating deep into the sandstone cliff.

Men were cutting the skins with long knives. It was very noisy in the cave: every sound echoed, and Tom could see little in the gloom… He just followed Alice, who soon found her father and brother. She took her father's arm and gave the message to him with hand-signs, because of the noise. Suddenly, the alderman bellowed like a bull, and every man, woman and child stopped working and turned to look at him.

"Come with me – every man jack of you!" roared Drury. "Bring your knives and follow me. We're going to the Shire Hall!"

They all trooped out. Tom thought they looked like a fierce army in their leather aprons, their faces smeared with dirt, and several men wielding frightening long knives. They marched along Narrow Marsh and up Bright Moor Hill, glad to be out in the sunshine although most of them knew nothing of where they were going or why. Tom, Alice and Sam paraded with the alderman at the head of the crowd – feeling very important but fearful too.

William Drury suddenly let out the clarion call: "Save our parliament! Spare our church!" This cry was repeated down the line and the people raised their improvised weapons, frightening a carthorse, who shied in fear, toppling his load and spilling vegetables which rolled in their path.

The protestors met up with a medley of crop-eared apprentices and gossiping servants outside the Shire Hall. George Hutchinson was there, standing on a mounting block, loudly addressing the gathering townsfolk:

"People of Nottingham…. Sir John Digby and Lord Newark

have come here today to steal away your weapons from the Shire Hall. The town's arms, muskets and ammunition are here for defence against anyone who wishes to disturb the peace. These arms are in the care of the Mayor, Alderman James, for the use of the militia and trained bands. Lord Newark says he wishes to seize them for the king – what do we say?"

"Save our Parliament! Spare our church!" chanted the tanners.

Alderman Drury followed George Hutchinson onto the mounting block.

"You all know me – I speak for the people of Nottingham. You remember the petition that many of you signed – the one that Master Hutchinson, here, and his brother took to the king at York? It stated that the king shouldn't levy taxes without Parliament's consent, that he can't despoil our churches with graven images, and that he must dismiss his idle, foreign advisors and listen to his own people. What did he do? He ignored the petition. Now – he sends Lord Newark to demand you hand over the town armoury, your only means of defence. He sends his soldiers into town…look behind you!"

He pointed to the men guarding the horses. They were not soldiers, but they carried weapons and looked as if they might use them, if provoked. Behind them was a large covered wagon, with two burly men on board.

"What do we say to Lord Newark? "

"Go back to Pierrepont Hall!" – cried an angry voice.

"He cannot hear you," shouted Alderman Drury. "He's in the Shire Hall with the windows closed. Shout louder!"

Tom gripped Sam's arm: "We need more people here – enough to bar the road, and stop them leaving with the weapons. Let's go and rouse the market."

Sam nodded, and all three of them ran to the Weekday Cross, where market traders were already busy selling produce from their carts: butter, eggs, pots and pans, hens, chickens, pigeons and geese. People were clustered outside a butcher's booth, and there was a cart selling fish from the Lincolnshire coast. Clearly, the people here knew nothing of what was happening on High Pavement and it would be difficult to grab their attention.

Then Alice noticed a pedlar selling broadsheets and occasionally banging a drum, decorated with pink ribbons. Impetuously, she caught his eye and a word was all that was needed. Alice and Tom found themselves hoisted up on one of the carts, with the pedlar beside them, banging his drum for all he was worth and shouting "No taxes. No papists. The king's men are come to Nottingham to seize your arms and take them. Follow this lad and lass and they'll show you the rogues at the Shire Hall. Go, with them to defend the town!" And he gave a roll of his drum.

There was a rush towards High Pavement. The wooden cart collapsed under them, and the young people fell on the cobbles, amongst a welter of running feet. They scrambled up just in time to see the pedlar seizing the opportunity to fill his pockets with eggs and dart down an alleyway.

Running back with the crowd, they saw several men trying to break into the Shire Hall, ramming their shoulders against the bolted doors. One of them was suddenly opened from the other side, and the men fell on top of one another in a tangled scrum of arms and legs.

Lord Newark and Sir John Digby strode angrily out of the entrance and through the rabble by the big door, closely followed by John Hutchinson and the mayor. The crowd jeered and booed them, as they mounted the waiting horses, and the taller man scowled at Tom's master. "I'll be reporting today's events to the king, John Hutchinson. Your name is already noted."

"If those men are Lord Newark and Sir John Digby, they're empty handed," Tom whispered to Alice, "That means we've won."

Alice's eyes danced, confirming Tom's conviction that, despite her Puritan costume, she was a girl of spark and spirit.

The royalists ignored the angry shouts, dug their heels into the horse's flanks and ducked the mud and rotten apples being flung at them. In a cloud of dust, they were gone, and the big, horse drawn wagon followed in their wake, empty of its intended load.

* * *

In the afternoon, Tom rode back to Owthorpe Manor alongside his master. He sensed he had earned a new status. He could see that John Hutchinson was quietly pleased with the turn of events. As they trotted along the lanes, Tom realised how events had turned upside down: he had set out to stop a small group of men forcing their will upon others, and had ended up doing this very thing himself.

CHAPTER 3

STRANGERS AT OWTHOPE

Tom saw little of his master these days. John Hutchinson was spending much of his time at Attenborough with his fiery cousin, Henry Ireton. It seemed to Tom that Mistress Lucy had become very tetchy and highly strung, but then, he remembered that she was expecting a child. Perhaps that explained it.

Early one morning when Tom was feeding the horses, John Hutchinson strode in and ordered Steadfast to be saddled and made ready for a journey.

"I'm going to Leicestershire," he explained, then checked himself. "I shall be away for a few days – don't concern yourself as to where. You might be questioned."

Tom did not like the grim expression on his face – it seemed ominous.

Then he heard rumours amongst the servants about the reason for the squire's sudden departure. Royalist soldiers had arrived in Nottingham and billets were being sought for them in the larger town houses. An officer had called at George Hutchinson's house, demanding accommodation. A troop of cavalry had been sighted at Stanton searching the houses of parliamentary supporters.

For a while, all was quiet. Then came the message that Mistress Lucy was to join Master John. The Hall was filled with bustling activity in preparation for her journey. Mr George and Mason, his manservant, came riding over from Nottingham to escort her and Tom heard Mason tell Mr Oliver that Nottingham folk were in fear, because rumour had it that the king himself was to ride there at the head of an army.

Mistress Hutchinson made a great show of demanding a range

of gowns to take with her, but soon they were stowed in the carriage and she and her escort were heading off up the lane in a cloud of dust. The household was much quieter in her absence, but filled with apprehension.

The very next afternoon, the sound of hooves brought Tom into the stable yard. A proud, well-dressed horseman was looking around. Then he noticed the boy.

"Can I help you, sir?" Tom walked over and caught hold of the horse's reins.

"Is your master at home?" the stranger demanded. There was a ring of authority in his voice but it was without menace.

"No, sir – he and the mistress are away." Tom remembered his master's warning about being questioned.

The man looked disappointed.

"That's unfortunate. You clearly don't know me, but I'm family – John's cousin, Richard Byron. Will he be back tonight?"

"I don't think so, sir. They did not say when they would be back. They will be away for a few days."

Richard dismounted. "Then I think I must leave John a message. Take me to Mr Oliver – he'll have quill and ink so I can write a note for my cousin."

Suspecting that the Byron family were strong supporters of the king, Tom was uncertain of the best course to take.

"If you will wait here, sir – I will go and find Mr Oliver."

Richard Byron ignored this, and strode forward into the house.

The steward appeared in the hallway, surprised by the unexpected visitor. Tom followed, in time to see Sir Richard give a slight bow and say: "Forgive my intrusion. The lad tells me that your master's away. I need to speak with him urgently, or at the least, to leave him a note. When do you expect him to return?"

Mr Oliver looked pale. "There's no telling, sir. He didn't even say where he was going."

"Not even to his steward! That's strange. His lady's away too, I am told. Do you know how I might find them?"

"Indeed I don't, sir." Oliver closed his eyes.

"Curious! Since my cousin is so secretive, I must pen him a note. Take me to .the study." Oliver led the gentleman away.

Tom reluctantly returned to the stable yard where he met old Ben, who shook his head and spat at the ground. "Wild lot – them

Byrons. What right have they got to come snooping as soon as the master and mistress are away?"

Tom thought this a biased judgement. Richard Byron looked a strong man who knew his own mind – but not one he would call wild.

* * *

While the household waited for the squire's return, there were other visitors at Owthorpe. This time, three royalist cavalry men, who came clattering into the forecourt, demanding that they be allowed to search the premises for weapons.

Mr Oliver met them at the door.

"This is a quiet house. You will find no arms here, except a fowling piece or two, and the odd sword, such as all gentlemen hold for their own protection."

The officer was brisk: "Barnes! Come with me into the house. Wilkinson – go search the stables and out-houses. Things could be hidden there." His underlings ran to obey his barked commands.

Tom was ordered to open up the stable loft. The soldier climbed the ladder and prodded the hay-bed with his sword.

"You'll find nothing there…" The soldier ignored Tom, and continued with his untidy search. He peered in amongst the horse tackle, upturned a barrel of oats, invaded the lads' sleeping quarters, prodded the pallets and scattered items of clothing – but found nothing of interest.

Soon afterwards, the three soldiers met up in the yard. The officer had seized a sword from the master's rooms and the man Barnes held four pewter dinner plates, saying that they could be melted down for ammunition.

"What about the family chapel? Try the door – and fetch the key if it does not yield," the officer shouted.

"You've no right to search a church!" protested Mr. Oliver.

The officer laughed, as he kicked the door open: "A fine place this – a rabble-preaching house! Where's the altar? No paintings, no figurines – only a great pulpit for preaching sedition and a table for rebels to gather. Your Master Hutchinson has a reputation for smashing images in the churches around here. Is this ranters' barn the sort of place he would have us all worship in?"

Finding nothing of any material value anywhere, the soldiers were soon remounting on their horses and cantering away, without a backward glance.

"Good riddance!" spat Ben. "It's that Richard Byron who sent 'em, I'll be bound. Cousin 'e is, and 'e means to get at the master, so 'e can grab this estate...you mark my words!"

CHAPTER 4

THE KING'S CUISINE

August 1642

Now that the master and mistress were away, life was quiet at Owthorpe and it was agreed that on certain days during harvesting Tom could help on the farm.

All the talk of the neighbourhood was that the king had come to Nottingham with his royal courtiers. The reason was uncertain, but rumours of war were in the air.

One market day, when his parents were busy in the fields, Tom was sent there with the vegetable cart.

As he was approaching the river, he saw Meg waiting for him at the finger post. "What are you doing here?" he demanded rather angrily.

"Coming with you to market. Mistress is curious to know all she can about the royal court, and when I asked permission to go to Nottingham market, she agreed, telling me to bring back any news I can. I've been waiting here for the last hour for you to arrive."

"But I don't need your help. The town's full of soldiers. I don't think it's safe for a girl..."

Furious, Meg jumped up beside him, seizing the reins from his hands. "I'm a year older than you! And I was sent marketing all the time you were doing your so called studies at that grand Nottingham school, so you'd best hold your tongue!"

Tom disbelieved her story about the countess, but he could see no point in arguing. It would only make her more determined to have her way. Secretly, he felt quite pleased that she'd come – perhaps he could find an opportunity to slip away while she was busy with customers and find out more of what was happening in the town.

People were streaming over the bridge, their carts piled high with belongings, which suggested an air of alarm.

Soldiers guarded Trent Bridge at both ends. It looked like an official picket, being supervised by an officer. Most of the travellers coming south were allowed to go by, but some were detained for questioning. They had to wait a while before they were allowed to ford the crossing way, as the long stream of people leaving the town continued.

Nottingham was alive with king's soldiers. Some were fierce looking and bristling with weaponry, looking as if they had been 'blooded' in the Dutch wars. Others were new conscripts, beardless youths, who seemed proud and yet half afraid of the weapons they were carrying. Windows were shuttered – a sure sign of trouble. It seemed as if ordinary townsfolk either stayed indoors or left with their bundles on carts. There was no market today. Instead, a group of raw recruits were drilling on the patch where the baker usually set up his stall.

Tom and Meg were uncertain what they should do. They saw one of the regular stall-holders – stolidly beginning to offload his milk churns onto the steps of the Weekday Cross. So, they ignored the bellowing officer, and began to display their vegetables on sacking, spreading them out on the cobbles, as usual. It was a full hour before they had their first customer – an old lady – who emerged from her house on Blowbladder Street. She hastily bought her wares and scurried back like a frightened mouse.

No one else approached for some time and Tom was intrigued to observe the small troop of young recruits being drilled in using firearms by their sergeant: He listened to the commands. "Prime your pan!" and "Wedge your bullet!"

Tom was used to using a fowling-piece, but these matchlock muskets were something new to him. They were long, fearsome looking weapons, which took some shouldering. Despite the commands, he hoped that this was just a preliminary and exercise and the guns were not being loaded.

Suddenly, a liveried gentleman appeared around the corner from High Pavement and, in a loud voice, ordered them to pack up their cart and follow him.

"Why? We aren't doing anything wrong!" cried Meg. "We always have a stall at this market."

The gentleman gave her a doomsday glare. "Would you deny the royal court?"

Even the loud-mouthed sergeant stopped his shouting to see what was going on. His recruits remained silent.

Meg and Tom were acutely aware that all eyes were upon them.

"Come!" ordered the footman. Hastily the pair repacked their cart, while the colourful gentleman tapped his buckled shoe impatiently on the cobbles.

They were led down Fletchergate, across Warsergate, and through Swine Green to the Earl of Clare's great house on the northern edge of town. This, as everyone knew, was where the king was staying with all his court followers, but why were they being taken there? The footman said nothing to enlighten them, marching them around to the servant's entrance. He called through an open window.

A sturdy cook emerged to inspect the vegetables on the cart. She sniffed the turnips and potatoes, nibbled the carrots, ruffled the feathers of the pheasants, chewed at an apple, bit into a cheese, dipping her finger in the milk churn and licking it lustily. Then she told the fancy footman she'd have the lot and disappeared into the kitchen, chuntering to herself: "This court'll be the death 'o me – I never know'd such stomachs!"

Meg and Tom were ordered to offload the cart and carry everything through into the scullery. Tom stopped to work out how much the produce would cost. The footman harried him: "No time for that now, boy – I will see you are paid, just as soon as all those wares are unloaded."

Good as his word, he poured a shower of coins into waiting hands, when they were done. Meg tipped the coins out into her apron:

"You count the bronze – I'll count the silver." They were both beaming at their bounty.

"Three cheers for King Charles and his court! That's what I say!" Meg exclaimed. "They should be staying at Pierrepont Hall – with our farm as the vitlers."

"Well now – we've sold our produce, so the rest of the day is ours! Let's walk across town and see what's happening at the castle!" Tom suggested.

"Since we are in a royal courtyard – I have a mind to sit here as long as I may, and watch the goings on. Everyone's so busy, they'll scarce bother about us."

"Well then, I'll take the horse and cart to the Drury stables – I know the ostler, and we can meet up again there and go home at the usual time."

* * *

There was a loud knocking on the door of Vault Hall. Alice was at work in the kitchen, when a distressed maid came bustling in.

"Oh miss, it's one of them royalist soldiers, a sergeant I think he said, he's at your door- an ugly man with a great black beard wi' crumbs on it. He says he's been sent to take our horses for the king's army. Did ever you hear the like?"

Both her parents were out and Sam was at the tannery too, so Alice ran into the stable yard, just in time to see her own pony, Patience, and two other horses, being led away by three burly soldiers.

She turned on the sergeant, who was standing watching. "Who gave you permission…?"

"We don't need no permission. We're under king's orders to collect all the 'orses in town for the parade this afternoon in the market square!"

"And when do we get them back?"

"Best ask the king, missy. If your papa'll join our force, he can ride his own steed. If he won't, someone else will."

"That pony's mine!"

"Then ride her in the square," the sergeant laughed. "We'd like a buxom lass like you in the king's colours. T'would be good for the recruiting sergeant."

There was nothing she could do, but choke her rage and say she'd report them to her father, who was an alderman. It sounded so weak.

"I couldn't stop them, Miss Alice," the groom was furious. "They just marched in and seized the poor creatures. They said they was goin' to all the town stables on the same errand. Plain thievin', I calls it!"

Alice left him, and ran out after the soldiers to follow them down High Pavement. She stopped at the corner of Weekday Cross. There was no point in doing this. She must run to the tannery to tell father. She turned and almost collided with Tom, who was walking towards her leading his carthorse.

"Alice," he cried. "Is there any chance of stabling Charlie at your place...?"

"Oh Tom," her eyes were wet. "Yes, bring him in quickly. It's for the best. They've emptied the stables, so he'll be safe. They won't come back our way."

"Who won't?" Tom was puzzled. He'd never seen Alice so upset.

She told him what had happened. "They've even taken my pony, Patience. She's much too small for a war horse! I think they just took her to spite us. Whatever can they use her for?"

"Those royalist soldiers don't respect anyone, or anything!" he said.

"But it's not just them, is it? The parliament men are little better," Alice cried. "They're taking horses as well. Oh, why must it be like this? We all lived peacefully as neighbours until a few months ago, now there's quarrelling and pillaging and cruelty all around us. Oh Tom, where will it end?"

"Who's to say? I only want to leave Charlie here for a few hours, but since you're in such a plight, it doesn't seem right..."

"Nay, he'll be no trouble. Bring him in quickly, before he's spotted. Take him to the loose box."

Tom complied and soon the horse was fed and watered, and Alice was stroking his white mane, lamenting her loss.

"Maybe you'll get Patience back in a day or two." Tom tried to console her. "Someone will probably ride her in the parade everyone's talking about and then set her free. As you say, she's much too small for a cavalryman, and not strong enough to pull carts. I thought I'd see this march-past or whatever it is, so I'll look out for Patience, and tell you if I see her. Better still, why don't you come with me, Alice? It's best to take stock of the enemy."

"Oh no, Tom. I've no enemies. Father's a low church man I know, but that doesn't make him a parliament man. He'll challenge anyone seizing arms or horses. There's no need for this stupid fighting – be it for king or parliament. We want to keep Nottingham free from this folly. That's the aldermens' view and mine too."

Tom looked at her determined face, and realised how resolute she stood on these matters.

"Well I've helped collect signatures for the petition against ship money," said Tom stoutly, "so I reckon that makes me a parliament supporter."

"And what about your sister, Meg?" Alice showed concern.

"Oh, she works at Pierrepont Hall, so she's no choice. Lord Newark's the king's representative in the county, isn't he?"

"But does she have a mind of her own? Do you, Tom? Are you just being blown by opposite winds?"

Before Tom could think of a reply, they were hailed by a youthful voice, "Tom, Alice, how do I look?"

They turned to see Jed Martin, a lad who worked in Drury's tannery. Usually ragged and bare-foot, Jed was now decked in a buff coat, adorned with ribbons, boots much too big for him, and a lightweight sword slung from a leather belt. Tom nearly laughed in his face. He looked ridiculous.

"What's this?" demanded Alice. "I scarce recognise you!"

"I'm one of the king's men now," Jed proclaimed. "Signed up yesterday at the Salutation. They giv' me a flagon of ale and this garb! Mine to keep. This is mi' own sword to 'ave as long as I'm in service. I've been doin' the pike drill, and they're goin' to teach me to fire a musket, honest… I'm paradin' this afternoon as one of Lord Newark's pikemen."

"Parading! Where?" enquired Tom.

"In the market square. It's the king's great rally before 'e raises 'is standard. All our troops is marchin'. Then we're goin' up to the castle. There'll be drums and fifes and all that, and the king 'isself is comin' ere with Prince Rupert – to declare war on the rebels. It's the biggest thing that's ever 'appened in all my life. You must come and see it, Tom!"

"Where is the king, now?" Tom asked.

"E was at Clare Hall – but 'e left two days ago to fight the rebels at Coventry or some such place."

"Oh, Jed. Don't get mixed up in this?" Alice broke in. "We're cousins, aren't we? You know how opposed your aunt is to all this fighting. No good can come of it."

Jed ignored her and gave Tom gave a knowing wink. "That's women's talk. Sergeant says the king's comin' back 'ere at any moment. That's why we're drillin' like demons. And after the parade, you'll see the banners flyin'."

"It's war then," Tom muttered, half to himself, his spirit sinking.

"Can't come quick enough for me!" Jed said, beaming from ear to ear. "I gets a shillin' – if I'm in at the action."

24

CHAPTER 5

STANDARD HILL

Monday 22 August 1642

The great parade in the Market Square began when a trumpet blast sounded. Tom was standing near the Malt Cross, and could see that a platform had been erected on the opposite side of the square for the mayor and aldermen. One or two of them were sitting there on chairs, but the mayor was clearly absent and so, he noted, was Alderman Drury.

"That 'll cause offence to the king," someone said nearby, "but John James has never been one to bow the knee."

"There's a man in mayor's robes coming up now. That's not Alderman James though," said another. "Who is he?"

Some one laughed nearby. "Why, I know that man. It's Hercules Clay, the Mayor of Newark. They've wheeled him in for the look of the thing."

"They say 'alf the soldiers they've mustered 'ere come from Newark. There's precious few Nottingham men 'ave joined the king's army."

Tom peered closely to see who was on the platform and recognised the two men who had tried to seize the town arms at the Shire Hall, Lord Newark and the High Sheriff. He felt proud he'd helped defeat them.

Another trumpet blast – and then a richly attired officer rode into the square mounted on a black horse, followed by a posse of cavaliers, wearing armour and steel helmets. A parade of drummers and pipers followed, leading a march past of men carrying long pikes on their shoulders. Amongst them he saw young Jed with a pike far to long for him to hold fully upright. It was pointing dangerously near to the man behind him. Jed had to skip every other step to try to keep up with the big men and at every hop the pike looked more perilous. Tom laughed out loud. After a short wait, the cavalry cantered past and there was Sir

Richard Byron, sporting a scarlet cloak and waving to the ladies on the stand.

Tom looked again in that direction and to his dismay saw Meg, near the platform, cheering and waving her kerchief. A feeling of revulsion shot through him. He could stand this no longer. Tom pulled out of the crowd, seething with anger.

Meg was riveted, with tears in her eyes, as she watched the brave parade pass. She saw the Newark Mayor cross himself, in high church fashion, and then a team of horsemen cantered by, flying a great streamer which read 'Give Caesar his due'. She cheered and waved, and was delighted that one of the riders turned, smiled and waved back to her.

"They are like animals – dressed for the slaughter!" Tom angrily exclaimed to Sam, as he returned to the Drury stables. "They couldn't get many men to sign up here in Nottingham, so they recruited boys and decked them up like turkey cocks."

"That's what the mayor told my father and he said that a lot of the men in the square are mercenaries from the German wars. There's some gentry from Newark, and the Welbeck and Newstead estates, and no doubt their retainers have been dragged along to fill out the ranks! My father reckons that the Nottingham men will show their metal once the king has gone…"

"You mean they'll join the parliament's army?"

"Not they! They've too much sense to start fighting, unless they're forced to defend their own families, of course!"

"But you'll join, won't you, Sam? You helped us beat Lord Newark out of town, when he came for the weapons and ammunition."

"I helped protect our town armoury, of course!" affirmed Sam. "I would have done the same if your man, Hutchinson, had tried to take the powder and arms away for some Roundhead army."

Tom's anger welled up. "John Hutchinson wouldn't do that. He's defending this town! His quarrel's against the king's tyranny and I support him to the hilt!"

Alice heard Tom's raised voice and came to join them in the yard.

Sam turned towards her. "We'll see when the time comes,

won't we, Alice? Our family will help protect the town from warfare in our streets, but we'll none of us take sides in the stupid quarrel – neither father, nor mother, nor Alice nor I. But we'll tell you what we two mean to do. We want to see which local men are really with the king, so Alice and I are going to the castle tonight to watch them raise the standard. Will you come with us, Tom?"

Tom hesitated. Sam's attitude had thrown him. He thought Sam would be solid for parliament. It was awkward. He'd agreed to meet Meg later. But the very thought of Meg angered him now. And if Alice was going..? He hesitated.

"Will the king's men let us in?"

"They've issued an invitation to all the townsfolk. They want as many there as possible." Alice explained, "Father and mother aren't going. It would look as if they were supporters, but they haven't forbidden Tom or me. They want to know who'll cheer the king round here."

"Yes, I'll come along," Tom said. "It's good to know who our enemies are."

* * *

When Meg met Tom again at the end of the afternoon, she was very surprised to hear that he intended to go to the castle to see the raising of the standard. Nothing could have pleased her more.

The sky darkened and a summer squall began to blow up, as they all four made their way across the town. A sudden downpour made them scurry for shelter under the overhanging roofs in Houndsgate, but it soon passed and a watery sun emerged.

The castle stood high on a cliff to the west of the town. Approached by a steep causeway and an ancient gatehouse, the old royal fortress had been disused for over a hundred years. Some of the curtain wall had fallen, and grateful townsmen had used the stones for their own purposes.

A crowd of revellers, several of them plainly tipsy, were lounging by the gatehouse, singing bawdy songs about Puritans and Roundheads. King's soldiers wearing helmets, metal breastplates and scowls on their faces, guarded the entrance, allowing no one through.

After a considerable wait, a royalist officer took control of the situation, ordered the revellers to hold their peace, and asked everyone to follow him in an orderly fashion. The crowd were led into the lower castle green, a great open space between the moat and the castle walls. They were ordered to walk up a grassy hill two by two, between lines of pike-men standing to attention. Tom had a sense of foreboding, as he walked beside Alice, followed closely by Sam and Meg. He realised that Alice was shivering, and he quietly took her hand. By the northern wall, a group of officers were waiting. They recognised Lord Newark and Sir Richard Byron – their finery still sodden from the sudden downpour.

"The Byron brothers are out in force tonight, all seven of them," Tom heard someone say. "They never miss out on a bit of pageantry."

"Time will show if they stick to their colours," muttered another.

Suddenly a trumpet sounded and a group of horsemen approached from the gatehouse. As they came up the hillock, the men bowed and women curtsied. This must be the King!

He was a small, frail figure, dressed in royal blue with an amazing head dress – a wide hat adorned with the whitest ostrich feathers they had ever seen. As he came more into view – they saw that his face looked sad and tired and his beard was greying prematurely.

Next to him, in stark contrast, rode a tall, elegant young man in bright Cavalier attire. He had a broad, confident smile and a white dog trotted proudly at his heels. Two young boys – dressed richly, but solemn and wide-eyed, flanked them as they surveyed the scene. Someone murmured close by: "That's the king's nephew, Prince Rupert of the Rhine, with the Prince of Wales and young Duke of York."

"God save the King!" shouted the crowd. Meg's voice chimed in, but the other three remained silent. This might have been noted, except for the fact that a general cry went up: "The standard!"

A troop of mounted soldiers rode through the gate towards them, their leader carrying a flag on a long pole. The horses broke into a canter. The leader carried the standard up the mound, held it high, saluted the King and presented it to him. A hole had been prepared in the ground and the King was assisted as he placed the standard in position.

Glistening new spades were produced, and two soldiers filled in the hole. But the standard was too tall for the flag to stand upright, so it had to be held in position by two troopers. Tom thought this rather spoilt the effect, and could not avoid a smirk. Meg glanced at him in disgust.

The King donned his fashionable pince-nez and perused a scroll, which had been handed to him. He frowned, shook his head, and called for quill and ink horn, so he could alter a word or two. He then handed the sheet to a herald. The man bellowed out: "This standard has been raised here in Nottingham on the 22nd day of August 1642, to summon all loyal subjects to hasten and take arms with King Charles, Defender of the Faith, against the traitor, the Earl of Essex and the parliamentary faction, who have defied the King and are threatening the peace of the realm!"

The Royalists cheered and Meg joined in, but Tom and the Drury family remained tight-lipped.

* * *

Later that night, Meg and Tom travelled back in their cart without speaking. They were too much in awe, and in any case, they knew that any words between them would have been in conflict, and neither wanted that.

Meg climbed down wearily at the gate of Pierrepont Hall, and turned to give Tom the money she still held from the sale of produce that morning. It seemed an age ago. As she wished him goodnight, Tom was surprised at the tenderness of her tone and by the lingering look she gave him. While she walked up the path, he remembered the closeness he'd felt to her in his childhood and realised that they now stood on opposite sides of a great divide.

CHAPTER 6

THE GATHERING STORM

When Tom reported for work the next day at Owthorpe Manor.
Old Ben was bemused by a new situation. "The master's decided
to stay in Leicestershire for some time," he told Tom, "and me
an' you've got to take all our 'orses to Master George's stables in
town. Seems they're all empty now 'cos the thieving army men
stole 'em for the king's parade an' never brought 'em back, so
we've gotta' go and stay in the mews cottage there, along o' Albert
Watkins, who's groom to Master George."

"How long will that be for?" Tom remembered the
threatening words, "John Hutchinson, your name is noted,"
which he'd heard from the Lord Lieutenant.

"I dunno. They say there's to be a big battle fought some time
soon to sort out all this mess between the king and 'is parliament.
By chance we'll 'ave to stay in town until we know wot's wot."

The accommodation in the mews cottage, behind the town
house was very cramped. Tom found that he had to share a bed
with Ben in Albert Watkins' bedroom. This was an unhappy
experience for all three of them, and they all hoped that the battle
would be soon be held so that life might return to normal.

When the battle eventually erupted, at Edge Hill in
Warwickshire, it proved to be a bloody affair, which solved
nothing. Although Richard Byron was knighted by the king for
his services, there were no clear winners, so the nation had to
recognize that a long civil war was likely to follow. Both sides
bedded down for the winter.

A local defence corps was being formed to protect
Nottingham, and Mr George, being one of the officers, told Tom
to join them and learn musketry. "It's not that you'll be sent into
combat elsewhere," he explained. "Purely defensive."

One afternoon, just after Tom had finished his training session at the butts, the household were summoned and informed that Master John and Mistress Lucy were to arrive there, from Leicestershire, together with their newborn baby boy.

The next day, their coach rumbled into the yard. The master opened the coach door himself and climbed out so that he could assist Lucy, as she carried the baby, who was swathed in white robes. Lucy was ecstatic, almost girlish again for the next few days, but John Hutchinson, though clearly overjoyed, was soon whisked into town politics.

Next day, Master John was with Tom in the stables, checking the condition of his horses, when the mayor called to see him and urged that he should accept the post of colonel in the new defence corps.

"Francis Pierrepont's already been made a colonel by the parliamentary bigwigs," said Alderman James, in his rough way. "He's a peaceable man who lives in the town but the councillors have their suspicions, because his brother's the King's Lord Lieutenant. It's a divided family, and there's those that thinks it's their father's plan to have sons on either side, so the estate won't lose out whoever wins. I'd be a deal happier if you was to be a colonel too, and keep an eye on things."

John said he would consider the matter, but Tom noticed a flash of pride in his eye and knew that he meant to accept.

Once John was commissioned, the musketry practice and drills were held more often, and Tom soon learned there were no favourites on Colonel Hutchinson's parades, particularly those in his own household.

The first test for the new soldiers came some months later. In February 1643, they were called to support an attack on the town of Newark, which had become the main Royalist stronghold in the area. Tom was left with the other servants to take care of the town-house, but Colonel John Hutchinson and Major George rode out of Nottingham at the head of their own local recruits. Mistress Lucy stood at the window with her babe in her arms to see them leave. The household held its breath. What would the outcome be?

Tom felt concern for Alice Drury who, with her mother, was particularly worried at the military turn of events. Sam had volunteered to join the local defence team, but they were very thankful that he was not asked to join the group that went to Newark. "My concern's for Nottingham," he told Tom. "I'll fight if need be to protect my home, but there's no way I'll be drawn into marching elsewhere for parliament." This sentiment was shared by his father and most of the other town councillors.

As it happened, the soldiers came back a few days later. They'd had a skirmish rather than a battle, and the injuries were light.

"The Newark defences were very lame," John Hutchinson declared. "A few ditches and a handful of men with muskets. We seized their cannons and brought them back with us and if the Lincoln men had not withdrawn, we'd have taken the whole town and held it."

The success made the colonel more confident and gossip talked of him as a local hero, which tended to increase his pride.

One day, when work was slack in the stables, Tom slipped out to go and see Alice. He tried to reassure her. "Everything's going to be safe. John Hutchinson's got the measure of the enemy, you'll see."

Alice was unconvinced. "Father believes his real loyalty's to parliament, not to the townsmen here. My nightly prayer is that Sam will not be sent away to fight. I've heard terrible things about that battle at Edgehill."

Tom returned, rather crestfallen, to face an angry Ben.

"Where've you been, lad? I told you to clean all the horse brasses – we must have them all shining tomorrow – now the master has been made up to town Governor."

"Governor? What does that mean?"

His anger abated, Ben plunged into this latest news: "Well, now – whilst you were skulkin' off yer duties, the army man, Sir John Meldrum, 'as been 'ere with a commission from the Parliament Committee. They've appointed Master John as Gov'nor of Nottingham Castle. 'E and Master George is to take command of all the soldiers there – to defend the town. That's one in the eye for Francis Pierrepont 'oo's supposed to be their commander. So you best polish them brasses bright, so as you can see yer face in 'em. Gov'nor of Nottingham Castle – oh my!" Ben shook his wizened head, smiled toothlessly to himself and went off to spread the story. Tom was bemused also, as he polished and whistled. Whatever did this mean? What would happen next?

Alice was surprised, one evening two months later, when her father announced at supper, "There's to be a special meeting at the Town Hall tomorrow, and I want Sam to come with pen and paper to take note of all that's said."

They stared at him in amazement. Hall meetings were for councillors and aldermen to decide the town affairs. There was a bench at the back for spectators, or strangers as they were known, but none of the family had ever attended except father, who had every right as an alderman.

"How 's this, father – is there trouble?" Sam asked.

"You'll know soon enough, so I may as well tell you now. That country squire, Hutchinson, is proud as a turkey cock now they've made him Castle Governor. He's laying claim to all our cannons from the town walls and ditches and wants to lodge them in the castle. Did you ever hear the like?"

Alice gasped.

"What's that you say, husband?" Mistress Drury dropped her spoon with a clatter.

"He claims that, if the king's men attack from Newark, our defences won't hold. I want you to write down all that's said, Sam. You've a good hand, and so you should have with all that schooling I've paid for. Master Salisbury's a fair weather clerk. But he can be slow and we need every word recorded – chapter and verse. We may need to report Hutchinson to a higher authority!"

"But I thought he and his soldiers were here to defend the town," their mother interposed. "We all helped to dig those ditches right round from the Toll Bar to the River Leen. Alice and I have calluses on our hands to prove it! Are you saying that Hutchinson is going to take our cannons and he and his men will hide behind the castle walls, if the Newarkers come here? I can scarce believe it so."

"No more can I, but the mayor has shown me a letter to this effect and he's summoned this special hall meeting. We must have Hutchinson deposed. That's why I want every word recorded – as evidence. Maybe they'll put one of the aldermen in command – or Francis Pierrepont, if we find he talks any sense!"

"But wasn't Hutchinson appointed governor by parliament?" enquired Sam. "How can the Town Hall dismiss him?"

"Not by themselves, it's true. We need to convince our M.P,

Gilbert Millington. We've every right to send a petition to the army commanders or to Parliament in London, if need be."

"Who's coming to this meeting?" asked mother.

"The aldermen and councillors, of course – and we've invited one or two others to sit on the strangers' bench – Parson Laycock and Dr. Plumtree and.."

"And who will speak up for the women and children?" she interrupted.

"Why, the ward councillors of course."

"All men – as usual! I shall be at that meeting!"

"You can't possibly do that, me' dear. It's a hall meeting."

She wasn't put off. "I'm sure if young Sam can be there, they can't stop me."

"Or me either!" Alice felt it was time she joined in.

"Whoa there, ladies. This is war – which is men's business!"

"It wasn't just men's business to dig those trenches was it?" Alice glared defiantly at her father. She had never dared challenged his word before. "If my mother and Sam are to be at that meeting then so am I!"

"There now, see what you've started!" The alderman looked accusingly at his wife. "Your mother is not going to be at that meeting, and you can't go neither, you silly goose!"

Mother thumped the table. "If there's to be fighting in the streets of Nottingham, who will bind the wounds? We're *all* involved, William. You'll need the women. Alice has got a clear head, so she will be needed too as a witness. We won't sit up at the table with the councillors. We'll sit on the strangers' bench with Parson Laycock and Dr Plumtree. If Sam is fit enough to scribe, we're fit to listen!"

The alderman knew when he was outflanked and reluctantly agreed. "But no talking mind. Strangers can't talk."

* * *

Next day it was a bright sunny morning and Tom Marriott and Sam Drury were due to be taught how to load a cannon in the Nottingham east defence ditch. Their tutor, Laurence Collin, was a wool comber by trade, but since he had gained experience as a combat soldier in the Low Country wars, Parliament had sent him to Nottingham to train their new conscripts.

"This here is a culverin," explained Collin. "It's a deadly weapon, with a point-blank range of 420 paces, and 2,100 paces random shot. It took eight horses to lug it here. It weighs all of four and a half thousand pounds. We seized it from the royalists at Newark four months ago. I was there and saw it used. We shall see they don't capture it and turn it against us again! Now – stand back lads – I'll show you how to load the beast."

"This here is a budge barrel," Collin indicated a circular wooden tub at his feet.

"We ladle out the gunpowder like this – careful not to drop a snatch – a spark will set it alight. I once saw a powder monkey like you blown sky high, when I used a culverin like this one in the Lowlands."

The boys swallowed and watched intently as Collin neatly measured out the gunpowder, with the care of an expert cook.

"Then you load the ball," he said, picking up a cannon ball, and holding it in his hand.

"You can make ten shots in an hour, if the pieces are strong like this. After forty shots, you must refresh and cool the gun. Let her rest an hour, otherwise she may blow in your face…"

"If the Newarkers come – what would we have to do?" enquired Sam.

"Every ditch around the town will need to be manned, so all men and boys will be needed. I'll be stationed here because this cannon is in my charge. There'll be two men from the Trained Band assigned to help me, but we'll need runners to bring the powder and shot along the line, and to carry the water buckets too. That's where you lads come in. You'll have to run low and keep your heads down – or they'll take pot-shots at you!"

"They're still digging ditches around the town – well over a mile of them, so I've heard – reaching all the way from the castle walls to the River Leen," said Tom. "You'll need a lot of lads to guard the guns there, day and night!"

"It's got to be done to protect the town," Sam responded.

Tom swallowed and said nothing. He'd heard his master deriding this plan – saying that a single line of ditches would not be enough to stop an all-out assault. The town was secure from the west, protected by steep cliffs and castle walls, but Newark lay to the east – that was where the danger lay.

A sudden yell, Tom saw what had happened. Sam had tripped

over a loose cannon ball, lying in the ditch. Laughing, Tom grabbed Sam's arm to pull him to his feet. Sam shrieked, "Let go, you fool!"

"Sorry what's the matter?"

Sam nursed his arm and said nothing.

"What's going on?" Laurence Collin was angry. "Who left that ball on the ground? Didn't I tell you how important it is to keep them all boxed?"

"I'm sorry. We didn't see it," Tom was contrite. "But Sam's hurt. He fell on his arm."

"You pulled it!" cried Sam. "I heard it crack."

Abashed, Tom walked back home with him. "I'd no idea how much you'd hurt your arm. Perhaps it's just badly bruised."

"No, it's more than that. I can't move my fingers. It's my right one too!"

Elizabeth Drury studied the bared arm, which was swelling up badly.

"It must be kept tightly bound," she said solemnly. "I'll make you a sling to hold it firm against your chest. It should mend, but it will take many weeks."

"But I must use it tomorrow," protested Sam. "Father spoke to the mayor and I'm to scribe at the Council Meeting."

"There's no way you can do that," Mistress Drury spoke with certainty. "Your father wants his own record made by one of the family. That's true. My schooling isn't good enough and neither is his. Alice must do it in your stead."

"Alice! But she's a girl. Father will never let her."

"I'll deal with father!"

CHAPTER 7

COUNCIL AT WAR

On the day of the hall meeting, Alderman Drury walked with his family to the Guildhall. Alice felt a mixture of humility and pride at her new assignment. Women were not normally allowed to attend meetings of the Council. Now she was not only to attend, but to act as a scribe. It was a daunting honour and she was determined to be equal to the occasion.

As the family approached the Guildhall, they saw the plump figure of Dr Huntingdon Plumtree hurrying to catch them up. He raised his hat and panted – "Good morning, Alderman, Good morning Mistress, and the young people too, I see. Excellent, why not indeed? This occasion affects us all, does it not? I felt I must come to this wretched meeting, though I'll have to sit at the back with you on the strangers' benches – stupid name that. Dreadful business this is of war in the town, and I'm called to see a patient who wants bleeding today too. Had to bring the leeches with me, so I can go straight on. Hope you're not afraid of leeches, Alice." He turned her with an apologetic smile. "I'll keep the stopper on, but not too firmly. They have to breathe, you know. Lovely specimens these, I caught them myself in the meadows, this morning, look!"

Yesterday, Alice would have squirmed. Today, she simply nodded.

At the Guildhall, they found the Councillors standing in angry huddles, complaining about John Hutchinson and the proposal to move the town guns. Some raised their eyebrows at Mistress Drury and Alice, but Alderman Drury immediately announced, "My son, Sam, was to have taken notes at this meeting, as you recall, but he's broken his arm and can't hold a quill, so the mayor has agreed that my daughter, Alice, will oblige."

The committee clerk, somewhat reluctantly, moved along his bench to make room for Alice. She felt herself blushing as she sat down at the long table around which the members were arranged. Several of them murmured but no one objected. Her father took his place beside the new mayor, Alderman Nix. Alderman James, last year's mayor, sat on his other side, looking red-faced and tense. Mistress Drury and Sam sat down quietly on the strangers' benches beside the vicar and several other men, who were already there. Dr. Plumtree put his jar of leeches on the floor between his feet.

At that point, a richly dressed elderly man pranced into the Chamber. He paused, glared at Alice and held up two delicate white hands in horror. "What's this?" he cried. "A girl on the member's bench and a woman amongst the strangers. What are you thinking of, Drury?"

"My lass, Alice, who is well schooled, is taking notes, Toplady. She has sharp ears and nimble fingers. I'll go over every word she's written tonight and make sure that everything that's said on this important matter is recorded."

"Ridiculous!" cried Alderman Toplady, with a wince. " In all my thirty years on the Council, I've never known anything like this. Mr Mayor, as father of the Council, I lodge an objection. No women and girls. Order them out!"

Dr Plumtree jumped to his feet. "I support the women, Mr Mayor. We need to record everything today most carefully. And your committee clerk, Mr Salisbury, has a shaky hand. He came to see me yesterday for a remedy."

"You've no right to speak, Plumtree, you're a stranger!" Toplady pronounced.

The Mayor banged his gavel. "Now then, alderman, take your place at the table. We all know Dr Plumtree. He's no stranger, but I must remind the visitors that they have no right to intervene in council business. I've already agreed that Alice Drury can be an additional note taker at this important meeting, but since you've raised the point – does anyone other than Alderman Toplady object to women at this meeting? " No one stirred. "You're overruled, alderman. father of the Council you may be, but you can't dictate. And now gentlemen, I declare this urgent special meeting open. We have but one item, the removal of the guns, and we await Colonel Hutchinson to explain himself."

They did not wait long. The door swung open and in marched Colonel Hutchinson with Francis Pierrepont. The Mayor and

Alderman James rose from their seats to greet them, while all the others remained seated. The Mayor indicated two high backed chairs, which had been placed beside the table, and the two men moved to sit there.

Banging his gavel with ceremony, the Mayor addressed them with some severity.

"Gentlemen, we welcome you to the Guildhall. However, we feel bound to tell you that we are most disturbed about your proposal to move the cannons, brought here from Newark and elsewhere, by our own men for our protection. The Council demands a full explanation. We will reserve further comment until we have heard your reasons!"

Alice, quill at the ready, poised herself to try to write down every word. Colonel Hutchinson stood up to face the meeting in a determined manner. Francis Pierrepont shifted uneasily in his seat.

"By your leave, gentlemen...and ladies," giving a nod to them both, "I'll speak plainly and I hope to cause no offence. This town's indefensible against a full assault by the king's forces. Lord Newcastle has over a thousand men at his command, including expert cavalry and seasoned soldiers, who've fought in the German wars. Your ditches and palisades stretch for over a mile and a half, encircling the town. There are fourteen cannons in them. You would need three thousand soldiers to man them efficiently and fortify both town and castle against attack. You have only three hundred. You'll have to put them in three watches to cover the full twenty-four hours. That's a hundred against a thousand. It must be remembered that most of your men are not trained as soldiers for such work – never before have they been in battle. They could not hold on indefinitely, throughout a long siege lasting weeks. What happens if the enemy seize your cannons in the ditches? I'll tell you straight. They will turn them on your people. That will cause havoc. It will be a total rout and probably a massacre."

The Colonel paused to let this all sink in. Alice was scribbling to try to keep up, but the committee clerk was not even trying. Like all the others he sat, staring at the speaker.

"But," continued Hutchinson, striding to the window and pointing outside. "We still have hope. There stands the castle, four-square upon a rock and circled by a moat. The site was chosen by the conqueror for its position. Suppose we place our cannons there? The enemy could be kept at bay for many weeks and our weapons would be safe. So, I invite you all, townsmen, women and children, to come into the castle grounds for safety. Take refuge there, behind your cannons, and help me and my soldiers beat the rebels and send them packing!"

Alice could not keep up. She found herself gazing at him too, fascinated and appalled. He commanded attention, but when he finished speaking, everyone started shouting. Alderman Drury and his wife both jumped to their feet, along with the councillors and spectators. "What about our houses?" "Shall we leave all our goods behind for rebels to pillage?" "That castle's an old ruin. Where will our families sleep?"

The mayor banged his gavel and called for order. "One at a time. Alderman Drury. I call you first!"

"I must remind Master Hutchinson that I was one of the first townsmen to support him when he stopped Lord Newark from taking our gunpowder and arms at the start of this miserable affair. I thought we'd agreed then that weapons are here for the protection of the people – not for the king and not for parliamentary soldiers who want to fight battles. You were appointed as Castle Governor – not Town Governor. The castle walls may still stand, but the buildings are ruinous and no fit place for townsfolk to lodge, especially the women and children." His wife and daughter shouted their support. He carried on regardless. "If we were all to go there, it would be an invitation to the king's soldiers to march into the town and fire our houses. I propose that we refuse this request from the Castle Governor to take our guns, and call on all honest townsmen to join the defence corps and help guard our ditches."

"It won't do!" Hutchinson was dismissive. "I saw how easily the town ditches were overrun at Newark because they were badly manned. Townsfolk who have not been properly trained as soldiers cannot be trusted. I'm not satisfied with the vigilance of the town watch – some of the men could be turncoats, if the going gets rough."

This last remark caused an angry roar from the assembly. Dr. Plumtree, who had the loudest voice, shouted out that he and most townsmen were as honest as the colonel. Hutchinson shouted back at him. Plumtree jumped up, knocking over his jar. The Mayor struggled to keep order, whilst Dr Plumtree and Sam dived to try to gather up the leeches. Sam scooped up two, with his good hand, but was dismayed to see two more climbing up the table leg, and was afraid to disturb the councillors by pointing this out, through all the uproar.

"I would remind the Castle Governor," the Mayor shouted "that he is not the only commissioned officer present. Sir John Meldrum gave me the rank of captain and I have two hundred loyal men at my command. Francis Pierrepont, you live amongst us, what have you to say?"

With obvious reluctance, Colonel Pierrepont rose to his feet.

"I've lived in this town for several years, and recently took a hand myself in digging the trenches. I'm prepared to stand on the defences as long as they can be defended, but the bare fact is there is no way they can be held against the combined forces of Lord Newcastle, the men from Newark and the other royal troops. We'd be outnumbered ten to one, and their soldiers are more experienced. Yesterday, I had the painful task of telling my soldiers that the odds were against us. I gave them three options – take the coward's choice and leave the area, fight the enemy from the castle walls, or man the town ditches and have your throats cut! My troop voted to a man to fight the enemy from the castle. I invite you all to come and join us. Bring your families and your valuables. We've ample storage in the caves below."

He was greeted with dismay. Many rose to protest, and above the din, Elizabeth Drury was heard shouting "I thought you'd more sense, Francis Pierrepont. How can all the old folk and the babes live amongst soldiers in that cold ruin?"

Alderman Toplady was incensed. "She spoke, Mr Mayor!" he cried, pointing, "from the stranger's bench. I've been thirty years on the town council, and never before heard a woman's voice in this chamber!"

"Well, it's time you did!" shouted Elizabeth.

"Here, here!" cried Alice.

Alderman Toplady jumped to his feet with a screech. Alice thought he was beside himself because she'd spoken, but then she saw a leech crawling on his hand. He hopped around the floor, like a demented dancer, shouting "There's one of those creatures crawling up my thigh."

Dr Plumtree rushed to his aid, captured it on his glove and popped it back in the jar. Then he did the same with the one on Toplady's hand.

John Hutchinson started speaking again, and Alice resumed her task of scribing.

"You asked me to come here and justify the moving of the cannons. This I have done. Remember, there is a greater issue than the safety of your houses. It is the safety of the nation. I am responsible to parliament for holding the castle fortress. The cannons don't belong to you or me – but to parliament. As I answer to my maker, no vote of yours will stop me saving them. I gave the command this morning!"

"What! This is a device to keep us here, while they steal our cannons!" roared Drury. Hutchinson moved to leave the room, but Dr Plumtree leaped to bar his way. "I denounce you as a traitor!" he cried. "You care not a fig for this town, only for yourself and your crop-eared troops!"

There was instant uproar in the chamber. The doctor was thrust aside. The colonels both marched out, followed by the angry councillors and spectators. Alice was caught in the press and found herself tumbling out into the street, where she had a glimpse of Tom waiting for his master and holding Steadfast's reins.

Hutchinson and Pierrepont quickly swung into their saddles. Dr Plumtree tried to grasp the governor's bridle, but Hutchinson lashed out with his whip.

"How dare you hit me!" the stunned doctor shouted, throwing the jar of leeches at the colonel. But the jar missed and John Hutchinson took no notice. With a flick of the spur, Steadfast moved forwards, and Alice saw the governor riding towards the castle, with Tom following on Hasty.

CHAPTER 8

WOMEN TAKE THE LEAD

As soon as John Hutchinson and his followers disappeared from view, Alderman Drury issued his command; "Surround the guns!"

Alice, Sam and Elizabeth joined the crowd, running down Middle Pavement and along Bridlesmith Gate towards the ditches. They were in time to see a team of soldiers and horses dragging a cannon along Cockstool Row.

The alderman placed himself in front of the troops: "Stop! I command you in the name of the town council to take this cannon back to where it came from."

"Stand aside!" A stoney-faced officer rode up and faced him.

"The town council's just voted against removing these guns, Laurence Palmer. We're sending a letter to Parliament stating that we have no confidence in the Castle Governor. You must leave the guns in the ditches until there is an official ruling from Parliament!" The alderman stood his ground.

Captain Palmer repeated his order: "Stand Aside. The town council has no authority in this matter!"

Alice was astonished to see her father fling himself on the gun barrel. She moved forwards to join him, but was thrown to the ground. Staggering up, she saw him being hauled up by two burly soldiers.

"Are you all right, father?" Sam was at his side.

"Obstruct our orders, would you? This is a military operation and I command this troop. Tie him up and bring him to the castle!" Palmer was fuming.

The crowd shouted angrily as Alderman Drury was bound to a horse, protesting all the time. He was then led under military escort to the castle.

"You won't get away with this," shouted Mistress Drury, "Not while I live and breathe!"

"What can we do?" Sam cried as he chased after the soldiers, but his mother called him back, begging him not to make matters worse. "Until now, it's the men who've run everything in this town and the whole country, come to that. Just look what a mess they're making of it. It's time for the women to take over. I'm going to call a meeting of wives and mothers. We'll get your father freed and show the men folk how to save the town. Alice and Sam, here's work for you both. Go and knock on every door in your father's ward. Say that their elected alderman has been arrested and all the women are to come tonight to Vault Hall after supper. I'm going to form a Women's' Watch."

"I'll help," said Dr. Plumtree, looking up from his task of recapturing leeches, that were now crawling all over the cobbles.

"No, you won't," said Mistress Drury. "No offence, but this is women's work. If they know men are involved, some of them won't come. We need all the women to face their men and tell them what needs be done to save the town. I'll lead this meeting and Alice will take notes. Sam can come. I don't mind lads, but no grown men. They're sure to try to take over and wreck everything again!"

With that, she stalked off, with Alice and Sam running to keep up with her.

* * *

The women came: young and old, matrons with children, tradesmen's wives, servant girls, pot girls from the taverns, one old dame of eighty and even the wives and daughters of some of the other aldermen. They were puzzled and agitated. There had never been a gathering like this before that any of them could remember.

They were invited into the parlour. Alice brought in drinks and found that there were not enough chairs for everyone. Some people were resting on the floor and she had to step carefully between them to pass the flagons round. Elizabeth was saying, "Between them, the men have made a mess of this whole business. It's our job now to pick up the pieces and decide where we go from here. We've worn ourselves out digging those trenches around the town, but without the cannons they are useless. Our men can't keep the Newarkers out and if they try they'll be cut to bits in the ditches. I know they're supposed to work in shifts, but if we value their lives, we must stop them going out."

"How?" several voices asked.

"You know your men. Keep them at home, with your food and your ale and other pleasures. Women's wiles, that's the way to do it. If we let them man the ditches, one day you'll see them go out and not return, and then who's to provide for the children?"

"My man says we're all to go and live in the castle," a young girl with a baby said.

"That may be his choice, but is it yours? Think for yourselves, each of you. How will babes fare in that broken down ruin? It may be fine for the able-bodied, but can we take all the toddlers and old folk? Are we to leave them behind? You must each of you decide. Don't just leave it to the men. My vote is for staying put. If the Newarkers come, bolt your doors and stay inside. They won't linger here. They'll run to the castle. Let them fight the soldiers there, not in the town. If we set up a look-out post in the old archway at the top of Vault Hill, we'll get warning of the approach. From there you can see for miles, down to the River Trent and beyond."

There was a buzz of approval.

"They might come by night, you wouldn't see them then," an elderly crone said.

"They'd need lanterns to pick their way across those marshy meadows, and they'd be seen from the archway. One thing more, we need to set up refuges for those who lose their homes. Any of you could get a door smashed in or your thatch set on fire. I've already spoken to Parson Goodall about this and he's said he'll let us use the side aisle at St. Peter's as a safe place in which to stay the night. I'm going to see Parson Laycock at St. Mary's tomorrow, on the same matter. We'll need different women on duty at each refuge every night. Alice, bring a quill and scrolls. You can make out a list of volunteers for each night of the week. This ward will be the first to be ready. Then we can speak to the church wardens and make sure that every ward in the town is covered too."

In the face of such danger, the women were empowered by these ideas. Many volunteered to do tasks that were new to them. Alice had more confidence now that she had something positive to do, and set about listing the names, the times and skills offered, and the food, blankets and equipment needed for the refuges, where these could be found and where they would be stored in readiness.

* * *

The next few days were tense, both in the town and the castle. The mayor set up a day and night watch. Under strong pressure from the women, he agreed that there would be no resistance in the town itself. He insisted though, that if the enemy were sighted, the castle must be warned.

Some families with a man already based there went to join him, and a few others left their homes and moved to the castle, but most stayed where they were. The women equipped the churches as refuges, with straw bedding and supplies. Sam and Alice prepared two refuges, one in the caves below Vault Hall and the other at the tannery.

They both took their turns at the archway look-out. Someone donated a spy glass and, with its help, they could see for miles on a clear day. Beyond the meadows, there was the whole expanse of the winding river, and on the far side, they could pick out the tower of Pierrepont Church, beside the hall. This was enemy territory now.

"The Newarkers'll come by boat and we'll see them coming," Sam spoke with authority.

Alice wasn't so sure. "They'll know we expect that, so perhaps they'll try to take us by surprise. They might find a path through Thorneywood and come over the penny footbridge."

Sam laughed. "They could never do that – with all their horses and guns? No, the river would be much easier and safer. They've things to transport."

All the same, Alice mentioned her concern to her mother and she agreed. "Most like, they could split their forces. We'll post a woman by the footbridge over the beck as a lookout."

That afternoon, Sam came to relieve Alice, who was on watch in the archway, and brought her serious news.

"Father's been moved. I went to the gatehouse today to ask if they would let me see him and the guard commander told me, he wasn't there any longer. He's been sent to Derby with some others, under an escort led by Colonel Ireton."

"Derby? Why?"

"They won't give a reason. Perhaps they think there's less chance of him escaping. He said that he was taken yesterday with some other Nottingham prisoners and Colonel Pierrepont's staying there for a while to keep an eye on things. I'm glad about that. Better him than Hutchinson or Palmer."

"Oh, Sam. Why can't he come home? He doesn't mean any harm. It's just that he wants to spare the town all this danger."

Sam shrugged his shoulders, and took the spyglass. He peered through it.

"The road's quiet," he said. "There's a man with a cart crossing the meadows."

Alice took the glass. "Yes, I see him – probably a market trader. Looks innocent, but I'll keep an eye on him, just in case." She turned the telescope to the west, towards the tower of Wilford Church, and the bluff outcrop of rock and woodland across the river.

"Nothing there."

"Give me the glass again. I'll watch the water-craft."

She handed it over, saying, "I don't know why you feel so sure they'll come by river."

"I've told you before." Sam was impatient with her. "They'll have guns. They can't lug them up the dales. They'll bring them on barges."

"Well, I've told my worries to mother and she's going to have a woman stationed at the penny footbridge, just in case. You never know, Sam. They could come from both directions."

Sam sighed and said nothing more. *He's unusually tetchy these days,* Alice thought. *Now father's away, perhaps he thinks that he should be in charge of the family, but with mother such a determined woman, that will never be.*

CHAPTER 9

THE CASTLE FORTRESS

Events at the castle moved swiftly over the next few days. Tom helped as the guns were fixed in position. Forty barrels of gunpowder and match-cord were safely stowed in caves. Fifty townsmen moved in with their belongings. Most of them were the more resolute members of the mayor's regiment. Several brought their wives and children with them, and tents were set up in the outer bailey to accommodate them, together with some pens for sheep, goats and hens.

Tom was very surprised to find Jed among the castle soldiers. He had last seen him wearing the king's colours on the day the standard was raised.

"We never got paid," Jed explained glumly. "It was all promises and came to nothing, so I moved over when the parliament lads attacked Newark. Slipped the lines and marched away with Hutchinson's boys. I'm still waiting for pay day here, though," he added ruefully.

There was a cold attitude about the men in the castle now. Some of them were afraid, but others were clearly looking forward to the opportunity to use the cannons that had been brought in.

Tom did not like the atmosphere. He remembered how, as a young boy, he and his friends had played "Sailors and Spaniards". The bigger boys always took the "Jack Tar" parts and the younger boys had to be Spaniards. He was small, so he nearly always got tied up and bullied. This time it was for real though: no longer just a game.

When he had the chance, Tom liked to escape the shouting sergeants, and the noise of clanging hammers. He would go into the courtyard where Lucy Hutchinson and her sister, Barbara, presided over the stew-pots, which were slung over an open fire. They had created a place of safety for the children by converting two old rooms off the castle-yard, making them cosy with woolsacks and cushions. Tapestries had been draped over the old stone walls and there were hanging baskets with colourful flowers and even a chirping bird in a cage.

Tom preferred the company of the gentler women, and liked to amuse the toddler, Jack. John Hutchinson and his brother, George, were so busy with their duties,that they seldom came to this little haven. Preparing for the battles to come was turning them into harder men.

"I don't like Captain Palmer," Lucy confided to Tom one day. "Yesterday, he asked John if little Jack had been christened yet. He had the gall to suggest that he might do it himself. I know he's in holy orders, but I'll hazard he bought that parish post in Gedling. John and I don't hold with infant baptism. Jack will make his own declaration of faith, when he's old enough to understand about sin and salvation."

This idea was a new one to Tom. He had heard that the Hutchinsons were puritans, but did not really understand what that meant. Nevertheless, he shared her dislike of the loud-mouthed captain.

Soon afterwards, the governor summoned everyone into the castle yard. John Hutchinson, flanked by his brother George and Captain Palmer, quietened the crowd, as the governor addressed them all.

"I've called you all to warn you that the enemy is approaching and that their men greatly outnumber ours. But we have the advantage of our position, here on the castle rock and we know that God is on our side! We are fighting for His true church. He calls upon you all to make a sacrifice, even as Christ did for you. The testing time is upon us, when the Evil One, like a devouring lion, is at our gate!"

"Your homes lie in the town, and you may be tempted to put family first when the enemy comes. You may see your houses burning. You may see your loved ones cruelly abused, but those who are loyal will stay at their posts, even if we should face a long siege. All this, I am resolved to do myself. If necessary, I will die for this cause, for my first loyalty is to my maker. Comrades, I invite you all to join me. Anyone who wishes can leave now! All I ask is that those who choose to stay, sign this pledge – that you will be faithful, one to another and to me, for we will stand together and hold this place – until death, if need be – without any parley or terms from the enemy."

He waved a large paper in the air.

"I have signed first – I lay it down here on this mounting block, so that those who wish to sign may add their names. Tomorrow, all who have signed will observe a solemn day of prayer and fast in token of our pledge. God save us all!"

Just a few people moved forward as commanded, others looked down as they walked away.

Captain Palmer seized the paper and was about to demand more signatures, when Major George intervened.

"Give them time, Laurence," he said. "We want no coercion."

* * *

The following day Tom and several others were set to work building a wooden gun platform on a small outcrop of rock half way down the sheer rock face. In order to reach the spot, they had to descend through a winding tunnel inside the rock.

Laurence Collin, who was leading the work party, told them that this cave was known as Mortimer's Hole. It had been used as a secret entrance to the castle many years ago.

"Why is it called Mortimer's Hole?" asked Tom.

"I'm told it's after a man called Roger Mortimer who was a traitor and held the castle at the time. Young King Henry the Third climbed up this tunnel secretly, and seized it. This was many years ago. We're not going to let anyone try to do this again. Our gun emplacement at the base will be manned to ensure no one surprises us," he added.

When Tom, Jed and the others emerged into the daylight, they found that they were perched on a little ledge of rock about fifteen feet above the moat at the base of the cliff. It was a good vantage point from which to observe the lanes approaching the castle. On the ledge there was a weathered dovecote, and the startled birds flapped about frantically, as if they knew that their territory was about to be invaded.

"We'll soon have this down!" shouted Collin, as he wielded

an axe above his shoulders, and started to hack at the base of the birdhouse.

"Careful! There might be some young chicks in there!" warned Tom.

Jed laughed as he batted the birds, which dived at their heads.

"No time for sentiment!" said Collin. "We must have this platform ready for tonight, so we can lower the culverin tomorrow. Those lanes will be blocked up with barricades, so we will have a double line of defence. Take this hammer, Marriott, and nail those planks together – be quick about it!"

By now, the doves had fled, to find a safer place to roost.

Tom set about his task with a heavy heart. He was baffled to understand how a God fearing man like Collin could be so uncaring. A cannon shot was a brutal way to die. One of the Rhineland veterans had given him some disturbing war-like advice, "You've got to hate the swine you're facing when you fire the shot or when you put the knife in!"

"Hold! There's an envoy coming!" Laurence Collin pointed across to the Brewhouse Yard. Tom saw a boat being moored at the Castle Quay on the River Leen. Three men were climbing out of it and one of them was carrying a white flag of truce.

"I know that man in the plumed hat!" Tom whispered to Jed. "It's Colonel Hutchinson's cousin, Richard Byron…"

Collin overheard: "Is it, by God!" He checked himself then, because although he was a soldier, he rarely swore. "He's Governor of Newark, and recently knighted for his work at Edgehill, You had better climb back up that tunnel, Marriott, and let the Colonel know – look sharp!"

Tom was glad to be of service. He ran back into the cave and was met by a wall of darkness. Coming down with all the others, and a lantern to guide them was bearable – this was quite another matter! He overcame his fear, as there was no time to lose. A flag of truce must be a good thing – surely?

A little grazed and dazzled by the sudden brightness of daylight, Tom emerged at the upper level and then ran across the castle courtyard towards the governor's headquarters. Lucy was playing at spinning-top with young Jack.

"Where's Colonel Hutchinson!" he panted. "Richard Byron's here – Sir Richard, I mean. He's landed at the quay, with a flag of truce."

Lucy looked annoyed. "He's not trying that trick again? First – he sends us letters, now he comes in person!"

"I thought it a good sign..." Tom faltered. "Perhaps the Newarkers are in some difficulty."

Lucy gave a hollow laugh. "If they had any problems, we would be the last to know. Cousin he may be, but Sir Richard has greedy eyes on our estate – and I'll vouch he's here again to press the old argument. If John will make terms, he can keep his lands and the governorship. Otherwise, he'll lose everything!"

John and George Hutchinson could be seen in the room beyond, engaged in earnest conversation. Lucy went to the door to tell them: "Byron's on his way to see you."

"I know – the look-out sent me word." John replied. "Go and see him, George. There will be no surrender. It's pleased God to give me this task, and I'll see it through to the end. Tell him – there is enough of a Byron's blood in me to scorn betraying my trust."

George nodded. "Aye – I'll tell him plain. If he will have this castle – then he must wade to it in blood!"

* * *

Tom felt gloriously free as he cantered across the Castle Park on John Hutchinson's pride and joy, Steadfast. For two weeks he had been cooped up inside the overcrowded castle and now at last he had been given permission to leave for the afternoon and exercise the governor's horse on the parkland.

It was a bright winter day, and he was determined to make the most of it. After two circuits of the pasture, Tom decided that he would like to go to the town and call on the Drury family. It was not out of bounds, and would be more exercise for Steadfast. Ever since the arrest of Alderman Drury, Tom had been uneasy about Alice and Sam. He wondered if they knew that their father was now in Derby. He would take them what news he could.

The hooves rang on the cobbles of Low Pavement, as they slowly climbed up the hill to the Weekday Cross. He knew that there was no market here today. Houses were shuttered and the town was subdued. Tom rode up the High Pavement, drew the reins outside Vault Hall, dismounted and pulled the bell rope.

Alice came to the door. Her face was worried, but she beamed a greeting.

"Tom, how are you? Have you heard anything about father? We all want to know what's happening at the castle."

"They've sent your father to the Derby garrison. Major Ireton took him. I think he'll be quite well treated there. Francis Pierrepont has gone there too to liaise with their military governor and I'm sure he'll put a good word in for him."

"Take your horse to the stable, and come in so we can talk properly. I'll see you at the kitchen door."

Tom was there most of the afternoon. He learned that Sam was out on guard duty and that Elizabeth Drury was ill in bed and much of the work she'd started was now being done by Alice and Sam. Tom was dismayed to hear how bad relations were between those who lived in the town and those based in the castle, each blaming the other for shortages of food and equipment. Despite the strict code of conduct laid down by Governor Hutchinson, the soldiers were being accused by the townsfolk of pilfering and drunkenness. Tom feared that much of it might be true, since he had heard some of the garrison bragging about the rich pickings to be found.

"There are so many empty houses," Alice explained. "Some people have moved into the castle with their men folk, but more have fled the town. I know there are so many empty houses because I knock on the doors to collect food and supplies for the refuges we've now set up. A lot of the shutters and door latches have been broken and there's been a deal of pillaging. It's mainly the old folk and those with young children who are left behind, and most of them are very fearful."

There was serious concern in her voice. Tom came away moved but excited by his meeting with her. He liked that girl. He liked her a lot.

There was still time for a canter over the castle parkland, and Steadfast needed the exercise, so he decided to do a few rounds. Full of his own thoughts, Tom took longer than he'd intended and quite forgot to watch the winter sun sliding down in the sky.

At last he noticed that it was beginning to set. Oh dear, he'd be in trouble.

When he got to the postern gate, it was locked and no one responded to his shouts. He had to go round to the gatehouse, and there he was greeted by a surly sergeant who said he would report him to the governor for staying out beyond hours. Tom realised that he wanted a bribe to keep his mouth shut, but he had no money.

"Look, I've got the governor's horse here," Tom argued. "I'll have to put it back in the stable."

"What's all this arguing about?" a voice bellowed. Captain Palmer was swaying in the guardroom door, clearly the worse for drink: "Oh, it's you, Marriott. I've had enough of your family for one night. What do you want?"

Although he was mystified by the remark, Tom decided he'd best ignore it. "I need to stable the governor's horse, sir."

"Bit late for that isn't it. Oh well, get on with it then."

Tom was admitted through the archway. He knew that the whole Hutchinson family were dining with the mayor that night, but Palmer's behaviour was outrageous. And what on earth did he mean by saying he'd had enough of Tom's family? He could not make sense of it. Once he had stabled the horse, Tom turned in.

"Jed was lookin' for you," said one of his barrack-room mates, as he dished out the evening mutton stew.

"Jed. What did he want?"

"I dunno. Said somethin' about your sister."

"My sister?" Tom was puzzled, and after his supper, went out to look for Jed. But the boy had completely disappeared – yet another mystery. He lay quietly on his pallet bed, turning things over in his mind.

Tom: *Why is Palmer so cruel? Why is there so much brutality? It's not just our side. It's the others too. They're just as bad. It's the war that does this. But there's more to it than that. This isn't just a power struggle between king and parliament. It's also a struggle between people seeking power for themselves. They're angry and bitter, and when things don't work out as they want. They blame their neighbours, and call them the enemy. This is a sickness, formed through the war but it's also fed by local feuds. Hutchinson versus Byron, Palmer versus Hutchinson, and so it goes on. Bound together, this has created a weeping wound which pains the land.*

CHAPTER 10

WATCHERS IN THE NIGHT

Alice Drury was startled to hear the banging. The hourglass showed that it was the third hour in the morning, and she and Sam were sharing the night watch in the archway spanning Vault Lane. They were peering through the south window towards the river when the knocking started. Alice moved to the north window and looked out into Weekday Cross. There was someone banging on the front door.

"What do you want?" Alice opened the casement and called "What do you want?"

"It's Meg Marriott. I'm soaking wet. Can I come in?"

Alice was surprised to recognise the girl from the vegetable stall in the market.

Sam moved to the window. "It's Tom's sister. Let her in," he said, and went back to his look-out duty. Alice lit a candle, and made her way down the winding stairs to the guardroom door, which adjoined Vault Hall.

She opened it and invited Meg in. The girl was shivering and her clothes were sodden. "You'd best get out of those quickly. I'll get you some of mine. Then you can explain."

She called to Tom and then led Meg up to her bedroom, fetched a towel and spread a dress and under-garments on the bed. Although Alice was shorter, the clothes fitted well enough.

"I'd fetch my mother, but she's out on patrol tonight. She insisted on going, although she's not well. We think there could be an attack from the Newarkers at any time. Whatever's happened to you, Meg?"

"I was locked in a prison in the castle. I had to swim the moat. I'd gone with a letter to Colonel Pierrepont from his mother, the Countess, but the duty officer said he'd gone to Derby. Then he started insulting me and it ended up with him shutting me in a cell."

"He locked you in? How did you manage to escape?"

"I thought I'd never get out. But then one of the gaolers helped me. He wanted to break free himself. He was supposed to be guarding me and the duty officer had gone to bed, so we managed to get out through a passageway. He showed me the way, but we had to swim across the moat. The youth says he's finished with soldiering. He's tried both the armies and never got his pay from either side, so he's making for his mother's in Shelford."

Alice thought that she might know who the young soldier was, but she took it in her stride. "We'll do what we can for you," she said, "but we're very busy just now. We've watchers posted at each town gate and there's a women's patrol in every ward. If the king's soldiers come, we've seven shelters for the families. One of them is in the caves here below this house. We've prepared food stores in case there's a long siege. It might be necessary to stay secure for a week or more, so we have a woman in every street who's promised to knock up her neighbours if the Newarkers come."

"Who planned all this?"

"The women's watch. The men drew up lists for manning the ditches. My mother told them that it was all useless after they'd taken away the culverans, so she set up the shelters instead. There's one in each of the seven wards. She organised food collections for them all, and tonight she's meeting the leading women in each of the town wards to see how things are working out."

"Are you one of the watchers?"

"I'm the scribe. I keep the notes." Alice was obviously proud of her duties. "I've been active with the women's groups ever since that Captain Palmer arrested my father. They say he's a preacher, but there's more hate than love in his heart."

"Palmer, that was his name!" Meg broke in. "That was the man who put me in the cell." She started to explain, but suddenly, there was a loud wail from the street outside.

They jumped in surprise.

"That sounded like our signal," Alice said. They went to the window and peered
out, but could see little in the darkness.

"The women were told to cry out if the enemy came and then to bang every door and give warning."

"Is that someone by your doorstep?" Meg pointed down. They saw a shadowy figure move away. Something like a bundle of clothes was left behind.

"I'm going down." Alice led the way down the stairs. Cautiously, she drew the bolts and opened the door. The still figure of a woman lay spread on the cobbles. With horror, Alice realised that it was her mother.

She rushed to stoop beside her. Her head flopped hopelessly as she tried to raise it, and a gush of blood streamed from a neck wound. Alice cradled her mother's head, as she tried to stanch the blood with a kerchief.

"Get Sam!"

Meg ran back into the house. Alice felt tears welling up but stifled them.

"Mother" she whispered, and for a brief moment Elizabeth opened her eyes. She struggled for breath. Alice's fear was transformed into energy and strong determination. She must save her. Everything depended on how she acted.

"Alice, don't mind me," Elizabeth gasped. "But quick, you must open the shelter...spread the word...the Newarkers ... they've come!"

Grief, anxiety to do the right thing, fear for the town: these conflicting emotions swept through Alice. Then she quietly took command of the situation.

"Mother, can you hear me?"

There was no reply. Suddenly, Sam was stooping beside her.

"She's passed out," Alice told him. "If I move, the blood will start again. I must hold her. Sam – rouse the neighbours. We need their help to bind mother's neck and move her into the house. And we must tell them they can take refuge here. Meg, you can help too. Quick, but be quiet when you pass the word. We don't want the soldiers on us."

Sam hesitated, appalled by the situation.

"Go on," Alice ordered. "Both of you. I'll cope with Mother. I must."

"Come." Sam seized Meg's arm and she followed him out into the street.

Sam started knocking on the doors. Meg watched what he was doing and then crossed the road and did the same . The message was simple. "The Newarkers are here!"

Some folk were ready to leave: a few houses appeared to be deep in slumber. Swiftly and silently, figures appeared; some muffled in greatcoats, others in night attire, some with babes in arms, others with aged parents. A line of refugees, clutching precious bundles, streamed up the hill to the safety of Vault Hall.

Neighbours came to help Alice, and gently she was lifted over the threshold and into the house and laid on cushions. Her wound was washed and dressed whilst she was asleep. When Meg returned, Alice remained at her side, still as a statue. She looked up.

"Meg, stay by mother," she commanded. "I must check the roster."

She went to a drawer, produced a scroll and, unrolling it, began to check all the neighbours she had seen enter.

"Is Bessie Charlton here? Can you go and check, Susannah. See if she and her babe are in the cave, and while you're there ask if anyone has seen old Reuben Sandby. I didn't see him come. Meg, did you check the houses in Listergate?"

"What about the castle? Has someone sent them word?" Sam enquired.

"Can't do that," was the terse reply of a grey-haired man in a striped nightshirt.

"Who says?"

"Alderman Toplady. 'E's guard commander tonight and no one dares cross 'im."

"Guard commander! He's being held at gunpoint in the Guildhall, so I was told," said a sturdy matron. "Bound to a chair with ropes. He can't command a dog."

"Be that as it may," said the man in the nightshirt, "'e's in charge, and one of the watch told me that 'e ordered them not to tell the castle if the Newarkers came. If we did that they said they'll fire all our thatches and set the town ablaze."

"God help us all," said a woman in widow's black.

"You'd best go down to the caves, the lot of you," said Alice. "Meg and Sam will keep watch up here, and I'll stay by mother. You'll find some ale down there to warm you, and there are skins and rugs on the floor." With muttered thanks, the neighbours moved towards the stone steps that led to the rock cellars below.

CHAPTER 11

THE MESSENGER

Tom was awakened by the morning drum roll known as reveille. This was the signal for the garrison to rise, and also marked the changing of the guard.

He stirred slowly, then suddenly gunfire rent the air. The barrack room was in turmoil. People dashed to the doorway. Another round of gunshots – then yells of pain from the gatehouse area and the thud of the great gates slamming together. Everyone in the barrack room dashed outside.

The castle yard was in uproar. Tom saw John Hutchinson running barefoot, in his nightshirt, towards the keep. He leaped up the outside stone steps to the new look out post on the roof. "There's shooting from the houses opposite," he cried, "To the guns. Man all cannons on the east wall. Return fire!"

All was confusion. Tom rushed to his place beside a cannon on the outer wall, to assist Laurence Collin and his team.

"What's happening?" Tom asked a grizzle-haired veteran.

"Newarkers, no doubt," the gunner replied. "They must have crept in after midnight and seized the town.

"Where's Jed?" demanded Collin,

"Dunno," said Tom. "I haven't seen him yet or last night."

"Not him too. There was too many of our men out last night. Blast that rat Palmer, and his guard. Look, the Newarkers 'ave got the houses opposite. You'll have to work double hard and do Jed's job as well as your own. Help me load this culverin."

"I saw them try to storm the gatehouse," said one of the gunnery crew, "They fired at us when our gates opened to let out the night guards. They'd have got in too, if we hadn't slammed the gates tight shut!"

"Stop gabbing, Marshall and help load!" Collin bawled.

They had to stoop low over the gun. Fire boomed from a cannon, newly placed on the tower of St. Nicholas's Church. It was raking the whole of the lower bailey, making movement across it impossible. The gunnery teams were imprisoned in the upper bailey by this fire and separated from the gatehouse team.

It took time to get Collin's gun ready for action and the first time it fired Tom was stunned by the noise it made. A roll of thick smoke enveloped all the gunnery team. Their eyes smarted and they found themselves coughing and spluttering, but gradually they got used to handling the situation.

Whilst Tom and two others laboured to help Collin, the governor called an emergency meeting in the keep. All morning Tom sweated as he lifted cannon balls, and helped to load the smoking culverin. Their shots were falling well short of the church tower, but they did breach the walls of some of the houses opposite, where muskets were peeping through windows and peppering everything within reach with deadly shot.

In this hurley burley a man, bent double to avoid the shots, came running with an urgent message. "Governor's orders. Tom Marriott to report to the keep immediately."

"I can't spare a man." Collin was angry. "Go, Marriott, but tell the governor that I'm keeping his messenger working on this gun team until you return. You're trained. I can't really spare you."

Surprised, but glad to be relieved for a few minutes, Tom ducked, as he hurried across the yard. Someone had seen movement, because a bullet flew past his head and lodged in the wall beside him.

John Hutchinson was in close conference with his brother, while nearby Lucy and Barbara were washing the bloodied arm of a wounded guardsman, who was moaning and wincing with pain.

"Can we get a message to Cousin Ireton? "George was saying. "He'd be a useful ally."

"No chance," the Governor replied. "He's been called to the eastern counties by that new man, Colonel Cromwell." Then looking up he said, "Tom Marriott, we need your services." John Hutchinson was peremptory. "As you know, our cavalry horses are all stabled in Castlegate and Houndsgate, and now they're behind enemy lines. We only have two horses here in the castle, mine and George's. I can trust you with Steadfast, and you know the road to Derby, so I am writing a letter to Sir John Gell, the military governor there, and you will take it to him. I'll give you another for Francis Pierrepont, who's also there. We're sending Mason on George's horse to Leicester. You'll go tonight, under cover of darkness. I can rely on you, can't I, boy? Lucy suggested I sent for you as you know the horse so well."

"Of course." Tom was honoured. He glanced at Lucy, who looked up for a moment, smiled and then returned to the gory task of extracting bullet splinters from the man's arm.

"You must realise the importance of this mission," the Governor continued. "We're hopelessly outnumbered. Over half our men are trapped in the town, and others in the gatehouse. We can't get to them because of the firing across the lower bailey and we can't man the cannons in the middle and lower baileys. For all we know, Lord Newcastle's army from the north may be on his way now to take over from the Newarkers. It's essential that the enemy are attacked from the rear, and only the Derby or Leicester Garrisons can do that. We'll slip you out of the postern gate when night falls, and God go with you."

* * *

The night ride to Derby was a frightening affair. There was an eerie, moonless sky, and very little sound from Steadfast's hooves, as they had been specially bound in cloth. Tom had two sealed papers, in his greatcoat pocket one was addressed to Sir John Gell, Parliamentary Governor of Derby, and the other to Colonel Francis Pierrepont.

A startled sentry challenged Tom from the bushes at Park Valley, but he did not stop. There was a bang and a bullet whistled over his head. Tom spurred Steadfast faster. He could hear the pounding of a rider behind him, in hot pursuit.

"Quick! Steadfast – we musn't let them catch us!"

Tom knew that everyone depended on him. If the town fell to the Royalists, there would be free passage for the king's forces over the Trent from north and south. He realised that the Duke of Newcastle's men from York might join with Prince Rupert's cavalry – perhaps the whole cause would be lost.

Tom bent forward, jockey style, and whispered encouragement in the horse's ear. In a blind gallop, he kept repeating the words: "We must get through, we must get through!" matching the rhythm to the pounding hooves. His thighs were rubbed raw and he felt his heart pounding. Only when the sounds of his pursuer ceased, did he dare slacken the pace. But this was not the end of their troubles.

Steadfast suddenly shied in fear but Tom clung tightly and did not lose his seat. A moment later he saw what caused it. The broken branch of a tree was caught between the two front hooves. Gently, Tom soothed the horse, slipped down, disentangled the branch and threw it aside.

They had been cantering dangerously on a dark night. He must take greater care. It was about twelve miles to his destination. He had ridden to Derby before, but that was in daylight and there had been no urgency. Trying to remember the landmarks and road junctions on the governor's map was no simple task.

Tom mounted again, engaging the horse in an easy trot. This was more sensible. The important thing was to get there safely. The next few miles passed without incident, although he went wrong and landed up in a sleeping farmyard, where a fierce dog was soon barking at his heels.

At last, Tom recognised an inn which he recalled was near to the town. Then he saw the glow of a watchman's brazier on the side of the road.

"Who goes there?" a gruff voice demanded.

Tom brought the horse to a standstill, dismounted, and was confronted with a flint-lock musket, aimed at his head. To his great relief though, he also recognised the orange sash of a parliamentary guard.

"I'm a messenger from the Nottingham parliamentary garrison. I've letters from Colonel Hutchinson for Sir John Gell and Colonel Pierrepont."

The soldier was suspicious and asked to see the letters. Tom passed them over and showed him the governor's seal. The man nodded and asked if Tom carried any weapons. His pistol was confiscated, and he was then taken to a guard hut, where other soldiers took him, under armed escort to the main guardroom carrying Tom's gun. The letters were handed to the officer on duty there.

"Sir John's away on a military campaign. Colonel Pierrepont should be able to identify you." The officer was cautious. "We can't be too careful these days!"

The escort marched him along the streets, until they came to a large mansion, guarded by more soldiers.

Once inside, he was shown into a wood-panelled parlour, where an auburn-haired maidservant told him that Colonel Pierrepont was not yet awake, and he would have to wait a while.

Tom felt tired and hungry. He asked if he could have something to eat while he waited. The girl led him to the servants' hall, where he joined others who were breakfasting in bowls of steaming porridge. Those around quizzed him about his errand, and then how things were in Nottingham.

Tom did not think it right to speak about the attack, so he simply explained that he was the stable-boy to Colonel Hutchinson and had been sent with letters.

"Who owns this house?" he asked.

"Well now there's a question," said one of the serving men. "It used to be a great gentleman's house, but he has fled with his family, and Sir John Gell's taken possession and brought his officers with him, but I doubt he has the title deeds."

There was a laugh from a plump cook. "Some of these military men have no notion of how to conduct themselves in a great house like this."

"That Mr Pierrepont from Nottingham is different though – he's a proper gentleman, he is. Not a jumped up monkey, like Sir John," the girl next to him whispered.

"Or a dull-headed Dutchman like Major Malanus!" said another maid.

"Do you know Colonel Pierrepont? Where does he live? I wager he's got a grand house!"

The cook was keen for Nottingham gossip. "Do they still have jugglers and gypsies telling fortunes at the Goose Fair? Are there lots of soldiers in the town? 'Ave you been in at the fightin'?"

All this tittle-tattle was cut short when Francis Pierrepont's step was heard coming down the stairs. Tom hurried out to meet him and was invited into the parlour.

The Colonel looked grave as Tom told him briefly of the attack. He then took the letter in silence, and scanned it before speaking:

"You say there is one for Sir John Gell too?"

"Yes, sir." Tom passed it over. Francis glanced at it and rang the bell.

"Ah, Marie – send for Major Malanus – tell him to hasten here at once!" He turned back to Tom, and spoke confidentially: "This is a bad business, Marriott, if Newcastle's men come to Nottingham as well as the Newarkers, There'll be no holding them. It appears that the Royalists are right up to the castle walls and firing into the yard…"

Tom nodded, "We'd intended to block off the approach lanes today. Yesterday we were putting up barricades at the ends of Castlegate and Houndsgate, but we weren't able to finish them – so now they're held by the enemy."

The door opened and a gaunt man, with thinning hair strode into the room.

"Malanus – there is an urgent letter here for Sir John. Nottingham's been attacked and they need reinforcements – fast! Go with this sealed letter immediately. Find him, wherever he is. Sheffield, I think. Tell him that I am going to Nottingham today with my own men, but they will need an army. Gell is to send us all the men he can spare!"

The Dutchman accepted the letter, and after a few short questions, he turned to go.

"Oh, and send Marie in. I need some breakfast." Francis looked kindly at Tom. "You must be hungry, boy, after that long ride in the dark. Come – eat with me!"

Tom did not like to admit that he had already eaten in the servants' hall, so just nodded and joined Colonel Pierrepont at the table. Gentleman and stable-boy talked as they ate, rank laid aside in the urgency of the hour.

"You say that Hutchinson took a roll-call, and there were only eighty men in the castle? That's terrible – where were all the others?"

"Sleeping in the town, sir. They were mostly local men." Tom replied.

"But that was expressly against orders. Who was the duty officer last night?"

"Captain Palmer, sir."

"Palmer! That parson fellow from Gedling! I never trusted him. I don't like his theology, or his manners – and now this! How do men like him get holy orders? That's what I'd like to know! He's well named. A few shillings in the palm, I suspect. He was never short of silver, that one. He bought his commission, too. It's his sort we are fighting to be free of!"

"He was the worse for drink when I saw him last night," said Tom.

"And he was the duty officer!" Francis was scandalised. "I tell you what, Marriott, when this battle's over, I'll have him stripped of his commission for yesterday's doings. Do you know why I support Parliament? It's because I believe in the rule of law, regardless of rank or privilege. That goes for the king, as well as his subjects. Too many people have squirmed their way into positions of power and then use it to trample others. What troubles me most is that I see this attitude on both sides of the conflict. There are too few honest men left in the kingdom. Remember that thought, young Marriott, when it's your turn in life to make decisions! Come with me now and we'll round up all the Nottingham men who are here temporarily. I've send the letter on to Sir John and it's up to him then to respond as soon as he can, with a sizeable force."

When they had finished eating, Colonel Pierrepont led Tom across the yard to a smaller building.

"This is where we house the malcontents," he said, with a smile. He opened the door, and to his surprise, Tom came face to face with a rather dishevelled Alderman Drury.

"You two know one another, I believe. Well, Tom Marriott can bring you all the news from Nottingham. You've cooled your heels long enough now, alderman! Come back with us and you can help save your town! I'm off to round up all the Nottingham men who came here with me. We'll leave within the hour."

As soon as he understood the situation, the alderman agreed to come and help. Once, Colonel Pierrepont had left the room, he smiled grimly at Tom.

"So, it's come to this. The town's fallen, just as I said it would, when Hutchinson moved the guns. He treated me like a rebel. But Pierrepont saw my argument and has always been civil to me. Well, I'll support Hutchinson now, since the town's in peril, but once it's quit of these royalists, I'll fight for parliament no more."

CHAPTER 12

BESIEGED

Cannon fire! Tom had difficulty in controlling his terrified horse. He was cantering through the woodland with Colonel Pierrepont's men, heading for the northern sally port. The attack was coming from the other side of the castle. Despite the fact that they were not in the line of fire, the noise was deafening, and so was the response. As the battle was raging on the town side, they were able to enter by the side gate, without being molested by the enemy.

"Thank God – you've got through!" The sergeant at the gate mopped his brow. "Are the Derby reinforcements following?"

"I've sent the message on to Sir John Gell – I've no doubt he'll be coming," Pierrepont replied.

"We need them sorely. Two of our men are dead and many wounded. We've got two watches with forty men in each of them against hundreds attacking us. We've only three officers here, the Hutchinsons and Cap'n bloody Palmer, and we've fourteen guns to man!"

Francis Pierrepont went immediately to report to John Hutchinson, and the others were soon assigned tasks. Seeing there was no way of reaching his family in the town, Alderman Drury volunteered to join one of the gunnery crews.

"You can help the diggers," the sergeant said to Tom. "The lower bailey was a no-go area yesterday because of enemy fire. They're digging a trench tonight, to enable safe movement and we've a stack of woolsacks to protect it."

"They 'ad us 'oled up in separate parts of the castle before we 'ad these trenches," the man digging in front of Tom explained.

All morning, he sweated in the trenches, till his clothes stuck to his back and his hands were covered with blisters. But as soon as Laurence Collin got word that he was there, Tom was called back to the gunnery platform.

Tom saw the familiar stout figure of Alderman Drury now working as one of the crew.

"Drury told me you were digging trenches. That's monkey's work. I can't lose an experienced hand. Help sponge out the hot cannon." Collin gave Tom a kindly pat on the back.

Enemy fire was still being aimed at them from the houses over the road, so they had to stoop as they plunged the long pole down the mouth of the cannon to cool it with the damp lamb's wool wad. The routine was the same as yesterday.

"The wad's drying out. Tom and Ginger, go and fill more buckets."

The two lads picked up the leather buckets and scurried across the yard to the well. Crouching and running with empty buckets was not difficult, but with full ones, it was precarious. A bullet hit the other youth as he returned. He dropped the pail and fell, clutching his shoulder. Tom arrived at his side at the same time as Laurence Collin, who quickly inspected the wound.

"That's bad. Can you walk, Ginger? Try standing, but duck for Christ's sake."

He picked up the buckets. "Tom, you go with him to the governor's house. Mistress Lucy will patch him up. He may rest there a while, but you must come running back. You're needed."

* * *

The governor's parlour was now completely transformed into a sick bay, with Lucy and Barbara acting as nurses. Lucy wore a blood-stained pinafore, which may once have been white. She looked at the lad's shoulder with concern.

"The bone's shattered and there are splinters of metal in the flesh. This will take some time to heal, but first we must clean the wound." She looked at Tom.

"Can you help him on to that?" She indicated a small wooden truck on wheels, with a make-shift pallet of fresh straw on it.

"I'm sorry, Ginger, but this is going to hurt. It has to be done for your own good. Here, bite on this piece of leather."

She took a sharp knife from a jug of hot water and deftly made an incision round the entry wound. Very carefully, she cleaned around the area with an alcoholic solution. When satisfied, she poured some liquid on the wound, which made him struggle so violently that the two women had to hold him down. Then he was given linen dressings for his arm and shoulder. His face ashen, Ginger was shaking all over.

"There now, you're all fixed. You can rest awhile in the bedchamber with the others." Barbara took Ginger's good arm and led him gently beyond the curtain. The groans of wounded men could be heard from behind it.

Lucy looked at Tom. "Nasty one that. It'll mend in time. It's good to have you with us again, Tom. I knew you'd make it to Derby."

Tom was soon back to his duties. The culverin on the church had started its deadly work again and masonry was falling around them. There was no let up till nightfall, when it was too dark to waste the powder and shot, and both sides were able to snatch some rest.

Even then, the crew had to sleep in the open by the cannon, taking it in turns to watch. Tom was so exhausted that he surprised himself by falling into a deep slumber on the ground, despite the cold. Every part of his body ached.

He was roused in the night, when Laurence Collin pinched his ear lobe and handed him a bowl of chicken broth. Tom realised then that he had not eaten since his two breakfasts yesterday in Derby.

Collin squatted down beside Tom on the muddy turf to eat his own share.

Tom looked up at the stars and around at the shadows on the gun platform. He shuddered in the frosty night air.

The broth tasted good.

"How long do you reckon we can hold on waiting for the relief to come, Mr. Collin?" Tom hoped that the fear did not show in his voice.

"As long as we have arms, gun-powder and vitals. Your Derby friends must be on their way."

"Do you think the Royalists will storm the castle?"

"Not unless Newcastle's men join them. The governor thinks there are about six hundred Newarkers. Six hundred against eighty – that's poor odds, but we hold the high ground. There were three lines of defence. They've crossed the town ditches, and seized our street barricades, but they'll never cross the moat, scale the cliff and the castle walls! No, they'll try to starve us out."

"I sometimes wonder what we're really fighting for, Mr. Collin. We're all Englishmen, after all."

"We're fighting for the people's liberty and God's cause, boy – freedom to be our own masters instead of serving dukes and earls and greedy monarchs – freedom to speak to God in our own way, and not just rattle out words from a prayer book – freedom from fear and want and the chance to build a new Jerusalem, as we're promised in the Holy Book. I've seen a kind of cruelty in the Low Country wars, which could make me ashamed to be human. I've also seen true courage and self-sacrifice. When folk are brought to their knees, it can bring out the best and the worst!"

Tom was silent for a while, pondering these words. Then almost in a whisper, he said, "And how do you think it will end?"

"Only the Lord knows that. My prayer is for a land at peace with itself. I'm not much bothered whether we have a king or some other sort of protector, as long as men and women can worship as God wants; as long as there's food for all our bellies, not just for gentry and yeomen farmers; as long as the children can play safely and the elderly walk without fear. I tell you, Tom Marriott, if I come out of this mess alive, and have enough strength to do it, I'll help build a better land: one with refuges for the sick and the old, almshouses maintained by a free church, not a popish monastery. That's my dream. That's what I'm fighting for, Tom Marriott."

"I don't know what I want to do after the war," Tom responded. "My elder brother will run the farm when my father's too old. I'd hoped to stay in service with the squire, either as groom or even steward, but now he's a changed man and I don't know. He's so much harder than he used to be."

"He has to be," Collin replied. "Managing an army of townsmen like we have here is no easy task. Most of the men we have here aren't soldiers at all. We're called a parliamentary army, but parliament doesn't know the name of a single man here. They have no say in the conditions of service, and provide no pay. We have to scratch here and there to get money and supplies. That's not right. The way I see it is this: we're all Englishmen with liberty of conscience, which comes from God. Parliament represents the people and the army is the servant of Parliament. So it is Parliament's duty to organize their army and provide us with pay and equipment, fit for our tasks."

Tom wondered how Laurence Collin had come by these lofty ideas. He was different from the other soldiers. He was self-assured and what he said sounded good common sense. He fell asleep again, pondering these things,

* * *

The next day there was no let up. The cannonade continued, but at least when the trenches were completed, it was possible to move right round the castle again and they became a united fighting force.

Tom stayed with Collin's gunnery crew along with Alderman Drury and Ginger, who, with his arm in a sling, ran messages. They worked in shifts, and to Tom's relief, his officer was Francis Pierrepont. The other shift had to endure Captain Palmer!

In the afternoon, they scored a considerable success, with a direct hit on St. Nicholas's tower, which was shattered. The enemy cannon there was put out of action! But soon the bombardment continued from behind street barricades.

Working together under constant gunfire created an incredibly strong bond among the team members. Colonel Pierrepont was always approachable and willing to lend a hand wherever it was needed. Tom developed a real respect for him and for Laurence Collin, whom the governor promoted to master gunner for the whole castle, so that he could supervise the other teams. William Drury worked like a bull and often had a quiet word with Tom also.

"Do you recall, I once offered you a job in my tannery," he said one night. "With your schooling, I thought you might learn to keep the books. You and Sam were always friends, but he's most likely to do the buying and selling, when I eventually hand over. You were always a promising lad. The offer's still open."

"Thank you ,sir, I'll bear it in mind."

Tom: *I remember the pressure that you put on me when I was leaving school. You spoke to my father about it, but I hated the thought of working in the stinking tannery then, and was very happy when Squire Hutchinson came up with his suggestion about the stable job. It seemed to be a blessed escape to go to Owthorpe Manor. But things have changed mightily since those days.*

The prospect was no longer one to be feared after these war experiences.

CHAPTER 13

RAISING THE SIEGE

For four days Alice and Meg were unable to leave the security of Vault Hall. Lawless soldiers were roaming the streets and they could hear sporadic shooting and the cries of frightened townsfolk. The story spread that whilst the Royalist officers were planning an assault on the castle, their men were looting the houses, especially any that were left empty.

The Drury home was crowded with refugees from the fighting, but Elizabeth, who would have directed operations, was confined to her room, weary and very confused. Sam and Alice took over the running of the household with quiet efficiency. Meg was impressed with the way they coped, spare bedrooms were allocated to the sick and elderly, but they decided to allow close friends and neighbours, who wished to stay overnight, to sleep on the floors in the parlour and the study. Others, who were less well known and trusted were given quarters in the rock cellars below, where there was a labyrinth of underground caves.

Alice asked Meg to help her make the women and children comfortable there, rigging up curtains to screen them and carrying down blankets and shawls to keep them as warm as possible. Porridge and hot broth bubbled incessantly in the great kitchen above and a team of younger women took it in turns to ladle it out and carry it round in jugs and bowls. Meg even devised some simple games that the children could play in their cramped conditions.

Each night, Alice led sincere prayers for peace and forgiveness, kneeling on the floor of the cave.

After three days of turmoil, the Mayor's wife, Mistress Nix, called at Vault Hall. Her husband was being kept a prisoner in the Guildhall, and Alice was touched that with all this anxiety, she had found time to call and ask after her mother.

"I've a great admiration for Mistress Drury," she explained. "She's been an inspiration to us all, and it's a tragedy that she's been wounded."

Alice took her upstairs, and was very pleased to see her mother looking a little better, although she was startled to see the mayor's wife.

"I should be up and about my business," she said, struggling to sit up. "It's too bad, my lying here, with all these people in the house needing help."

"Don't you worry yourself, Mistress Drury. Alice and Sam have everything in hand. People tell me that Vault Hall is the safest place in town. That's why I'm here, to thank your family. Who would have thought it? The Royalists have seized the churches and turned the refugees out. St Nicholas's is a battleground, with a canon on the tower. People are coming here for sanctuary instead, and they are getting it, prayers and all."

Alice heard her mother whisper that this was what she would have expected of her children, brought up as good Protestants. She blushed, but was saved from further embarrassment by a maidservant coming in with a message for Mistress Nix, "Please, ma'am, there's a Royalist officer at the door and he wants to speak to you."

Alice went downstairs with the mayor's wife. A richly dressed officer stood in the doorway.

"What do you want now, Colonel Cartwright?"

"Sir Richard must speak with you urgently." He spoke with extreme politeness.

"Doesn't he know that I am attending a sick lady, an alderman's wife, who was grievously wounded by your men? Sir Richard will have to wait until I am ready to receive him!"

"Pardon me, madam, but that's not possible. We wish to stop this senseless killing – to stop the bombardment of the town from the rebels in the castle, and…"

"Then the answer is simple. Release my husband and go! The whole pack of you!" Mistress Nix struggled to control her fury.

"Unfortunately, we can't, madam. We have orders from the King of England to garrison this town. We can stop the cannon fire from St. Nicholas's church, though, and that will save many lives. In order for us to do that the castle has to surrender. The mayor's written a letter on behalf of the townspeople asking Colonel Hutchinson to stop his slaughter. Your husband and Sir Richard want you to take this letter to the castle personally. Hutchinson will have no option but to receive you. Please can you come with me to the guildhall without delay. Your husband will confirm all I am saying."

"My husband is your prisoner," Mistress Nix was icy. "If I do consent to come with you to the guildhall, it will be in response to his request, and not to any demand from Sir Richard and his bullies from Newark."

With that, Mistress Nix swept past Colonel Cartwright, marched out and strode up the street so fast that the officer, resplendent in top-boots and spurs, had a hard task keeping up with her.

* * *

Tom was the first person to see the re-enforcements coming from Derby. He was taking his turn as a look-out on the roof of the old keep, the highest part of the castle, when he saw the line of horsemen emerging from the trees of the castle park. He had been told it might take four days to release a sizeable force from other duties. There was no mistaking it. Here they were!

With a word of explanation to his fellow look-out, Tom ran down the winding stone stairway to the large barrel-vaulted chamber below. John Hutchinson and Francis Pierrepont were there with maps of the castle and the town spread out on the table before them.

"They're coming, sir!. The men from Derby!" Tom panted.

"At last. Praise God!" The governor jumped to his feet. He ran up the stairs, with Tom at their heels.

"They're at least a hundred strong!" exclaimed the governor.

"And more – over there, sir!" shouted the other look-out, pointing south. They all turned round to see a posse of horsemen approaching Trent Bridge. But were they friends or foes?

A burst of fire aimed at the riders from the newly built royal fort on the far river bank decided the issue.

The governor smiled. "It must be Charles White, with his men from Leicestershire," They saw wave upon wave of horsemen following behind. Two of them fell from the opposing fire, but the others did not waver. "They've come just in time, our supplies are running very low. Tom, run to the gatehouse and tell Major George to watch for the red flag. He'll understand. Then, tack the horses."

76

George Hutchinson was inspecting the horses that had come in with Tom from Derby. They were drawn up in a line behind the gatehouse. His eyes glowed at the news.

"The relief's arriving. As soon as we get the signal, we'll be through the gate to join them," he called to the horsemen. "Remember, our objective is to get Byron while he's in the house opposite. If we can take him alive, we have a hostage. If he tries to run away, I'll hack his legs, cousin or no!"

Tom looked up to the roof of the Norman keep and waited for the signal. The top-most storey had crumbled, long since, but the floor of the highest chamber now formed a roof. Some of the stonework had been shaped to form battlements. They waited in a tense silence, men alert, horses champing at the bit. Then they saw the flutter of a red flag.

"Now!" shouted George. The bolts were thrust back. The great wooden doors opened and the drawbridge thundered down.

The horses charged over it. Beyond, Tom caught a glimpse of Sir Richard. He was standing beside his horse, talking to the mayor's wife. She turned and fled, and a paper fell from her hand, landing on the cobbles. The bridge clanked up again and all was blocked from view.

Curiosity overcame Tom. Breaking all rules, he ran to the parapet to peer over. Sir Richard, back in his saddle, was in close combat with George Hutchinson, swords glinting as they clashed. The frightened horses were prancing around each other.

The duel looked evenly balanced until a sudden thrust from George unseated Sir Richard. He fell to the ground. Another swipe towards his leg, accidentally caught the horse. It squealed and tried to run, blood streaming from the wound.

Sir Richard, on his feet now, dashed into the nearest house to escape. His plumed hat fell on the cobbles. George pierced it with his sword and scooped it as a trophy.

The drawbridge crashed down again and George galloped back into the castle, followed by three of his horsemen. He held his sword high in the air. Sir Richards's black hat was still attached, and the red feathers drooped down like a slaughtered bird.

CHAPTER 14

THE FORT AT TRENT BRIDGE

It was clear to everyone in the castle that the fighting was fierce in the streets. They could hear the cries of those who were wounded. Several sallies were made from men in the garrison, who eventually recovered some of their horses from the stables in Houndsgate, but they grumbled that the best horses had been taken by the enemy.

The musket fire from the houses opposite had ceased, so Collin stood the gunnery team down for a while. "We don't know who we are firing at," he explained.

Tom, squatted down again on the gun platform beside Alderman Drury who had advised him, "We may as well get all the rest we can and let those men from Derby and Leicester bear the brunt for a while."

But Tom was impatient to know what was happening and kept peeping out between the battlements.

"Make yourself useful," Collin told him. "Run to the canteen and bring us all some gruel."

After the brief repast, Tom resumed his watch through the battlements. The street beyond the moat was empty of people. The noise of fighting still came from Houndsgate and Castlegate, but there was no activity on St. Nicholas tower.

Suddenly, a boy's figure came running towards the moat. The boy was waving his hands and peering desperately towards the battlements. Then Tom realised; it was Sam.

Tom popped his head over the parapet and shouted "What is it, Sam?" He took no notice of the order to sit down again, because Sam turned eagerly in his direction. "The Royalists – they're firing the thatch of houses in Castlegate," he shouted, and dashed away.

A few moments later, Laurence Collin swung the team back into action, reloading the cannon and aiming it directly at the area mentioned.

"That was brave of Sam," said the alderman "and of you too, Tom. Wish I'd seen him."

Before nightfall, the bulk of the Newark soldiers were driven out of Nottingham by the two relief forces, but a small group rallied and Tom heard that they were holding out in the fort they had built by the River Trent.

"We must clear the rats from the whole area," he heard John say to his brother, "but the cowards from Derby and Leicester won't help us. I've offered them the use of our cannons, but they say they that they've played their part and they're going home. So, it's left to us."

* * *

A banging on the front door alerted Alice. She ran to quiet the noise, concerned because her mother was sleeping at last, after three days and nights of incessant pain.

It was her neighbour, Widow Gosling, full of the news, "The Newarkers are fleeing! An army's arrived from Derby and they are beating them out of the town!"

"Thank God!" Alice cried. "But please keep the noise down; Mother's managing to sleep." Alice lost no time in passing the good news to Sam, Meg and the neighbours still sheltering in the house. Meg wanted to collect her horse and take the cart back to the farm as soon as possible. They waited a while, until the clamour of running soldiers had subsided, and then ventured forth. Sam escorted Meg back to the inn to collect the cart. The refugees began to return to their own homes.

Alice crept quietly upstairs. Her mother was half awake now, so she told her everything.

Elizabeth received it calmly, but she was very tired. She tried to smile. "Thank you for all that you are doing," she murmured. "You're a good girl..." But her words trailed off. She was in another world again.

A deep sadness overcame Alice. She knew she should be rejoicing, but her worries were overwhelming. Would her mother pull through? Would Sam and Meg be all right? Where was her father? She knelt down and sent up a silent prayer for everyone in the town; her family, her neighbours, Tom, the soldiers, even the enemy. "May there be peace again, and no more killing!"

* * *

John Hutchinson ordered a roll-call in the castle, and it soon became clear who had deserted. Most had gone, without leave, to join their families in the town. Jed was amongst them. No one knew where he had gone, and Tom was quizzed, but could not help. He told George Hutchinson that he had been on duty under Captain Palmer on the night of the attack and was last seen in the early hours by one of the other lads. Palmer paid the price for letting so many go home that night. He was reduced to the rank of lieutenant.

The Royalists holding the fort remained an irritant. On the next Sunday morning, Tom rode with the governor and officers to a thanksgiving service at St. Mary's, conducted by Parson Laycock. John Hutchinson was to read the lesson.

Tom had to stay outside to guard the horses, which were tethered to the iron rings on the wall, by the gate. After the service, Mr. George, Colonel Pierrepont and Lieutenant Palmer collected their mounts and rode back to the castle. Slightly puzzled, Tom waited for his master.

It was some time before the governor emerged. As they rode back, he explained, "I took the opportunity to climb the tower and view that fort. We'll storm it from both sides tomorrow and beat them out."

That night, a meeting was summoned of the whole company and the colonel outlined his plan of action. No one was to leave the castle. The next day a group were set to work loading a cart with woolsacks. These were taken to the meadows, where the men built a barricade before the fort. The Royalists peppered them with bullets as they did it, and several wounded men were brought back to the castle for surgery. The ground was now prepared for an assault.

Tom watched the soldiers leave, march through the long grass and take up their positions. Two horsemen rode first carrying flags. They set up their Parliamentary colours on either side of the newly dug trench.

"Why are they doing this so openly, inviting attack?" Tom asked.

"That's the plan," Collin told him, "to encourage an engagement on the north side. Another force will approach the fort from the lanes at the rear and surprise them."

Next day, Tom saw the bloody corpses and the wounded being brought back into the castle. "They rushed us as soon as the governor left the barricade to collect the cannons," one of the wounded men moaned to him.

The wounded were taken to the chapel, which had now been converted into a field hospital, full of groaning bodies. The governor's lodging was now much too small for this function, and Lucy called Tom to help her. Dr Plumtree had been sent for, and he had come, grumbling "Of course, I'll help. But this is all the fault of the governor and, when I'm through, he'll have my bill for mending all the heads he's broken – on both sides that is. If he won't pay, I'll send my bill to Parliament or to the King - whoever wins! A plague on them both, Roundheads and Royalists. This war's a scandal!"

The assault on the barricade made John Hutchinson all the more determined to win this conflict over the fort. The next day, Tom was lying in the muddy ditch, with soldiers, some sixty yards from the wooden fort, which was now being bombarded by Laurence Collin's culverin, its nozzle peeping through woolsacks.

They took it in turns to man the gun for three hours at a time, and tried to rest in the narrow ditch when off duty, but as light began to fade, it was decided to stop, wait until the early dawn, and then make a sudden assault. Tom had never been involved in any hand-to-hand combat, and had not been trained for it. He dreaded the prospect. It was one thing to be in a team that loads a culverin and helps to fire at an enemy sixty yards away and quite another to charge a fort with a drawn sword and kill or be killed.

Tom was too cold and unhappy to sleep at all that moonless night. He lay in the dank mud, his fingers and toes dead and his whole body tense, dreading the morning. Collin, being a seasoned soldier, had no difficulty in snatching sleep when the opportunity provided. He lay breathing gently alongside Tom, providing a little warmth and comfort. Tom knew that he would spring to life at a moment's notice and be ready to face whatever peril lay before them.

Tom began to doze fitfully. Then suddenly, he was aware of

the outline of a dark figure inches away, on the other side of the woolsack facing him. Was it friend or foe? The next moment, there was no doubt. The figure reared up before him, knife in his hand, and aimed straight at Tom's face.

Tom dodged, seizing his musket. The man lost his balance, slithered down the bank, swung round and tried to stab again. Tom hit him with the butt of his gun. Wham! The man yelled and dropped the knife. Others were fighting around him, now. The man he'd hit picked up the knife again and made another lunge. A bullet flew past Tom's shoulder, and the grisly-bearded man fell gasping. Collin had shot him through the throat. He writhed for some moments on the ground and then lay still.

A clash of swords made Tom look up. Above him, on the edge of the trench, George Hutchinson and a Royalist officer were fighting for their lives, by the side of the culverin.

Collin swung round and rushed up the bank, sword in hand. The Royalist fled. In a few moments the field was clear.

"Good work, Collin," John Hutchinson was suddenly beside them. "They came for the cannon and we sent them packing. Come the dawn and we'll get our own back!"

* * *

A grey dawn was beginning to break. Tom was watching the dark shadows of the fort taking shape before them. What did the day hold for them all? He turned and edged himself further away from the gruesome corpse lying in the trench, his glazed eyes staring heavenwards. Tom shuddered again.

"We made a break in their walls last night, and that's where we're going in!" The governor was resolute. "Collin will go first – you will all follow as soon as I raise my sword."

They waited in eerie silence until the pale morning light revealed the gap. Tom's heart was pounding. Then, he saw the colonel raise his arm half way and they all moved forward – slowly, stealthily. Tom saw Laurence Collin make a burst forward, rush up the bank and plunge through the gap in the barricade. There was no fire from the fort. John Hutchinson raised his sword high and led the sudden charge. Together they ran forward – eyes on the gap, hands gripping muskets, knives in their belts. Still, there was no fire.

Tom scrambled up the mound before the fort. He rushed through the break, following others. Then they all pulled up in surprise. The fort was deserted. All that greeted them was a group of startled sheep, penned for slaughter. There was a shout of joy from some of the soldiers. Others looked disappointed. John Hutchinson raised his sword again. "They've fled – the cowards!" he cried. "They knew we were coming and didn't dare face us. We've won, boys. We've cleared the whole town of the vermin!"

* * *

Tom trudged wearily back to the castle. He had lived on nerves for two days. He'd had no food and felt thoroughly chilled. The vision of the dead Royalist kept flashing before his eyes.

As he approached the gatehouse, he was suddenly cheered by the sight of a small figure in a white cap and dark cloak. Alice Drury was speaking to the duty sergeant. He hailed her, and she turned, smiling.

"Tom, I came to ask if I could see you." A slight blush flushed her cheeks, "I wanted to be sure you were safe, and I've got news of Meg."

"Meg. What about her?"

"She stayed with us when the Royalists were here. She helped me with those taking refuge in our caves, but when the siege ended she went home to the farm."

"But what was she doing in Nottingham?"

"Didn't you know? She came to the castle with a message for Colonel Pierrepont. Captain Palmer put her in a cell, but Jed helped her escape."

"Jed. I don't know anything about this. I know he's missing. It's difficult talking here. Sergeant, I'll vouch for this girl. She's the daughter of Alderman Drury, who helped us with the guns. Can she come into the castle yard?"

The sergeant nodded, but told them to stay within his view and keep it brief.

Alice explained how Meg had arrived sodden after swimming the moat and how she'd stayed at Vault Hall until the trouble ended.

"But what brought her to the castle?"

"The Countess sent her with a letter for her son."

"But Colonel Pierrepont wasn't here. He was in Derby. I had to ride there to bring him back."

"And father too! I know all about it." Alice's eyes shone with gratitude.

"I only did as I was ordered."

"We were so relieved when he came home, Sam and I. We didn't know if he was dead or alive and mother was ill. We're all very grateful to you. Father knows I've come to see you, and he asked me to remind you there's a place for you in his business, if you wish to leave the colonel's service."

Tom saw a gleam in her eyes. Alice wanted him to work with the family. It was tempting. But he was still in the pay of John Hutchinson – not as a soldier, he thought grimly, but as a stable hand – if he was asked to fight again, that would be the last straw. He'd slip away to Vault Hall.

"I'll think about it," Tom said. "I don't know what the future holds – none of us do. I hate this fighting, but I've been lucky so far, and thank God, I haven't had to kill anyone."

The sergeant called that their time was up.

"Look after yourself." He squeezed her hand.

"And you," she said and there was a slight tremble around her mouth. She turned and walked away. He saw her pass through the gatehouse, her black cape disappearing through the archway.

Tom ran to the parapet and looked down at the cobbled street below. She walked down the lane towards the corner of Houndsgate, and then something made her turn and look back at the castle. He waved. She saw him and waved back. Tom was elated.

CHAPTER 15

THE ASSAULT ON SHELFORD MANOR

Tom rode towards Shelford with great reluctance, in the wake of Colonel Hutchinson's troops.

It was a bright summer day and he wished he was out with the hounds rather than fighting this war. What right had his master got to order him to go with the soldiers and look after their horses during the battle at Shelford? It promised to be a bloody affair and he wanted none of it. Not even guarding horses.

"You're looking wretched this morning, Tom." Laurence Collin rode up alongside him.

"I'm a stable-hand, not a soldier," said Tom. "I know I trained for the town militia, but that was for self defence, not attack. I fought with your team when the castle was bombarded, but I didn't enjoy the assault on the fort and I don't like this. I told Master I wouldn't fight, so he said I must come to tend the horses."

"It'll soon be over," said Collin. "The tide's running our way, since we won at Naseby. The Royalist garrisons are falling everywhere now. Bristol, Oxford and Newark are the only towns they still hold and Shelford's an outpost for Newark, so we have to take it out first. Colonel Stanford was offered fair terms for surrender. He's chosen to defy us, so he'll get what's coming. But, I reckon it will all be over here by nightfall. Think of it as I do. One more step on the road to a new Jerusalem!"

Tom looked at Collin. He'd seen the man's attitude change as the war progressed. When they'd first met, Collin had been a brash soldier, but now he had mellowed. He justified the war as a fight against the powers of darkness, and carried a Bible as well as a sword.

Talk was cut short when shots rang out. Two of the horses in front of them shied. One reared up and its rider was thrown to the ground. Tom managed to hold his seat, amid all the confusion.

"They're firing from the tower!" shouted one of the men, pointing up to Shelford Church. Tom could make out some movement in the battlements above.

More shots whizzed by. Colonel Hutchinson jumped from his mount and ran to the door of the church. It was locked.

"Fetch the battering ram!" he ordered.

Shots rained down. Most of the soldiers sheltered behind trees, while four of them rammed the church door with a tree trunk, ready shaped for such a purpose. After several attempts, the lock broke and they and the Colonel forced their way inside. Tom heard shouts, and then his master appeared again, his face flushed with anger.

"They refuse to come down from the bell-tower," he shouted to his men. "We'll smoke them out!"

Everyone was ordered to gather brushwood from the hedgerows and carry it into the church. A pile of timber was soon stacked under the trapdoor leading to the belfry, and then Hutchinson produced a tinderbox.

"We have a fire below you," he roared, "You men have a choice. Come down and surrender or we'll set the trap alight and you can roast!"

Angry voices could be heard arguing above. The hatch was raised and a wooden ladder dropped down. One by one, they climbed down, to be seized by soldiers who bound their hands and feet, pushing them roughly on to the flagstones. There were three men, a woman and a boy. The boy was Jed.

"What have we here? A turncoat!" Lieutenant Palmer kicked Jed in the shins and sneered. Tom noted the sadistic glint in his eye. "This youth was in my troop, sir. It's the whelp who deserted guard duty and let a prisoner escape on the night of the Nottingham raid."

"If that's so, Lieutenant, you had best deal with him!" Hutchinson did not even look at Jed. Tom was dismayed as he saw Palmer seize the boy roughly, pulling him away from the others, who were huddled together in fear.

"I'll leave you in charge of this rabble, Palmer. I must go on to meet with General Pointz. Mark my words, though – these prisoners may be of use to us! Shelford's well defended, with its earthworks and redoubts, but there must be some weak parts in the fortifications. See if you smell something out!" So, saying, the Colonel strode out of the church.

Pleased with his new power, Palmer strutted up and down before the prisoners, looking at them as if they were vermin.

"A nest of vipers, – country hobble-de-hoys who thought they could defy the armies of Parliament! Well – we'll teach you better. You thought to gun us down did you? Well, I've a few tricks up my sleeve too. We missed out on roasting you in your turret, because you came out squealing like pigs. We still have the firewood and tinder. How about setting you alight, like that traitor Guy Fawkes? But we'll begin with gentler methods…a lighted match between two fingers may suffice. Come now – who's the first to be sizzled? We just need to know where the weak points are in the defences…"

Nobody moved.

"Dumb are we? Lost your tongues? You've all still got them, I see – we can soon fix that!"

One of the soldiers grabbed hold of Jed's tongue, pulled it and let go.

"What do you know about the earthworks – sniveller!" Palmer leered at him. Jed was unable to speak.

"Bring me the tinder-box, Marriott! We'll soon have this tongue wagging!"

Tom stood rooted to the spot.

"Bring me the lighter!"

"No, sir – I won't!" Tom stood his ground.

Palmer's eyes glared: "Are you disobeying an officer?"

"This is a church. I thought you were a man of God…sir."

"We are at war, Marriott. Bring me that tinder!"

"We've no right to torture prisoners, sir, and I'm not one of your soldiers. I take my orders from the colonel!"

So saying, Tom turned and ran out through the church door. Colonel Hutchinson was mounting his horse.

"Pardon me, sir – but Lieutenant Palmer's going to torture those prisoners…"

Hutchinson looked at Tom with annoyance.

"I didn't hear that. Palmer must do as he will. Information will save our men's lives!" He spurred his horse, and went his way.

In that moment, Tom decided; he would leave Hutchinson's service. He watched the Governor as he galloped away and shook his head in dismay.

That isn't the squire I used to work for, he thought. *The war's completely changed him – and I know why Palmer's bullying Jed. It's because he was demoted.*

No one had followed Tom out of the church. He was alone. He turned his back, burning with anger and frustration. If they were going to torture Jed, or any others, he would have no part in it! He felt helpless to stop it – and for the first time in his young life, he knew the taint of cowardice. Is this the right thing to do – to turn away? What would his father have done?

Farmer Marriott was a stern man, but honest. He had a strong sense of right and wrong. Many times he had shaken his head over the war, but seldom had Tom heard him take one side or the other. Some of his father's words came back to him now: "Keep your head down – and your eyes open."

He stopped walking away. As he found a hiding place behind a hedgerow, his mother's advice came to him: "Be patient , bide your time" He would not participate. He would not run away. He would watch…and wait.

Above the hedge, Tom could see the flag flying from the roof of Shelford Manor, and he could also see the church tower. Was that movement on the battlements again? Yes – some of the parliamentarians had climbed up there to view the field. It would be wise to stay put for a while.

When they had gone, he decided to find a better vantage spot, so climbed up a sturdy chestnut tree, rich in foliage, which hid him. From this position, he could see a lot: the Manor House, with its earthwork and palisade defences, the church nearby, and beyond them the glitter of a clear stretch of the river. There were several horses tethered to trees on the opposite bank. Some Roundheads, who had presumably ridden them, were busy lashing boats together, endways-on, to form a bridge to span the river at its narrowest point.

He looked at the church again. The prisoners had been brought outside now and John Hutchinson had come back to join them. They were surrounded by soldiers and questioning seemed to be going on. He could not see if Jed was among them. Did they really mean to use torture, or just to threaten it?

His anger still simmered, but he realised now that there were practical difficulties about escaping. He could see that sentries had been posted on the approach roads, and others were patrolling the surrounding fields. If he was caught trying to run away he would be classed as a deserter too, even though he had never enlisted as a soldier. Was it worth the risk? The only escape route seemed to be across the river. The bridge of boats was now completed. Would a quick dash across be possible, now that the soldiers had moved on to another task?

He carefully climbed down and lay flat on his belly. He slowly wormed his way along the hedgerow. He made for a gap in the hedge, which opened out on to the field next to the church. He could just make out John Hutchinson's voice: "You know more than you are telling us! Sling a rope over the tree – and let him swing!"

"No, no, please, sir!" Jed gasped. "They've not yet completed the defence wall. I've seen a gap to the left of the house – by the knot garden!"

Within minutes, the soldiers ran off in the direction of the garden. Tom could hear a whimpering sound by the yew tree, on the other side of the hedge. He counted to ten, and then pushed through the thicket.

Jed was trussed up and badly bruised. He lay curled up by the base of the tree. Tom cautiously crept closer, careful not to be seen.

As Jed became aware of someone approaching, he winced in fear.

"It's all right, Jed – it's me, Tom." He took the knife from his belt and quickly cut the rope cords, noting the friction burns on the boy's wrists and ankles and the recent burns on his fingers.

"They've all gone over to the knot garden. This is our chance...stay close to me!"

Tom led the way back to the gap in the hedge, down into the dry ditch, which drained into the river in wet weather. The ditch ran alongside the hawthorn, so this provided good cover. They ran along, until they came to an inlet of the river.

The bridge of boats was unattended. Gingerly, Tom led the

way. He half expected gunshot to hit them, but they were lucky. Most of the sentries were on the approach road to the manor now, so they were not seen. But the boys did not dare to stand upright. It took several minutes of crawling on their bellies along the boats, which bobbed from side to side, especially when the weight was transferred from one boat to the other. Eventually, they made it.

They ran crouching towards the cover of a copse of trees. It was only then that Tom saw where the horses were tethered. He realised that by an incredible stroke of luck, no-one was with them. Having a natural way with animals, Tom approached them quietly.

They were not alarmed. Soon he had the confidence of a dappled grey and with help, Jed clambered from a tree stump on to the back of a black mare.

Tom mounted the grey and they set off in a bouncing trot into a lane with deep hedgerows.

Distant musket shots sounded from the manor grounds! The bombardment had started then. They could hear shouts and screams, as the raiders rushed the gap in the defences. No-one would notice them now, they thought, everyone would be too preoccupied. Digging their heels into the horses' flanks, they cantered, and then galloped as if for their lives.

They turned to glance back from the brow of a hillock. A flash of fire sounded from across the field. They must have been seen on the hillock by a watcher. But they were too alert to be stopped now. They bounded forwards again.

Eventually, they came to a breathless halt at a crossroads.

"Which way?" Jed asked anxiously.

It was a good question. Tom looked at the finger-post; one arm read "Nottingham", another "Shelford" and a third "Southwell 10 miles". Clearly, there was no going back. If they went to Manor Farm, the soldiers would soon find him there and it would put Tom's family at risk.

"We'll go to Southwell!" said Tom, without knowing where it was. They pressed forward at a gentler pace. The name was vaguely familiar. He could not think why – and then he remembered. His mother's sister had married an innkeeper there. It was several years since they'd met. Probably she would not know him, but Southwell seemed the best hope for shelter.

CHAPTER 16

A TURN OF THE TIDE

Elizabeth Drury died on the day that Shelford Manor fell into Colonel Hutchinson's hands.

Alice gazed sadly at her mother's alabaster face. She had helped the servants to wash her body, dress her in her favourite black dress and lay her out on the big four-poster bed. All this had to be done soon after the death and before the limbs became rigid. It was a labour of love, the last one she could perform for her mother, and strangely healing. Father and Sam had been in the room to view the body and whisper their last farewells. Now, Alice was exhausted and very sad, but there was a kind of peace, sitting beside the body in the silent room. Alice did not fear for her mother. She had a quiet conviction that although something of her spirit lingered in the home, her soul was now in heaven and at peace –'The peace that passes understanding.' Her mother had striven for peace all her life, both in the family and amongst neighbours. At the last she had a kind of victory about her.

"Well, Mother," Alice found herself murmuring, "you are at rest now. All the enemies have gone away and the town is at peace again, as you so dearly wished. This dreadful war is all but over. Thank you for the wonderful example you set for us all. I'll carry that memory with me all the days of my life. That I will."

* * *

There was much to be done. Alderman Drury was bereft – a quieter, changed man and more considerate of others. Elizabeth had been a power of strength to him and he had not fully appreciated it. Sam still suffered from his weak arm. It had never fully recovered from the break and still hampered him. Most of the household work fell to Alice, who instructed the two maidservants and prepared the funeral arrangements.

Alice thought the funeral service at St. Mary's a poor affair. So many had died in the recent conflict that Parson Laycock held a combined funeral service for sixteen people. The old church was crowded, and more came for Elizabeth's sake then the others, as she was admired for her initiative in forming the Women's Watch.

The family stood with other bereaved people by the church door as the congregation filed out and several of the women who had taken refuge at Vault Hall took Alice's hand. "She was a true Christian woman," and "She should have had a funeral of her own," were frequent comments.

A letter was delivered for Alice a few days later. It was brought by a waggoner, who had brought skins to the tannery from Lincolnshire. It was a rare thing to get a letter, and Alice supposed that it offered condolences, but she did not know the hand. Puzzled, she broke the seal. It was from Tom.

"Alice, I write from the King's Arms in Southwell, where my aunt is hostess, being married to the landlord. This is to let you know that I have left Colonel Hutchinson's service. I had words with him at the time of the fall of Shelford. The war has changed him into a cruel man, and I would not be part of the plan to slaughter those people, so I made my escape. I am now employed here in the stables and also with me is your cousin, Jed.

Please do not tell any of the soldiers because they might come for us, saying we are deserters, but that is a charge I deny. I never enlisted as a soldier, although I had a hand in the enlistment of others, which I now regret. Jed was brutally treated, but is now well and safe. Perhaps you can get word quietly to his mother. I am writing also to Manor Farm on my own behalf. We are well fed and cared for here and both kept very busy, as the Scottish army have a camp nearby, and use this inn much. We both feel it best to keep well away from Nottingham, until this sad affair is ended.

I trust you and your whole family are keeping safe and well. Please thank your father for his kind offer of work, which I have considered, and give him the note I have enclosed. Regards to Sam and my respects to your mother,

Your servant always, Tom Marriott."

An enclosed paper was addressed to her father, but as it was unsealed and fell open on her lap, Alice made bold to read it.

"I wish to thank you, sir, for your kind offer of employment. I have now left John Hutchinson's service, and am free to take this offer up at your convenience, although I think it would be wise for me to remain in Southwell until hostilities cease, since there are those who might wish to put me back under military orders.

I hope you will not mind my making a request. You told me that I might be trained to keep the tannery books. This I am willing to do, but fear it would be tedious for me to be overmuch indoors, being used to an open air life. Would it be possible for me to join Sam in learning something of the buying and selling side of your business? This I would greatly appreciate. Perhaps with the two of us in this work, we could help to expand the trade into other parts?

Forgive me, if you feel I'm impertinent to raise this, but I request an interview with you, so that things can be thoroughly discussed. Your obedient servant, Tom Marriott."

A glow of pleasure warmed Alice. Tom was man enough to spell out his wishes. She would try to persuade her father to agree to them. It was good to have news of Jed, too. She would go to see Jed's mother as soon as time allowed.

* * *

Mistress Martin wept when Alice came to Shelford with the good news.

"Bless the boy...and there was I thinkin' my Jed might 'ave been shot or hanged. They were so angry with 'im those Nottingham soldiers. I managed to escape myself in all that mayhem at the Manor House...Oh terrible things they did. There was a great slaughter and others were burned in the fire that took hold of the building, but I'd no notion what 'appened to Jed.

I've scarce ventured from the cottage door these last two weeks for fear of those Roundheads. Oh, it's a sad, sad business, when all decent folks want to do is be able to feed their bellies, and keep out of trouble. Jed should never 'ave gone for a soldier, but it was the silver shilling that tempted 'im – first with Parliament and then with the King's men. And two shillings was all 'e ever got. There was no wages, although the sergeant kept promising, but nothing came of it. I told 'im not to, but there.. lads are a law to themselves and will not be ruled by a woman. An' then they came for me, the king's men that is. They said they wanted a look-out on the tower, and what wi' me doin' the cleanin' there and knowing the bell-tower and having the key, I agreed.

Another shilling that was and Jed came with me, for he was back from the castle, where that Captain Palmer frightened the life out of him. A brute, that man is, an' 'im supposed to be a preacher man. So I was sent up the tower with Jed and the verger and the gravedigger, all being good church folk, you see. We had a telescope an' the gravedigger was told to fire a shot with his gun, as a signal like, if we saw anyone on the road. Well, when we saw that troop, he said it would be a waste of a good bullet to shoot it in the air, an' it would be just as good a signal to wait until they came closer and then aim at the enemy. There was no 'oldin' 'im. 'E'd no fear, I recon it comes of diggin' all them graves. But that shot finished us off. Oh, 'e were so mad, that Colonel 'utchinson, his face was purple, and then that Palmer with 'im too, and talking of flames and 'ell-fire. Oh, you're a good girl, Alice, you've brought cheer to my 'eart, walking 'ere wi' this news, like the angel on two legs you are. And Jed keepin' the 'orses at an inn all this while an' me thinkin' 'im dead. Well, I never."

All Alice could do was listen.

* * *

"Well, alderman, what do you think we should do?" asked John James, once more installed as the Mayor of Nottingham. Do you want John Hutchinson to step into his dead father's shoes as the Member of Parliament in the vacant Nottingham seat, or do we nominate someone else. I wondered about you, William. You stood in for me and went to York, when you were Deputy Mayor when I refused to meet King Charles in '41. Would you like to be one of our representatives in Parliament?"

"No, I would not," William Drury was adamant. "I'm a plain speaking man, not a mincing lawyer. Those endless wrangles of theirs would plague me to death. I've a tannery to run and a family to mind without a wife, but I tell you now, if you nominate

Hutchinson, I'll vote against you. I've never forgiven him for moving our guns to the castle and leaving the town to the mercy of the Newarkers, as well you know, and I've never forgiven him for that cursed edict he placed on us all after the town was saved by the troops from Leicester and Derby, and not by him and his soldiers, as he likes to pretend."

"Yes, but all that's in the past, William. Who are we going to nominate as our M.P. that's the question?"

"Call it the past, if you will, but it still rankles in my mind. Have you forgotten the curfew he declared on the whole town at nine o' clock at night until six in the morning, with a rattle of drums and a bugler to tell us the time? Fines and imprisonment for all who sold liquor between those times, and what's more, rewards for those who reported their neighbours. That stirred up a storm of trouble. Who in the blazes does he think he is – God almighty? He did this because he had managed his men so badly that some of them went out carousing when they should have been on watch. That's how the Newarkers seized the town that night, when he was down town himself. Hutchinson was appointed governor of the castle not the town, but that didn't stop him browbeating Alderman Nix when he was mayor and was fool enough to comply."

"I agree with all you are saying, William, but if we don't nominate Hutchinson who's it to be – Toplady, Hardmeat or Plumtree…"

"None of them. Toplady's a dandy, though he's a rich and powerful one. He fancies himself too much already, and I dread what he'd be like in Parliament. Hardmeat is an ignoramus, and Plumtree is a fool. If you want my advice, you'll nominate Francis Pierrepont. He's an honest man, and there's few to be found these days. He doesn't step out of line. His brother William is already an M.P. for somewhere or other, and the eldest brother, Henry, sits in the Lord's. But the good thing about Francis is, he lives with us in the town and we can talk to him and he'll listen. He won't override folk like Hutchinson does. I watched them both when I was in the gunnery team at the castle. The men all trusted him, and I trust him too, and that's saying something these days."

"Francis Pierrepont, he's a possibility I suppose, but there was a time when I didn't really know which side he was on, with his father an Earl and a brother who was the King's Lord Lieutenant for the county. You remember the time he came to seize our powder and arms at the start of all the trouble."

"Will I ever forget it? I was there, outside the Guildhall shouting, 'Save our parliament. Spare our church.' But that was Henry, Francis had nothing to do with that. He wasn't on either side. He'd too much common sense. Times have changed, John. As I saw it then, Hutchinson was defending the town's armoury, in the name of Parliament, from the King's interference. I was speaking up for the town and defending a free church against papist ideas.

Power can corrupt, John, I've seen that happen. Hutchinson was a different man then. He was a young idealist. But we've all changed through this war. I've changed. You've changed, and so has Francis Pierrepont. The ground has shifted beneath our feet. It's a strange world, we're living in now. Not what it was, or perhaps ever will be again, but my vote goes for Pierrepont because he's gone through the fire and kept his integrity. That's more that you can say for most of us."

The Mayor nodded. "You're a stubborn old man, William, tough as the leather you tan. I'll trust your judgement again, and nominate Francis Pierrepont, if he's willing. Then we'll see how the vote goes in the Guildhall."

CHAPTER 17

ROYAL DISGUISE

Tom wakened early on a bright May morning in Southwell. He remembered that there were some important guests at the King's Arms today. Now that he had parlour duties, there was much to be done. He hurried down to the kitchen where Bess, the cook, was bustling about, tending her pots and pans, and looking very hot and bothered.

"Who are these visitors?" he asked her.

"I reckon they are somethin' to do with that strange Frenchman who's taken our best room. If you want to know more, you'd best ask your aunt. I doubt she'll be any the wiser. 'E's a weird man, that Mon-sewer Monteval, with all 'is comings and goings, and 'is meetings with the 'eathen Scots – 'e let slip last night to expect three visitors of quality. 'E went out after dark, and no one's seen sight nor sound of 'im since. I never did trust those Papists!"

"How do you know he's a Catholic?"

"All French folk are Papists, like our poor deluded Queen. Why else would 'e wear that great cross around his neck? Now, then – let's 'ave less prattle. There's pots to be washed, and birds to be prepared for the oven. Go an' fetch some water from the pump, and make yourself useful!"

Tom picked up a wooden pail and stepped into the yard. He did not mind Bess's bickering. She was a simple soul, and he was grateful for the work and shelter that his aunt and uncle had found for him and Jed too. The boys had repaid the hospitality by hard work ever since that memorable day six months ago when they had arrived exhausted and saddle-sore.

He remembered the red sky they had all seen that night, and the expressions on the faces of the men in the bar, as they exchanged glances and spoke of Shelford burning. Some of the locals were filled with fear, whereas the Scottish soldiers, who behaved as if they owned the town, were gleeful and making merry.

His aunt had taken the two boys aside and, with tears in her eyes, had spoken softly: "Well, you're my nevvy, and this lad with his blistered fingers is your friend. While there is breath in my body, you're not going back to those brutes!"

It was a busy inn, serving the local folk and recently the high-ranking officers of the Scottish Covenanting Army, who had taken possession of the Bishop's Palace across the road to use it as their headquarters. They despised the ancient Minster, calling it a Papist steeple-house, and using it for stores and stabling for the horses. The villages saw this as a sacrilege, but were unable to prevent it. They became accustomed to seeing the blue lowland bonnets of David Leslie's cavalry in the streets, and hearing the guns pounding Newark, eight miles away.

* * *

Tom was filling buckets of water when he was aware of hooves behind him. Three riders were advancing through the archway to the inn-yard. The first was a large man wearing a scarlet cloak, followed closely by a man in buff, probably a servant, then a cleric – in raven black, and looking very tired.

Jed appeared and went to catch the leading horse's reins, bending his knee for the rider to dismount. The second man swung lithely from his saddle. The clergyman sat still – as immovable as if he were cast in bronze.

Tom left his task and walked over to the clergyman.

"Can I help you down, sir?" he asked with a slight bow.

The man turned his beaky head toward him, all the weariness of the world carved deep into his face. At once – Tom knew that he'd seen this man somewhere before.

Without a word, the man climbed painfully to the ground. He steadied himself by clasping Tom's shoulder. In a quiet, halting whisper, he uttered his thanks and turned away.

Tom knew for sure now – this shadow of a man was the King. He was clean-shaven. The greying beard would have given his disguise away, and he had lost weight, gaining wrinkles in his face.

The officer in the red cloak broke the silence: "Is there a Frenchman lodging here?"

"Yes. Monsieur de Montrevil" – answered Tom.

"Take us to him boy, and get these horses stabled."

"Monsieur went out last night and has not returned... He told us to expect visitors, so there is food prepared..."

"Then lead on. I, for one, am famished!" King Charles regained some authority at the mention of food.

Jed led the horses away, while Tom ushered the three visitors into the best parlour. His aunt and uncle were already there to receive them. Tom realised immediately that they had no idea whom they were entertaining, for their first attention was given to the man in the red cloak, whilst the King was left standing by the door. Tom quickly offered him a seat, which he took gladly, leaving the others to do all the talking.

"I fear our host must have missed us in the morning haze. We were to have met at the river crossing. Still, we're here now, and very hungry and thirsty. I think some mulled ale would be welcome first, would it not – Dr Hudson?"

The King nodded his approval.

Tom left the room to bring the ale. Fortunately, his aunt followed and so he was able to tell her who 'Dr Hudson' really was.

"Lawk a mussy! Are you sure?" she exclaimed.

"I saw him in Nottingham – on the day the standard was raised.

"Did you now? What am I to call him? Do I curtsey and say, Your Majesty?"

Tom urged her to do no such thing. He had seen more of the war than his aunt.

"We must call him Dr.Hudson, as that's the name he wants to be known by. Anything else might put him in peril – especially as the Scottish army are in the town."

"Aye – you're right, of course. My, such a to-do! I must whisper the news to your uncle."

With that, she was gone. Tom returned to the parlour. Monsieur Montrevil entered too, full of apologies for missing the rendezvous. Orders for the meal were taken and then it was made clear that the visitors wished to be alone.

Whenever it was necessary for Tom or his uncle to enter the room, the four men conversed in whispers. The one who appeared to be a servant stood by the window, looking for anyone entering or leaving the inn.

Although the King ate most of the food laid before him, his

eyes rarely looked up. Afterwards, when the four had finished the meal and were gathered round the fire, smoking their clay pipes – he sat with his head resting in his hands, as if it were too heavy for his shoulders alone to carry. Halfway through a conversation in French between Montrevil and Redcloak, he butted in with just four words, an order, "Go – fetch them. Now."

The Frenchman got up, gave the King a slight bow, and went out of the room. Tom, who understood little of what was happening, kept a watchful eye through the kitchen window.

He saw Montrevil depart in haste on horseback. In a short while, he was back, accompanied by three high-ranking officers of the Scots Army. He had seen one of them before – he recognised the steel helmet and weather-beaten features of Colonel David Leslie, a senior officer who frequented the bar and used to talk to the Frenchman but he did not know the other, a wiry older man in a blue Scots bonnet. Yet somehow, this man had an air of authority.

Leaving one officer with the horses, the three men entered the parlour. Tom and his uncle knocked on the door with trays of drinks, their curiosity on full alert. But Montrevil signed that they should leave immediately, and they withdrew to await another summons.

It was a considerable time before they were called upon, and throughout this time, while they waited in the outer room, they heard murmurings and occasionally high words from the parlour. Eventually, Montrevil opened the door, and commanded them to come into the parlour. No more drinks were required.

The King was standing facing the door, his back to the fire. He looked more regal and composed. There was no doubt about his being the senior person now.

"We invited you into this room landlord, because we are going with these gentlemen to the Scots encampment they call Edinburgh, outside Newark. We have work to do there, which will bring peace to this country at last. Before we leave Southwell, we wish to thank you for an excellent meal. Perhaps in years to come you will be able to say to your guests that you entertained the King at this crucial time in the nation's history, and he complimented you on your culinary skills."

A gentle smile accompanied the bows and curtseys, and the King, clearly satisfied with his negotiations with the Scots, exuded the air of one who had won a famous victory. He left the room with a flourish of his cape, leading the way to the horses.

The others followed, but Tom noticed that Redcloak looked uneasy, and the Scots officers stared grimly in front.

Once in the yard, it was not Colonel Leslie, but the elderly man in the blue bonnet who gave the order to ride on, and the last Tom saw of King Charles was a mounted figure riding through the inn-yard archway, escorted by armed Scots soldiers on either side. He had the uncanny feeling that in the last few moments the power had shifted yet again.

CHAPTER 18

HOLLOW VICTORY

That evening, there was revelry in the bar at The King's Arms, and Tom was kept busy supplying the Scots soldiers with drinks. He had difficulty in understanding their jests because of the brogue but, when opportunity seemed right, he questioned one of the men who had proved friendly on an earlier occasion.

"Why are you all in such high spirits?"

"Och, everyone will know in the morning, when Newark flies the white flag," the man replied.

Another blue-bonneted man sitting next to him laughed out loud.

"That stupid king thinks he's done a deal wi' us, and he'll ride north to come an' rule again in Holyrood. We've had our fill of they Stuarts, I can tell ye. He may have been born in Dunfermline castle, but that nae makes him a Scot."

"Aye, Lord Leven's a canny commander and there's nae way he'll allow his Covenant Army to march back over the border, with Charlie at the head. Yon fool thinks he can sell Newark for a throne. He'll ne're do that till thistles grow on rose trees," said the first man. "It even makes me sorra' for the Newark folk. They've put up a bonny fight an' now they're bein' sold like slaves in an Arab market-place. When Newark falls, Oxford will go and that's the end o' the rule o' the royalists. The war's all but won."

"And what will you do, then?" asked Tom.

"Och, we'll gae home to Fife, and my guess is we'll take Charlie boy wi' us as a sort of mascot, unless we sell him to Cromwell and the Ironsides down south. Lord Leven will decide.

I'm nae a soldier. No more is Andy here, we're farming folk, but we joined the Covenant army when our landlord called on us to fight for freedom o' worship, an' now that's safe, we've done our job, and it's back to the plough i' Balgownie farmtoun in Culross."

So, the blue-bonneted old officer, who took the King captive, must have been Lord Leven, mused Tom.

The next day, the news broke. Newark had suddenly surrendered. The end of the war was in sight.

This was also the day that the carrier brought a letter to Tom at the inn. He was surprised to see his name written in his father's hand, as writing was not something Farmer Marriott did very often.

"Dear Tom," he read "We trust you are well, amidst all these troubles. Your mother sends her love to you and her sister, and thanks her for finding work for you at the inn. We are well, though tired. It is hard here with so many soldiers camped around us, demanding food and fodder for their horses. This is to tell you that we have heard from Meg. She is in Newark, staying with the Clay family. The mayor is dead of the plague, and Meg will not leave his children in that dreadful place, where there is cannon fire and deaths every day. God knows what will become of her, but if there is any way you and your aunt and uncle can get her help and supplies, we know you will. God bless you, son. Your loving father."

The words "and Mother" were scrawled below.

It was the first letter Tom had ever received from his parents. He was so seldom away from home and they were not great hands with a quill. He was deeply touched.

So – Meg was in Newark, and the Clay family were ridden with plague. What could he do to help?

He shared the letter with his aunt but she was not able to suggest anything. She clucked over it and shook her head in dismay, being worried because the inn was in turmoil with all the soldiers cheering and singing in the bar.

"And those infernal bagpipes, they'll wake Old Nick himself," moaned the landlord.

When he had a chance to slip away, Tom saddled a horse before his irate uncle could stop him.

"If Newark's surrendered, I'm going to fetch Meg!" he called over his shoulder.

"You're a young fool, lad – the town is sick with plague!"

His uncle's warning went unheeded – he was well away and crossing the market place. A straight lane led past the deserted minster, which was now being used by the Scots army as stabling for their horses.

Tom found the road to Newark packed with Parliamentary soldiers and others. It seemed that the whole population was gathered there: pike men and musketeers from Nottingham and Derby, cavalry from Leicester and Warwickshire, Scots foot soldiers with a few officers on horses. Some had their friends and families with them, dressed in their best attire, and villagers turned out to wave and cheer them – more because of the end of the fighting than to celebrate a victory, Tom thought. People were feasting and drinking outside the taverns.

When he passed through Upton, there was dancing on the village green and some of the young farm wenches had climbed on to one of the supply wagons to join the revellers.

When Tom crossed the bridge at Kelham the road took him across the island close to the Scottish camp called 'Edinburgh'. No sentry challenged him. It wasn't until he came within sight of the grey walls of Newark Castle that he found the road barred. A Parliamentary army was being lined up ready for their march into the town. The men were assembling in columns behind their banners, and a drum-major was allocating places to each platoon.

"Tom Marriott! By God's grace!" Tom heard a friendly voice and recognised Laurence Collin, who asked: "What in heaven's name brings you here?"

"I've come to find my sister, Meg. She's in Newark somewhere. I hope to get her safely home."

Collin looked concerned.

"That'll be no simple task. No one's allowed into the town until the garrison has marched out. They'll be coming through the castle gate, over the bridge and down this road. When they've passed, we're marching in. Only those in the columns can enter, then the gates will be shut until tomorrow. Perhaps I could enquire about your sister?"

"Thank you – but it isn't safe. She's with a family who have the plague."

"God save us all!"

Tom was desperate: "I must find her. Can I enter with the regiment? I have served under the colours."

"You left us, Tom...."

"I left because of the cruelty at Shelford. I know you had nothing to do with that, Mr Collin. But I remember you telling me about the new Jerusalem there'd be, after the war. Well, my sister has stood by that young family at great risk to herself. She's trying to give them a future..."

Collin put his arm around Tom's shoulder. "And by His grace, she shall. Tie your horse to this tree and come with me."

He led Tom to the head of the column, where George Hutchinson was deep in discussion with a Scottish officer.

"Here's Tom Marriott reporting back for duty. He's the lad who rode to Derby, and brought us help in our time of need."

"And the lad who came to warn me on that first day when Lord Newark came to seize our ammunition. I remember your deeds well, young man. Where've you been hiding yourself these last twelve months?"

"At Southwell, sir. I've been working at The King's Arms, where some of the Scots officers stable their horses."

"That's the truth," piped in a Scots voice. "This is the verra lad who stabled the horse the King rode in on..." It was the soldier from Culross speaking.

"Then welcome back to the Nottingham regiment!" affirmed Mr George.

"Here – wear this orange neckerchief like the rest of us, and fall in behind Collin's men."

"Here they come!" cried the Scotsman. "Och! An 'tis a bonny sight ta see!"

A boy with a drum walked proudly through the castle gateway. Musketeers and pikemen followed him. They all appeared hollow-eyed and sallow-faced, but they marched with dignity. Behind them came the cavaliers, mounted on slow-stepping horses. Among the officers, there were two familiar faces: the grim features of Henry Pierrepont, and Sir Richard Byron. Although the soldiers were obviously tired and bedraggled, they held their heads high and marched with dogged determination.

They lined up in three columns and stood waiting for the Parliamentry army to enter the town.

Tom put on his orange necktie. He took his place with the gunners. There were three troops in the Nottingham Brigade; each being led by a mounted officer. Colonel John Hutchinson led the first one, Major George, the second, and the third was led by Lieutenant Palmer. As ill luck would have it, Tom was in the third troop. Just before the order came to march forward, Palmer rode along the line to inspect the men. "Marriott! The deserter! How, in thunder, did you get here?"

"Major George Hutchinson told me to fall in, sir."

"I don't believe you, boy. If he did, then he obviously didn't recognise you!"

Palmer grabbed the orange necktie, and ripped it from Tom's neck.

"I can have you hanged for desertion, boy!"

"It's too late, with respect, sir. The war's over."

"The lad's right, Lieutenant," Collin intervened. "And look – your column's moving."

Palmer realised he had delayed too long. The leading men in his troop had begun to cross the narrow bridge over the River Trent, and there was no room for him to move forward to lead the column. Cursing, he pushed his way through the throng of mounted men, to get ahead. He had missed the chance to lead his troop into Newark. The men at the head of the column had seen to that.

The slim file of men marched over the temporary wooden bridge, and through the castle gate into the town. Silent bystanders watched with glum faces as they passed along the narrow lanes into the Market Place. Here, they lined up in ranks before the Town Hall, and then were stood at ease. The principal officers were placed on a high balcony above the main doorway, among them John and George Hutchinson. Palmer had not made it. The speeches had begun.

Tom peered up at his former master. He recognised that glint of triumph in John Hutchinson's eye. He did not like it. Tom had no stomach for speeches, or for facing Palmer. So, with a nod to Collin, he slipped away before anyone had chance to stop him, and was lost in the crowd of spectators.

"Excuse me – can you tell me where Alderman Clay's house is?" he enquired of an old man.

The man looked astonished.

"The late mayor, God rest his soul, has been dead these last two months."

"Yes – but where is his house?"

"It used to stand right there." The man pointed to the ruined shell of a building behind where they were standing. "That was his shop – best mercer in Newark was old Hercules. Where've you been? Everyone knows about how this place was burnt."

Anxiety gnawed at Tom.

"But what about his family? Did they escape?"

"Be better for them if they had. Most of 'em 'as gone down with the plague.."

"But where…?"

"I don't know who's left of 'em. Not many. Most of the plague folk 'ave been sent to the 'ouses bottom of Millgate – far away as possible. They should a sent them to give the plague to the Roundheads, that's what I says – not kept 'em 'ere to infest the town. You're a prize fool if you go down Millgate. Leave 'em be there – they're all dyin' anyway."

Tom didn't wait to hear any more. He had been disgusted and not a little frightened by the old man's ramblings. He must find Meg. He had to get her away from all this.

Millgate was a narrow lane, with yards off it, running down to the waterside. A very sick-looking woman told him: "The plague yard is at the very end – all the doors are marked with a black cross."

He could smell the stench as he approached. A young girl with running sores on her face and neck, held out an empty bowl as he passed under the archway. He looked around in despair at the squalor of the yard, where haggard men and women sat on dirty benches, waiting for death to claim them. Putting the kerchief to his nose, he approached one of the men without getting too close, calling: "Excuse me, Sir. I am looking for the Clay family…"

"You'll no find 'em in 'ere…"

"Why? Surely, they are not all dead!"

"Oh – they 'ave friends in 'igh places. Them's too grand to come an' die with us! " The man sneered and spat on the ground. "The last I 'eard of the mayor's brood, they wus livin' in a stable be'ind the Saracen's 'ed."

With a hasty word of thanks, Tom ran from this hellhole, still with his nose and mouth covered. Back by the castle, he paused to ask for the Saracen's Head.

He found it, in the Market Square – right back where he had started!

John Hutchinson was now haranguing the troops. Even at this distance, Tom thought he could hear a note of triumph in the commander's voice. He had no time to waste. He ran into the yard and asked the first person he saw if they knew the whereabouts of the Clay family.

"You'll find them in that end outhouse." She shook her head sadly, "They're not allowed out in the yard, poor souls…"

Again, Tom put the necktie to his face, and ran across the yard, to be faced by another door marked with a black cross. He knocked boldly on the door.

"Don't be afraid! It's me – Tom."

The door creaked slowly open. Thank God! Meg was pale and gaunt and looked much older, but there were no sores.

All they said to each other was: "Tom" and "Meg". They had never felt closer.

* * *

Some hours later, Tom and Meg were trudging south along the road from Newark. Tom was leading his horse, riding on its back were three sickly children belonging to the Clay family.

Nick walked beside them. There had been no reason to stay in Newark. There was talk of plague-stricken families being rounded up and caged in the castle. That sounded like a death sentence and Meg was sure it was best to leave the town before the order came. They were heading for Manor Farm. Tom feared spreading the disease, but Meg was determined that she would not leave the children, so they decided in view of father's letter that this was the right thing to do.

"We won't go to the farmhouse in case they carry infection. None of them have the plague marks, but we must be certain." Meg was resolute: "You must ride ahead on the horse when we get near to warn mother and father. They must decide what's best. I think we could stay in one of the outlying barns until all's well. Nick and I will stay there with the children to see them through. The fresh country air will help."

There was hope in her voice and selfless determination. Tom noted the change in her.

"It won't be very comfortable in a barn."

"Nor was it at the stable behind the Saracen's Head, but these are the children who survived; the weaker ones didn't. Two of them were taken to the pit on the death cart. It came round every night and the man used to shout 'Bring out your dead!' It's strange how you get used to such terrors..."

Meg's words were cut short by confusion over a delay on the road. The stream of Newark refugees was held up by an approaching coach. Walkers had to step into the ditches to let the horses go by. It seemed an insult. Here were gentry riding against the tide, but there was nothing the walkers could do but grumble and stand aside, to be splashed with mud. Tom was angry, and was about to shout an insult, when he saw Meg's face light up with pleasure.

Then he saw that the Pierrepont Coat of Arms was blazoned on the doors.

"It's Bartlett," Meg cried. This meant nothing to Tom, but suddenly the coach stopped, and there was Francis Pierrepont gazing at them through the carriage window. He opened the doors to speak to them and there was concern in his eyes.

"Tom Marriott, the last time I saw you was at the siege in Nottingham, and Meg, I heard you'd left my mother's service and were helping the mayor's family in Newark. Are these waifs his children?"

"You remember Nick, he was at Pierrepont Hall too. There's only the the three boys left, together with a young servant girl. The mayor and the others died in the plague," Meg explained.

"We're trying to get to Manor Farm. We've walked all the way from Newark, but I don't think we'll make it before dark."

"I doubt you will. Isn't it better to stay in Newark tonight, and set out early in the morning?"

"Oh, Mr Francis, there's no going back. The whole town's diseased with plague."

"Oh, I'm sorry. I'd no idea." Francis Pierrepont gazed closely at the pale, exhausted younger children, huddled and shivering in cloaks on the horse – then at Nick, Meg and Tom in turn. He looked up at the darkening sky, and stood thoughtfully in the mire, whilst refugees pushed past them.

"Here, Bartlett," he called "lift those little mites into the coach, and you get in with them, Nick. You look half starved.

Meg and I will sit with the coachman, and Tom, you can ride the horse. We'll be at your father's farm before sundown."

Bartlett did as he was bid and the cumbersome coach was turned round in the lane, causing another hold-up. When all were settled, off they went – on the road south. Meg thanked Mr Francis profusely. This kindness was so unexpected, a complete breaking of traditions between masters and servants.

"I wasn't looking forward to those victory celebrations at Newark," Francis Pierrepont smiled. "I've seen too many broken heads and broken hearts. Perhaps taking you lot to Manor Farm is the best thing I've done in this dreadful war. Now it's to end and the hardest task of all lies ahead – building the peace. Pray God we are equal to it."

He turned to speak to Tom, who had been riding alongside them, but he was not to be seen. Tom was riding in front, spurring on his horse, and leaving the rumbling coach and the straggle of refugees behind him. He was filled with a new urgency – keen to be home first, to see his parents, tell them the news that the war was ending, that he had no longer in servitude to Parliament and that Meg was coming home too, but they must prepare for the arrival of sick children.

When the coach turned the corner at the end of the lane, Meg saw both her parents standing and waiting, ready to open the rusty old gate.

BESIEGED

CHAPTERS

Meg

1

PRELUDE TO WAR

Nottingham 1641

As he rode up Malin Hill on his black mare, Nick thought the whole town looked menacing. It had been hard work keeping up the brisk pace set by his master, Lord Newark, who was riding in front with the high sheriff. Now that they were in the cobbled streets of the town, the pace was slower, but the scowls on people's faces showed that they were not welcome visitors. A lumbering horse-drawn covered wagon had joined them at the entrance to the town. Now it followed them, keeping at a discrete distance.

They drew rein outside the Shire Hall. Lord Newark or Mr. Henry, as Nick and the other house servants knew him, dismounted, and he and the Sheriff banged on the closed wooden doors. "Open in the king's name," they cried, one echoing the other. Nothing happened.

Nick, Travers and the sandy-haired man who had come with the sheriff, were left holding the five horses, whilst a crowd of gawping townsfolk gathered round.

"Where's you from?" "Who's the big man wi' the plumed hat?"

Nick and Travers ignored the questions, until a butcher's boy shouted out: "They're all asleep in there. I'd try the tradesman's entrance, if I was you."

Then everybody started to laugh and jeer, and Nick was embarrassed.

Mr. Henry went red in the face, banged on the door and shouted all the louder. Still nothing happened. The high sheriff, prompted by the cries, marched through the archway and round to the stable-yard at the back. Mr. Henry followed and presumably they forced an entry, because raised voices were heard from within.

They waited and waited. Then three others arrived, the mayor in his robes, a tall determined young gentleman and a burly tanner, who was identified as an alderman by someone in the crowd. All these disappeared through the side archway. Shouting was heard from behind them. Then suddenly, everyone was swamped by an angry mob. Nick was surrounded by threatening people, brandishing cudgels and long knives chanting "Save our parliament – Spare our Church!"

Nick had no idea, what everyone was angry about. All he knew was that he must keep a tight hold of the reins of the two horses he was holding, as they were clearly frightened and might shy.

He heard Travers angrily protesting: "Keep back. You'll frighten the horses. We mean no harm."

"No harm," shouted one. "Hear that. They've come to steal our weapons, and they say it's no harm."

Suddenly the great wooden doors opened and Lord Newark and the sheriff reappeared looking angry and very downcast. The mayor and the tall man briskly followed them out and stood on the steps as if to see intruders off their premises.

Mr. Henry and the sheriff remounted their horses.

"I'll be reporting to the king, John Hutchinson, and your name is noted," shouted Lord Newark, glaring at the younger man. He dug his spurs into the flanks of his horse, and they all left at a rattling pace.

Nick kept his head down, as pelts of mud hit the fleeing horses. But all the time he was asking himself. *What's going on? What does this mean?* His head throbbed with questions.

CHAPTER 1

FEUD AT PIERREPONT HALL

Young Meg was the first person at Pierrepont Hall to see Lord Newark after he was rebuffed by the Nottingham townsfolk. His horse clattered past her on the lane leading to the hall, and she could hear him muttering foul things. He leapt angrily from his steaming horse. Throwing the reins towards the stable boy without as much as a word, he strode purposefully into his family home, banging the doors behind him.

'Who's bitten him today?' thought Meg. She went straight to the servants' hall to pick up the gossip. There was a huddle round the big wooden table.

"Whatever's happened?" asked the cook.

"Rebellion, that's what!" replied Travers, Lord Newark's serving man. "I was holding the horses with Nick, so we saw it all. Mr Henry had the king's commission to go into the Shire Hall and claim the muskets held there, in case of emergencies. And if this isn't an emergency, my name's not George Travers. That upstart John Hutchinson and the mayor defied him. Then an ugly crowd arrived with sticks and knives and started shouting insults at us. It got worse, and we could hear high words between Hutchinson and my lord and, in the end, he and the High Sheriff had to leave empty handed. Oh, he was right furious was Mr. Henry, and then the crowd started throwing things – cobble stones and mud. The horses were plunging and neighing, terrified they was. We could hardly hold them. We was lucky to get away, and Mr. Henry holding a king's warrant and all. It was a bad business."

"It's that John Hutchinson, that's behind all this trouble," said one. "Our Mr. Henry may have a sharp tongue but 'e's trying to keep the king's peace."

"The important thing is that we have no fighting in these parts," said the head steward. "If the king wants to fall out with parliament, that's his affair. Let the dandies fight it out in London, if they must. It's their quarrel, not ours!"

"The king's not in London – he's in York", chipped in Isaac, the footman.

"Let them fight in Yorkshire then!" continued the steward. "They are all dullards there. We'll keep our own counsel, if we've any sense – and there will be no political talk in the servant's hall…understand? " He glared at Meg, who had been whispering to Nick.

With that, the servants were dismissed and set about their tasks, and the next time that Meg and Nick were able to exchange glances was across the midday table, when they required to assist there.

Mealtimes were usually noisy occasions for the Kingston family. Her ladyship usually held forth at great length, often complaining about the servants, and the two eldest brothers would argue as if they were still at their places in Parliament. Frances, the youngest son, would try his best to keep the peace, whilst the old earl muttered quietly to himself. Today, it was as if someone had died. Plainly, the family were deeply troubled about matters which could not be discussed with servants in the room. The Earl of Kingston, a sombre figure, dressed in black with cream lace jabot, looked tired. There were grey shadows around his eyes that Nick had not seen before and his hand shook as he reached for his wine glass.

Lady Pierrepont sat dejectedly at the opposite end of the table. She had little appetite, and just picked at the food on the platter, making feeble sallies into conversation about the weather and the latest styles of dress being worn, but nobody showed any interest. Lord Newark was gulping down his food as if there were no tomorrow – Nick was kept busy, bringing him extra portions from the main dishes. Facing him, in cold disdain, were his younger brothers, William, a swarthy serious man, looking every inch a determined member of the rebellious House of Commons, and the more slightly built, fair skinned Mr Francis. They communicated with quick glances – their eyes speaking what their tongues could not.

"Am I glad that's over!" exclaimed Meg when she and Nick finally reached the kitchen after the mealtime ended. "I've never seen them like this before…there must have been a row between Mr. Henry and…"

"What did I say? No gossiping in the servants' quarters!" Walter, the steward had overheard them.

Grumbling to herself, Meg left the room to go upstairs, back to the chamber where she was busy letting out yet another of the countess's dresses. As soon as she picked it up, she saw that one of the little decorative flowers stitched on the skirt was missing.

Of course, she remembered now, she'd seen it hanging loose and picked it off, so that she could sew it on again properly. But where was it? There was no sign of it in the room. She remembered she had popped it in her pocket and gone to fetch a bigger needle, and then the countess had called her and told her to take a message to the earl, who was in his study. Meg felt in her pocket. It was empty, but her fingers slipped through a large hole. It must have fallen out, but where? It was not on the floor. She must find it. The Countess would be furious. She'd say she could not possibly wear the dress without it.

Meg tried to remember exactly where she had been. After the study, she had come back into the room. Then the mistress had called again and sent her to cut some flowers in the garden. She was returning with them when Mr. Henry had ridden by. Then she went to the servant's hall, then the dining room. She must retrace her steps and find it.

It was all to no avail. There was no artificial red flower in the garden, on the path, in the hallways, in the servants' hall or the dining room. She asked several of the staff, but no one had picked it up. Meg was getting desperate. She knew she'd be in trouble. The only place left to look was the earl's study and she had no right to go in there unless she was summoned. She had only been in the room on that one occasion. She must try to go again unseen.

Meg listened at the closed study door. There was no sound, *Good I must be quick.*

The door creaked as she opened it gingerly, just enough to peep inside. The afternoon light shone with the colours of the rainbow, dappling a wall, lined with leather volumes. A huge globe stood on the estate charts and there was a scatter of papers on a side table, but Meg's eyes were darting across the polished wooden floorboards. Ah! There it was – thank heaven no one had moved it! She pounced. Suddenly, there were voices from the passage outside They were coming nearer. Desperately, she looked round for somewhere to hide. The only place was a big oak chest by the window. She jumped in – just in time – there was enough space for her to crouch down.

Then the voices were in the room. Although she was cramped in the chest, a large keyhole let in some air and through it she caught glimpses of the earl and his sons.

"I've asked you to come in here," the earl was saying, "so that we can talk things through in private. I will not have disputes in front of the servants!"

For a moment, his sons were quiet and Meg scarcely dared to breathe. Then she heard William's voice.

"I'm sure I have no desire to quarrel with my brother, father." William was bitter. "Henry does not seem to understand. The ammunition in the Shire Hall is the property of the county. It should not be removed!"

"My commission's from the king himself!" retorted Henry. "It's clear and specific. I've been appointed Lord Lieutenant for this County and have instructions from the highest authority in the land to go with the High Sheriff to obtain the ammunition. I'll not be put off my sworn duty by bands of trouble-making tradesmen and tanners!"

"Then – what do you intend?" demanded William. "If you go in tomorrow with the militia, there'll be fighting, and people killed. It could spark off a civil war. Oh, I know it sounds absurd, but tempers are running high on both sides – it only needs a flashpoint!"

"I am sorry to remind you, brother – this county is my responsibility, not yours!" Meg could hear Henry pacing the room now. "You may be an M.P., but please remember you represent Much Wenlock – not Nottingham! Look to your own people – and leave me to my duties here!"

"Your brother's right, William," the earl intervened, "you should leave Nottinghamshire matters to him…."

"The place is of no consequence – it's the principle that counts!" continued William. "The same argument must be raging now all across this land. Every county has its powder and arms and its own militia. They're there for the protection of the people, not for the king to use as he wills. You're not his blind follower, Henry – you spoke in the Lords against his demands for a ship tax."

"I did," agreed Henry, "but I drew a line when you and your Puritan friends started to claim that the bishops had no right to sit in the House of Lords, and I 'm taking a stand on this too."

"Now that you have been promoted, you mean!" William countered.

"Silence – both of you!" the earl interjected. "That remark was uncalled for, William. You two give me a headache with your brawling! Give Francis a chance to speak. You live here all the time, my son. Tell us plainly – what do you think will happen if Henry goes back with a posse of militia?"

"I dread the outcome." Francis spoke quietly, but with authority. "There could be all out slaughter – and I am not talking of a few broken limbs! Do not suppose that barells of gunpowder, suits of armour and a piece of parchment with the royal seal will calm the town. It will provoke them, rather."

"Not in this shire!" affirmed the old earl. "Nottingham has long been a peaceful place, and so it will remain! If trouble in the town spreads, we would be drawn in – it would drive a wedge between us as a family!"

"There might be another way," Francis said. Meg strained to hear him.

"The mayor, Alderman James, is firm for Parliament, but there are others in the council who could be persuaded to argue for a compromise – Toplady, for one. He's rich and his voice counts. Suppose the council agreed to grant one or two barrels of gunpowder to the king – perhaps as a loan? I could take soundings – discreetly, you understand. You would need to let things cool, Henry – if you act in haste, it could ruin everything…"

"Thank you, Francis – do what you can." The earl was resolute. "My advice to you, Henry, is that you go to Newark. You, William – go to Much Wenlock or London. It's best you go your separate ways. We will communicate by letter, so that we all know the temper of the times. Perhaps there's no great harm done if we sit for a while in opposing camps, so long as we don't come to mortal blows." The earl's voice shook. "My concern's for this estate – one of you will inherit after I am gone. I've not laboured all these years to see it taken from us. No one can say how this folly between the king and parliament will end. After the dust settles, there'll be a reckoning. Some of our neighbours look now with envious eyes on what we hold. Francis – you go into Nottingham and stay in our town house – and keep your eyes and ears peeled and take those soundings you spoke of and bring me a report. For myself, I'll remain here – my gout troubles me much and I must protect this household and this land of ours."

Meg could hear a despairing sigh, as the old earl concluded: "When I am forced to take up arms with the king against parliament, or with parliament against the king – let a cannon ball divide me between them!"

After she was certain that they had left the room, Meg climbed out of the chest. Her legs ached because they'd been so cramped, but she hurried back to her duties.

Thank goodness, she'd not been missed.

But later that afternoon, as she stitched the flower back on to her lady's dress, the earl's last words kept reverberating through her mind.

CHAPTER 2

GREENWOOD DALE

Meg felt rather jealous when she saw Nick setting out for a spell of bird watching in the woods across the river. He had told her that Lord Newark had said he could have the day free. She had been very surprised because Mr Henry was never generous to the servants like Mr Francis could be, but now that the weather had turned into bright sunshine, here she was stuck in the house trimming another of the Countess's dresses.

Looking through the big leaded window, she saw him go down to the water's edge and untie the little green boat, which had a rope over it fastened to trees on either bank. She watched him climb in, stand up to grasp the rope and then propel himself hand by hand over the water. It was a slow process which always fascinated her.

If only she was free to go with him. He would have to be back to help serve the evening meal, full of his adventures, describing the birds he had seen and the wild flowers growing in the woods. Nick was not like the other boys she knew. Her brother Tom would romp around bird nesting and then come home with his prizes, but Nick would never do that. He respected wildlife. His reward was to observe it all and then his face would light up when he explained what he'd seen with an enthusiasm that was absorbing.

If she could only finish all her duties in time, and no one was looking, she'd slip outside to meet him, before they were needed to serve the meal. She'd climb the elm with the rope tied to it and hide in the foliage to surprise him.

* * *

Nick had used the rope twice before. He liked to escape from the gloomy hall into the woods whenever he could. It reminded him of the countryside near his father's home in Newark. Pierrepont

Hall was so vast and grand, that he sometimes felt stifled. He was used to the bustle of a country market town, and in Newark you were always close to the river and the meadows. It was his uncle, Edward Twentyman, who had taught him about the birds. As a young man, his uncle had worked as a gamekeeper for the Earl of Exeter, who had a big house in Newark, and now he was keen to pass his knowledge on to an enthusiastic nephew.

Nick still missed his home, although since mother had died two years ago and grand-mamma had moved in to supervise the little ones, nothing was the same. He'd been glad to escape the chores of working in his father's shop, so when he was told that Lord Newark would like him to work at the great hall, it sounded much more exciting than trading in cloth and sheepskins. At first, living in an Earl's 'palace' was so different and daunting that he had no time to be homesick, but now that he had been there for a year, he was beginning to miss his younger sister Dorothy and the tribe of little ones. The latest news was that his father had been elected as the new Mayor of Newark. Nick wondered how he would combine this with his business. Might he be called back to help? How would he feel about it? A walk in the woods, would give him a chance to consider.

His thoughts were interrupted by the flash of a moorhen. Nick dropped to the ground and crawled gently through the grass. If he was careful, he'd be able to see the bird. There it was, scratching near the base of an ash tree. He nestled down quietly to watch, listen and smell the woodlands again.

✳ ✳ ✳

"Where've you been, boy?" a girl's voice challenged him.

Nick looked around and could not see anyone.

"Where've you been?" the demand was repeated. Then he saw her, balanced on a branch of the elm tree, several feet above his head.

"Oh, it's you – you startled me?"

"You haven't answered my question."

"I've been watching birds in Greenwood Dale, and there are rabbits, dozens of them of them in the fields, hopping everywhere. I followed a track over the hill and down the other side, and there were bushes growing there all in flower, and the air was full of flutterbys."

Meg laughed out load. "You mean butterflies."

"Oh yes, of course I do. We always call them flutterbys at home. My father called them that by accident one day. He often tumbles over his words when he's speaking quickly, but my mother said it was very apt and clever of him. So we've always used that word in our family."

Meg gazed at him curiously. "Yes, it's a good name, and where did you go next?"

"At the end of a very long lane there was a drinking well by a cottage and the water was delicious, so cold – like water I've never tasted before."

"That's St. Ann's Well. The old folk used to say it had healing powers."

"Is that where the pleasure gardens used to be? I've heard Mr Henry speak of them."

"They've been closed a long while. The gentry used to go riding out there before the troubles, and there's a maze too, cut in the turf."

"I must go back and have a better look some time."

"You can come with me, if you like. I know the old man who lives in the cottage. Zachary, he's called. He's the keeper and he and his wife buy vegetables at my market stall in Nottingham."

Nick looked at her curiously. She was a determined sort of girl, with fair hair and freckles.

"Come and join me, here", she commanded.

Nick looked round. There was no one to see, so he scrambled up and perched beside her on the branch, which creaked a little under the double weight. "I'm not sure if this can take us both," he said.

Meg laughed. She had bright, white teeth and her eyes crinkled.

"I didn't know you had a market stall."

"My parents do. They rent a farm at Stragglethorpe, and I used to go to market with them, when I lived at home."

"So what brought you to Pierrepont Hall?"

"Years ago, my mother worked here. She was on friendly terms with some of the maids. One of them left and the Countess needed another, and Blanche put a word in for me, so to speak."

"And do you like it here?"

"I like some things, learning about the fashions, and the proper way to set a grand table. But mistress can be very demanding and I don't get days off to go into the woods like you."

"It's not often I do. This is only the third time I've been allowed a day all year, and Mr. Henry's got a sharp tongue, so I have to be very careful. He's going away on some business next month, and he doesn't like his servants doing work for other members of the family, so I might get some days off then, if I do. I'll try and explore all those woodland paths. There are so many of them."

"Boys get all the favours. It's not fair. Do you think there's going to be a war?"

"I don't know. Mr Henry says that the best way to prevent a war is to prepare for it and scare the rebels off."

"And do you think he's right?"

"I don't know. I suppose so."

"What does your father think? Is he for parliament, like all the Nottingham merchants?"

"Oh no. He's a Royalist. They're all Royalists in Newark, and he's just been elected as the Mayor."

"Good for him and good for Newark." Meg bounced up and down excitedly on the bough. It cracked, and they were both toppled abruptly into the long grass.

Meg thought this was a huge joke. They dusted themselves down and glanced anxiously towards the Hall. No one was on this side of the building so they did not think they had been seen.

"We'd better be getting back," said Nick, and aware that they might be observed them from the windows, he started to walk up the slope to the great house.

Meg walked along the river bank for a few minutes and then approached it from a different angle. She did not want tongues wagging.

CHAPTER 3

ENTERTAINING THE KING

August 1642

"What is to be done? What is to be done?" cried the Countess in alarm, when Meg went into her dressing room a few days later. It was clear that she did not expect a reply, and would have been most upset if Meg had had the audacity to make a suggestion. She was just in one of her tizzies.

Meg was getting used to this now and carried on with the business of buttoning the back of her mistress's gown without comment. In the sitting rooms the Countess was unusually quiet, but it was in the privacy of her boudoir that she gave vent to her acute anxieties. It wasn't really surprising, Meg thought, with the family divided. The Earl brooding in his study, Mr Henry assembling a local fighting force for the King, Mr William locked away with the parliament men and Mr Francis trying to keep the peace in Nottingham.

"Does that seem comfortable, ma'am?" Meg asked when she had finished the buttoning.

"Nothing seems comfortable, child," retorted Lady Kingston. "Comfort is a thing of the past, but the dress is very tight. You must have shrunk it in the wash."

"I'm sorry if I did that, ma'am. I am always am most careful," said Meg, remembering the large dinner that the Countess had eaten last night.

"Oh, well, it will do well enough, I suppose. Here am I cooped up in this place, with the family going off in all directions and I am unable to go anywhere. No visiting, no balls, no guests to amuse us. Everyone is afraid of what may happen next. And then there's Mr Henry gone to stay in Newark, whilst he's recruiting for the King. Even talk of the servants being rounded up as soldiers and made to march up and down. Who is to wait on us? I hear that our horses may be taken away to pull guns around. Did we ever hear the like? I suppose we will have no carriages soon and all have to trudge about in the mud like farm labourers."

When Meg went back into the servant's hall, there was an even greater stir.

"Mercy on us!" The cook was in dismay, "The Royal Court coming to Nottingham. Where will they lodge all of them courtiers and soldiers? Will they all come here and expect me to devise London delicacies?"

"No fear of that," the steward hastened to assure her. "I'm told that they are being accommodated at the Earl of Clare's house, Thurland Hall, in the centre of town."

"There's a blessing," said the cook. But Meg was disappointed. She'd dreamed of the Royal Family coming to Pierrepont Hall, and being able to decorate one of the dresses belonging to the fabled Queen Henrietta Maria, who was reputed to be decked with pearls and rubies.

On Saturday morning, Mr Francis appeared, having ridden in haste from Nottingham to avoid being pressed into joining the king's forces. From his manservant, the staff heard that the town was thronging with soldiers, drumming for recruits in the market square. Master Henry was in charge of the recruiting at the Salutation Inn, and young Nicholas Clay, scholar that he was, had gone with him to write down the names of new volunteers.

"There's no doubt that war's intended," Bartlett, the coachman, affirmed. "I'm told that they've ordered Robert Large to make a great banner to fly from the castle. They calls it the King's Standard. Wherever you sees that flyin' you will know that the King's nearby – him and all his cavalry!"

Meg was excited by this talk, and envious of Nicholas Clay, who had been chosen for such an important task. Why should it always be men and boys that got the exciting things to do?

She was determined that she would think of a way to go into Nottingham herself – soon! She might even catch a glimpse of King Charles or his gallant nephew, Prince Rupert of the Rhine.

Next morning, Master Henry rode up to the Hall. Meg, who was changing bed sheets at the time, peered through the window when she heard the hooves and thought he looked splendid in his new russet coat, and his wide rimmed black hat, with a huge ostrich feather tucked into its band. And there was young Nicholas behind him, looking much older now. He sat tall in the saddle and was flanked by two soldiers in breastplates and plumed helmets.

The Earl greeted his eldest son with a smile. Then without saying anything, he led him through the house to his private study. Nick dismounted, and was swept away into the servants' hall by an excited group of folk from "below stairs." The cook plied him with ale and apples, and the others all crowded around, eager with questions.

"Have you seen the King?" "What's to do in Nottingham?" "Is there goin' to be civil war?"

Nick was quite overwhelmed. He couldn't answer all at once. His part was limited to attending to Master Henry's immediate needs and sometimes acting as his scribe.

"I d-don't know", he stammered "Master Henry spends all his time in conference with people and I'm not in the room. I do know he's very angry because there are so few recruits. When the menfolk heard the King was coming, half of them chose to be out of town… the road over Trent Bridge is filled with carts and horses: folks are trying to get away. Some are taking their children and chattels too! They all have their excuses: sick relatives and such, but the truth is that no one wants being charged for the upkeep of the court and they don't want to be drummed into the royal army."

"Have you seen the King – or any of his family?" Meg managed to make herself heard.

"Only at a distance – Master Henry and the High Sheriff received the King when he arrived at the county border. I caught a glimpse of him when he came to Newark – he's smaller than you'd expect, with a pale sad face. Prince Rupert, now – he's a sight to see! He smiles at everyone. They say he's noble and brave and a great commander of men."

"Nicholas!" A loud command came from the entrance hall. It was Nick's summons to go with Master Henry and the soldiers.

* * *

That night, when Meg brought the washbowl and water jug into her mistress's bedroom, she found the Countess in a reflective mood.

"We live in sad times, child. Few men are prepared to show their faces when their king needs them." The Countess dabbed her face with a lace 'kerchief.

Meg seized her opportunity. "If you please, ma'am…I wonder if you will be needing me tomorrow. My father is busy with his harvesting, and it would be a great help if I could take our dairy produce to the weekday market, as the king's men will be needing extra food…?"

The Countess looked at Meg with eyebrows raised: "Do you think this wise, child? The town will be crawling with courtiers and soldiers."

"My brother will go with me," Meg quickly added, "He's helping at the farm this week as Mr Hutchinson's away."

"Mr Hutchinson will do well to stay away! They are traitors to the King – he and his meddlesome wife! Don't talk to me of traitors. Well – if you want to go to the market, I'll not stop you. Come back next day without fail and tell me all you've seen. I wish to know everything! T'is a sad thing when a Countess cannot go to the Royal Court, and has to pick up gossip from a country maid. This is what we have sunk to in these awful times! What is a body to do?"

Meg was dismissed with a small flick of the hand.

* * *

Early next day, Meg walked down the lane from Pierrepont Hall to the crossing with the Nottingham Road. There was a haze on the fields, and swarms of gnats in the air, which gave the promise of a hot day to come. It was a good two miles' walk, and Meg knew she had to be at the finger post by seven o'clock if she was to be on time to meet Tom as he drove the cart to market. He would be surprised to see her. Her only fear was that her mother might be on the cart also, and tell her to go back to the hall saying: "Nottingham is no safe place for a young girl at such a time!"

What nonsense! Tom was allowed to go, and he a full year younger! Parents always kept girls in the background when exciting events were happening. Meg remembered how she had to beg her parents to let her go out to work at all. They would have kept her on the farm, if they'd had their way!

As she approached the Nottingham road, her heart missed a

beat. Five gaudily dressed King's men were loitering around the crossroads, jeering and laughing at the passers-by. Some were townsfolk, their carts laden with family goods, hurrying south from the town. Others were women and children walking on foot. All looked harassed. One woman shook her fist at the soldiers, who scoffed at her. Then a farmer's cart appeared heading to the market. A red-faced sergeant held up his hand and stopped it and his men began to offload the produce.

"How dare you!" the farmer shouted. "These 'ere vegetables are goin' to be sold at Weekday Cross. You've no right to take 'em!"

"Hold your peace!" retorted the officer. "We're under king's orders. This beggarly town has not housed and fed us as it ought – and if peasants refuse to pay the king's levies, then my men must take their fodder as and where they will!"

"What do you know about our affairs? I pays the rent – and am a loyal subject of 'is majesty King Charles!" the farmer protested.

"Then, if you are loyal, you won't object to feeding his soldiers." The sergeant replied. "Now then, you'll see. Drive your cart to our camp, just over there."

One of his men took the horse's bridle, and roughly jerked the animal's head. The farmer jumped down to the ground and began struggling to take the reins from the soldier's grasp. The sergeant drew his knife and so the angry farmer was forced to follow.

"What are you staring at, Merrylegs?"

Meg flushed to see one of the soldiers leering at her ankles and the peep of her best red stockings. The man laughed, as he ran to catch up with his comrades.

Meg sat down on the grass by the signpost to wait for Tom. She hoped he would not be long, and worried about whether it was wise to take the cart to the market on this day.

The stream of people leaving the town was relentless – they came singly or in family groups, some riding, some walking and some pushing barrows piled high with their personal belongings, a stream of refugees. Were they leaving their homes temporarily, or for a longer time? Perhaps they don't know, she thought. There were very few folk going towards the town – and thankfully, no more soldiers.

Here was Tom looking quite cross! He reined in the cart, full of market produce.

"What are you doing here?" he demanded.

"Coming with you to market – I've been allowed the day off work, and have been waiting for the last half hour for you."

Tom began to protest that he did not need her help, and that it would not be safe for her to go with him. Meg, not to be dissuaded, quickly jumped up beside him, and seized the reins from his hands.

"I'm older than you! I was marketing while you were still at school, so you'd best hold your tongue!"

Tom could see no point in arguing – it would only make her more determined to have her way. Secretly he was pleased that she'd come – he'd probably leave her with the produce to sell, while he slipped away to find out what was happening in the town.

Meg's high spirits sank when she saw soldiers guarding Trent Bridge at both ends. They looked like an official picket, supervised by an officer. Most of the travellers were allowed to go by without stopping, but they picked out some men for questioning. Meg and Tom had to wait a while before they could cross the river, while the stream of people continued.

Nottingham was alive with king's soldiers. Some were fierce and bristling with weaponry, looking as if they had been "blooded" in the Dutch wars. Others were new conscripts, beardless youths – who looked proud and yet half afraid of the weapons they were carrying. Windows were shuttered – a sure sign of trouble. Ordinary townsfolk ducked inside their doorways or were departing with their bundles and carts.

There was no market today – instead, a troop of raw recruits were drilling on the patch where the baker usually set up his stall. Tom and Meg were uncertain what they should do. They saw one of the regular stall-holders stolidly beginning to offload his milk churns on to the steps of the Weekday Cross. So, they ignored the bellowing officer, and began to display their vegetables in sacks, spreading them out on the cobbles, as usual. It was a full hour before they had their first customer – an old lady – who emerged from her house on Blowbladder Street. She hastily bought her wares and scurried back like a frightened mouse.

No-one else approached for some time and they were

intrigued to observe a small troop of young recruits being drilled in using fire-arms by their sergeant:

"Prime your pan!" "Lodge your ball!"

Meg was familiar with a fowling-piece, but these matchlock muskets were something new to her. They were long, fearsome looking weapons, which took some shouldering. She hoped that they were not loaded!

Then a surprising thing happened. A liveried gentleman appeared around the corner from High Pavement, and in a loud voice, ordered them to pack up their cart and follow him.

"Why?" We are not doing anything wrong!" cried Meg "We always sell our produce at this market."

The gentleman gave her a doomsday glare. "Would you deny the Royal Court?"

Even the loud-mouthed sergeant stopped his shouting to see what was going on – his recruits remaining silent.

Meg and Tom were acutely aware that all eyes were upon them.

"Come!" ordered the footman. Hastily the pair repacked their cart, while the colourful gentleman tapped his buckled shoe impatiently on the cobbles.

They were led down Fletchergate, across Warsergate, through Swine Green to the Earl of Clare's great house on the northern edge of town. This, as everyone knew, was where the king was staying with all his court followers. They were curious to know why they were being taken there. The footman said nothing to enlighten them, marching them round to the servant's entrance. He called to someone through an open window.

A sturdy cook emerged to inspect the vegetables on the cart. She sniffed the turnips and swedes, nibbled the carrots, ruffled the feathers of the pheasants, chewed at an apple, bit into a cheese, dipped her fingers in the milk churn and licked them lustily. Finally, she told the fancy footman she'd have the lot – disappearing into the kitchen, chuntering to herself: "This court'll be the death 'o me – I never knowed such stomachs!"

Meg and Tom were ordered to offload the cart and carry everything into the scullery. Tom stopped to work out how much the produce would cost. The footman harried him: "No time for that now, boy – I will see you are paid, just as soon as all those wares are unloaded."

Good as his word, he poured a shower of coins into waiting hands, when they were done. Meg tipped the coins out into her apron: "You count the bronze, I'll count the silver." They were both beaming at their bounty.

"Hurrah for King Charles and his court! That's what I say!" Meg exclaimed. "They should have come to Pierrepont Hall – with our farm as the victuallers."

* * *

"Well now – we've sold our produce, so the rest of the day's ours! Let's walk about the town and see what is happening up at the castle," Tom suggested.

"Since we are in a royal courtyard now – I've a mind to stay here as long as I may, and watch the goings on. Everyone's so busy, they'll scarce bother me."

"Fine – I'll leave the horse and cart at the Drury stables – I know the ostler, and we can meet up again there and go home at the usual time."

Tom went to adventure round the town. Meg perched herself on a hen coop, and started to observe all the comings and goings.

CHAPTER 4

RAISING THE STANDARD

Standard Hill
Monday 22 August 1642

Meg stayed by the kitchen door as long as she could. It was clear that a great feast was being prepared at Thurland Hall. A brewer's dray was brought into the yard and unloaded, and then a man arrived with a cart buzzing with flies. When it was emptied, Meg saw pigs' carcasses and a side of beef being carried into the kitchen.

A footman spotted her sitting on the hen-coop and ordered her to go away. Disappointed that she had not seen any of the queen's ladies-in-waiting, Meg decided to make for the Earl of Kingston's town house in Stoney Street, where she knew she would be able to pick up some of the servants' gossip.

Nicholas Clay was the first person she saw, coming down the steps from the front door, and talking eagerly to a girl of about her own age. For a moment Meg felt a flash of jealousy but then he saw her and introduced his twin sister.

"Dorothy's come to Nottingham, with my father and family, to see the raising of the king's standard. It's the official sign that the king's declaring war on the rebels and my father's been invited to officially represent the people of Newark. We're all staying with my uncle, who lives here, in Chandler's Lane."

Nick's reserve was gone in his excitement about the momentous events and Dorothy chatted with Meg as if she were a close friend.

"Come back with us to my uncle's house," she urged. "We are to have a meal – you can join us, and then come on to the parade in the Market Square. All the king's men are marching."

"I'd be delighted. But I didn't know you two were twins."

"It runs in the family. We've got two little ones as well."

That afternoon, Meg stood by the Malt Cross on Long Row

with a large family. Nick and Dorothy, Will, Ned and the twins, Bessie and Tim (aged 4), complete with grand-mamma, uncle and aunt. They watched a colourful parade of soldiers and militia.

A platform had been erected under the trees on Timber Row for the high sheriff and his party. The younger children jumped up and down with glee when they saw their father, Hercules Clay, among them.

"My father says that the Mayor of Nottingham has refused to be here," whispered Dorothy. "Only two of the Nottingham aldermen are present – it's a snub to the King. The Mayor and gentry of Newark are all here, with our militia and trained bands, but there's few signed up from Nottingham – it's a disgrace!"

"What are trained bands?" asked Ned.

"Groups of men who've volunteered to serve as soldiers," Nick explained.

"Tim will be soldier too when big," piped little Tim.

A few minutes later, the high sheriff and his party mounted the stand.

"That's father in the blue plumed hat!" Dorothy told Meg.

He was a broad shouldered man, with a serious, lined face, standing beside Lord Newark. The younger children waved and shouted, and were quickly subdued by their grandmother.

A loud trumpet blast announced the cavalry, led by a dashing cavalier, resplendent in silk and lace, a huge ostrich feather adorning his broad-rimmed hat.

"Richard Byron," breathed Barbara and Meg's heart missed a beat.

* * *

Tom was standing on the opposite side of the square, but he recognised the richly attired cavalier who had suspiciously visited Owthorpe Manor when his master was away. He looked across at the platform and saw the two men who had tried to seize the arms at the Shire Hall.

"These are the enemies," he thought. This realisation sent a cold shiver down his spine. "And those local lads in the trained bands. They look like turkeys dressed up for slaughter."

Then he saw Meg, cheering and waving her kerchief and he pulled out of the crowd, seething. He had to get away.

Meg was riveted, with tears in her eyes, as she watched the brave parade pass. She saw Nick's father cross himself, in high church fashion, when a team of horsemen passed flying a great streamer which read "Give Caesar his due". She cheered and waved, and one of the riders turned, smiled and waved back to her.

When Meg met up with Tom again at the end of the afternoon, he surprised her. "Sam and Alice Drury are going to the castle tonight to see the raising of the king's standard and I'm going with them. They want to know which local people are joining the King's party."

Nothing could have pleased her more. "I'll be there, too," she announced with some defiance.

The sky darkened and a summer squall blew up, as they crossed the square and made their way towards the castle.

It stood high on a cliff to the west of the town, approached by a steep causeway and an ancient gatehouse. The old royal fortress had been disused for over a hundred years. Some of the curtain wall had fallen, and grateful townsmen had used the stones for their own purposes.

A crowd of revellers, several of them plainly tipsy, were lounging by the gatehouse, singing bawdy songs about puritans and roundheads. King's soldiers, wearing helmets, metal breastplates and scowls on their faces, guarded the entrance, allowing no one through.

The gathering crowd were herded into the lower castle-yard, a great open space beyond the ditch. In a ragged line, they made their way between two lines of pike-men towards a grassy hill by the northern wall, where a group of officers were attempting to keep control. Meg recognised Henry, Lord Newark and Richard Byron – their finery dripping from the sudden downpour.

Then Meg saw the entire Clay family, standing with other distinguished guests, on the other side of the hillock. Meg caught Nick's eye and he waved to her.

Suddenly a trumpet sounded and a group of horsemen approached from the gatehouse. As they came up the hillock, the men bowed and women curtsied. This must be the King of England!

He was a small, slim figure, dressed in royal blue with an amazing head-dress; a wide hat adorned with the whitest ostrich feathers Meg had ever seen. As he came more into view – Meg saw that his face looked sad and tired and his beard was greying prematurely.

Next to him, in stark contrast, rode a tall and elegant young man in bright cavalier attire, and a broad, confident smile. A white dog trotted proudly at his heels. Two young boys – dressed richly, but solemn and wide-eyed, flanked them as they surveyed the scene. "That's the king's nephew, Prince Rupert of the Rhine, with the Prince of Wales and young Duke of York," someone said behind her.

"God save the king!" shouted the crowd. Only Tom, Sam and Alice remained silent. Their silence might have been noted, except for a cry that went up: "The standard!"

A troop of mounted soldiers rode out of the gate to the middle bailey, their leader carrying a flag on a long pole. They broke into a canter, crossed the green and rode up a grassy mound, where they drew reign and the leader presented the standard to the King, who received it with reverence. He was assisted to place it in a prepared hole in the ground. A brand new spade was produced, and two soldiers filled in the hole, but the pole was too tall to stand upright and the flag was too heavy to fly, so it had to be held in position by two troopers. This rather spoiled the effect, and Tom, sensing significance, could not avoid a furtive smirk. Meg glared at him. How immature, he was!

She watched the King don his fashionable pince-nez and peruse a scroll, which had been handed to him. He frowned and shook his head, called for quill and ink, so he could alter a word or two, then handed the sheet to a herald. The man bellowed out: "This standard has been raised here in Nottingham on the 22nd day of August 1642, to summon all loyal subjects to hasten and take arms with King Charles, Defender of the Faith, against the traitors, the Earl of Essex and the parliamentary faction, who have defied their liege lord and are threatening the peace of the realm. God save the king!"

The princes and the officers all cheered, and there was further support from the loyalists in the crowd. Meg joined in, but Tom and the Drury family held their peace, staring stolidly ahead.

* * *

Later that night, Meg and Tom travelled back in their cart without speaking. They were too much in awe, and in any case, they knew that any words between them would have been in conflict, and neither wanted that.

Meg climbed down wearily at the gate of Pierrepont Hall, and turned to give Tom the money she still held from the sale of produce that morning. It seemed an age ago.

As she wished him "Goodnight", she surprised herself at the tenderness of her tone and by the lingering look Tom gave her. As she walked up the path, Meg remembered the closeness she had felt to her younger brother in his childhood and realised that they both knew that they now stood on opposite sides of a great divide.

CHAPTER 5

CALL TO ARMS!

Newark 1643

"Nicholas Clay, you're coming back to Newark with me!" Mr Henry was crisp and curt. Nick was delighted to be going home, but he did not understand why.

"You did a good job collecting recruits for the king in Nottingham," his master continued, "even if half of them have sloped off again in the last year. The men of Newark are made of sterner stuff, and as we can't hold the Nottingham river crossing for the king, we must secure the one in Newark."

Nick remembered that his father had told him that Newark was important for the king, as it stood on the great north road from London to York, and had a river link to the port of Hull.

Henry Newark saw the smile in his face. "Yes, you can stay with your family," he said, before Nick put the question, "but you must attend me in my quarters at Lord Deincourt's house, whenever I call you to The Friary."

* * *

Dorothy ran out to hug Nick, as soon as she saw him coming back home, carrying his wooden box of belongings.

"How did you travel?" she asked.

"I came in the Pierrepont carriage with two other servants."

"You'll never leave us again, will you Nick?" demanded young Will, who'd followed Dorothy into the street.

"You mustn't go away again," said Dorothy, "so many of our workers have gone to be soldiers that father needs your help in the business."

"Good," said Will, "The days seem so long with grand-mamma hushing us all the time."

"It's not so easy," said Nick. "I still work for Lord Newark. He's brought me here to help recruit more men for the king. I'll be living at home as long as he wants me to, but I'm still under his orders. That's all I know."

"Father must insist," said Dorothy. "He's working himself to death between his duties as mayor and running the business too. Surely, the king's got enough soldiers now. The whole town's alive with them. They're always drilling in the market place."

They entered the shop, and immediately Nick was surrounded by four more little ones. The twins, Tim and Mary, clambered all over him.

"Welcome home, Nicholas, my boy!" Hercules Clay emerged from behind a pile of ledgers on the counter, rose and shook the lad's hand as if to pull it off, words excitedly tumbling out:

"I'm so glad, you're here – so glad. Times are hard – short of staff – mayoral duties you know – meetings about the war – and then the shop-work and the children to see to. I need your help, lad – need your help. You can start with the book–keeping. It makes my head ache – lost my clerk – gone for a soldier – and we must keep these young pups in check – too much for grand-mamma." Eyeing the youngest, he cried "Climb down, Tim – decorum, Mary. Remember, you are all children of the mayor now, not just a mercer. You must set a sample to other children in what you say and do. You must mind your qs and ps."

Will tittered and Nick felt embarrassed for his self-educated father, who in his eagerness to say the right thing, frequently jumbled his words without realising. Nick blushed, remembering that when Mr. Henry had been talking to Sir Richard Byron last week, he had referred to him as "the son of the mayor, Mr Circulees Hay," and they had both laughed genially.

"You will find us all very busy here, Nicholas – very busy.

143

The king has been here – yes, indeed. I was introduced to him, myself and he told me that he has made Newark his principal base in the region, to protect the north road, you know. We have our own town militia now, too, and your brother's mother, Uncle Edward, is appointed to be their commander."

"I watched them this morning drilling with muskets in the Market Place," shouted Will.

"And there are so many grand ladies and gentlemen arriving now, that Sir Richard has been made Town Governor and he has his quarters immediately opposite our shop", said Dorothy.

"I watch the officers come and go from the nursery window," shouted Ned.

With all this noise around her, baby Bessie wakened and began to howl.

The excitement was cut short when Grand-mamma opened the parlour door to object to all the noise. Hercules disappeared again behind his ledgers, and the old lady ordered Dorothy to take Nick up to his old room, which had been hastily vacated by Will, who complained again that he was too big now to go back to sharing a bedroom with Ned and Tim.

* * *

Daily, Nick walked from his father's house in Stodman Street to get instructions from Lord Newark, who was sometimes at the Friary with Lord Deincourt, sometimes with his son, Colonel Sir Charles Leake and sometimes with the governor. If he was not needed, Nick went back to help in the shop.

One cold February morning, his grandmother had set him to checking the trading house ledgers, when a red-faced messenger came bursting into the counting room, his voice shaking with fear.

"The governor's sent me to fetch the mayor! We must rouse the town – the rebels are coming! Their army's gathering at Beacon Hill!"

"Who's seen them, Toby?" grand-mamma demanded.

"The officer of the watch. The militia's being mustered now. Lord Newark says we must send out the town crier to alert everyone, There'll be shooting for sure! All able-bodied men are to join a muster in the market square. All women and young 'uns to stay inside with doors and windows barred..."

"Father's out of town – and I don't know where the crier is!" Nick interrupted.

"There's no time to search for him," Grand-mamma affirmed. "Young Nicholas – this is work for you. Take the old drum and beat it around the streets." She pointed to a dusty drum hanging over the doorway. Nick hesitated. It had always been treated like a sacred memoriam to past valour. Nick had never been allowed to touch it – until now! As a child he had longed to bang it, but his father had always refused. Nick quickly climbed on a chair and carefully lifted the drum down. The stretched hide surface was well worn and dirty, some of the tassels were frayed with age – but it was intact, and there were two drumsticks tucked into the barrel-rope.

"Your great uncle was the last to beat that drum – when he was ensign to Captain Russell in the town militia. Now it is your turn – go now around the town and beat it with all your strength. That'll bring folks to their doors!" She turned again to the messenger. "You go along with him, Toby. Tell the men to bring pitch-forks, spits, spades or whatever they have to hand – and the women to bolt their doors. We'll send those rebels to the devil! Who do they think they are coming here from Nottingham or Lincoln, defying the King, and threatening this town? One thing's certain – Newark will stay loyal."

Nick ran out into the street, Dorothy and William hard on his heels.

The four younger children were jumping about with glee because Nick was making the drum go "Boom! Boom! Boom" – loud enough to waken even the dead! This was a glorious adventure. Grand-mamma struggled to catch them and force them back indoors, She called out to Dorothy and Will. Dorothy came back in, but there was no catching Will.

Nick headed across the road to the governor's house. Mr Henry had just arrived, and hearing that the town crier was nowhere to be found, sent Nick to parade the streets, shouting the message: "Call to Arms. All men assemble in the Market Square!"

Toby and Will were told to knock on doors telling all women and children to stay inside and lock the doors.

The youths made their way noisily down Stodman Street, into Castlegate, and were soon joined by a throng of tradesmen and apprentices, many carrying sticks and staves, and one farmer a fearsome scythe. All those who had served with the militia or been drilled in the trained bands hurried to the Market Place, where officers were attempting to assemble a fighting force. The elderly, and women with children, hurried inside and bolted windows and doors.

At the corner of Bargate, a sergeant from the Militia joined with the youths and started up a clarion cry: "For God and the king!"

This was echoed behind them, as more and more men and youths joined their progress. A pack of excited dogs barked around Nick's heels in Kirkgate – they had to be beaten off by the apprentices. In Appletongate, a woman had a fit of hysterics, and a crazed old man sank down to his knees outside the church, calling upon the wrath of God. By the time the procession arrived in the Market Place – the area was filling with armed men – some with swords and muskets, but most with improvised weapons. Breastplates and helmets were in short supply, so these were worn by the trained-band leaders.

Sir Richard Byron, the Town Military Governor, was speaking to the assembled men. Beside him, Lord Newark stood on the top step of the market cross, looking sternly at the assembly. The militia and trained bands, mainly local men who had volunteered for action before, were drawn up in lines facing them, with their pikes and muskets held high. Behind them, a motley gang of tradesmen, farmers, and youths, armed with an assortment of farming implements and tools, were craning their necks to hear.

When Nick came into the square, the governor was just finishing speaking. Lord Newark followed him on the top step of the market cross to speak to them all.

"People of Newark. I'm proud to be with you at this hour. When the king was last here, many of you joined forces with him – and some of you fought bravely alongside us at Edgehill. Now the peril is near at hand and I call on your loyalty to king and country again – only this time it is different – it's to defend your own town. We are told that rebels from Nottingham and Lincoln are gathering on either side of us, intending to attack and destroy us. Why? Because the road to the north lies through Newark, and our castle commands the river crossing. We will not let it fall!"

Shouts of "Aye! The swines! We'll have their blood!" from the assembled men. Mr Henry had to shout louder to be heard above the din:

"The rebels have seized the south, but the king's forces are stronger in Yorkshire. Newark is the key to the north – we not only fight to protect his majesty, but also his church – it is in God's name that I call on you to protect your liberty and laws. Your troubles are my troubles – I will stand by you and we will share this danger together. The militia has been well drilled and each man knows his duty – Go now and perform it bravely! God save the king!"

A unanimous cheer echoed around the square.

* * *

Nick, his grand-mamma and the younger children were virtually prisoners in their own home for the next few days. The Mayor spent much of the time in the governor's house, opposite, calling home whenever he could to check how they all were. He gave the family strict instructions not to step outside and they had no desire to, as they could hear gunfire, shouts and sometimes screams from the streets outside.

On the afternoon of the second day, the water pump broke in the yard. This was a crisis, and eventually Grand-mamma decided that the ban on going out would need to be broken. She sent Nick with a jug to one of the town pumps in Balderton Gate.

At the corner, he found the road was closed. Muskets were protruding through cottage windows, and there was shooting into the street.

"What's going on?" Nick asked, one of the local militia, who barred his way.

"Go back. It's not safe here. Rebels have burst through the defence lines!" he was told briskly.

At that moment a shot rang out and he saw a man fall on the cobbled street.

Staying no longer, he ran back.

When the mayor came home, he was cross that Nick had ventured out, and said he'd arrange for water to be collected from the governor's house.

"They're rebels from Nottingham, followers of that upstart,

147

Hutchinson," he told them. "but our militia beat them out of town. It was alarming, but they got their deserts and now they've run away to nurse their wounds."

Even after the enemy were gone, there was strong evidence of the fighting, with some mutilated bodies lying in the streets, and several of the houses turned into blackened ruins. Men and women were walking in a state of shock – their excitement turning to bitter anger and grief. People blamed the governor because they had not been given enough warning. There had been no time to prepare for the onslaught. A grim resolution grew to repay the brutality being suffered.

* * *

Pierrepont Hall May 1643

The countess was more impatient than ever when Meg arranged her hair, this morning.

"That will never do, child! Don't you know that the queen is coming and I mean be presented to her in a few days time!"

"I'd heard she's landed in Yorkshire." Meg replied. "The servants say that she's bringing re-enforcements from France, but I didn't know she was coming this way, or that you are to meet her."

"Of course she must join the king in Oxford and that means crossing the Trent. Mr Henry has written to tell me that he's coming up with forces to join her army, and he'll escort her south. She should cross at Nottingham, but that wretched man, John Hutchinson, holds the bridge with his rebels, so she will go to Newark instead. There's to be a great rally of loyalists there, and the queen has invited the earl, so, of course, I will go with him. We must be in Newark in two days time, and Sophia and you are to come with my best silk gowns."

This was the first Meg had heard of it. "Will we be there long, ma'am?"

"How should I know? It depends on the queen's pleasure. She may stay a while, or she may ride on, and then there's the question of what the earl will do. He may be pressed to command an army and he is so gallant that he may agree, who knows? Anything may happen."

* * *

The house where the earl and countess were to stay in Newark was too crowded to accommodate extra servants, so it was arranged that Meg would lodge at the mayor's home, although she would still be attending her mistress daily to assist her. Meg had never felt happier or more needed. She was confident that one day soon she would see the queen.

Newark was buzzing with noblemen, their ladies and servants. High-ranking officers rode the streets on magnificent horses, bringing much work for the blacksmiths and the saddlers. The provision merchants and the tailors had never been busier. Coins changed hands, and the town exuded an air of hope and prosperity, quite novel to the locals.

The church bells pealed in celebration of the day the queen of England and her entourage arrived in the town. Sir Richard Byron, resplendent in his role as military governor, officially welcomed her. The Earl and Countess of Kingston were also there in the select party, with Lord Deigncourt and Colonel Leake – but Meg was not. She was cleaning and starching her mistress's best gown for the splendid evening ahead. To her great frustration, she could not even see anything through the window, boxed in as she was in an upstairs attic room.

When the earl returned that night, rumours spread around the servants that he had accepted command of the Royalist East Midland Army.

Meg told Nick that the queen had been heard to say that now she had no fears for the fall of Gainsborough. Her gallant Earl and his Cavaliers would hold that stronghold for the crown.

"The countess is delighted that the dithering is over," Meg told the children. "No one but the queen could have won his loyalty?"

CHAPTER 6

THE QUEEN'S COMMAND

Newark – June 1643

It was a stifling, hot summer day. Meg threaded her way through the crowds in the bustle of the busy Newark market place. The countess had sent her to buy some silk ribbons. It was strange to jostle with the country women on such an errand. There were no such fripperies in the lodgings, and her mistress had been insistent that she purchase them so that her costume would be complete when she was presented to her majesty that evening.

"Will this do, ducky?" the plump stall-tender held up a rainbow of ribbons. The girl hesitated, the shade must be just right, or her mistress would be cross.

"Let me have a closer look – the colour must be exact – my mistress is dining with the queen tonight."

The words slipped out and Meg immediately felt embarrassed. Why should she mind? Everyone knew the queen was here, staying with Lady Leeke in Kirkgate.

"So – I'm selling to the Royal Court, no less! There's something to tell my old man…'ere ducky, I'll cut you a snip – you take it to compare with the dress, and you come back an' tell me if it matches."

Later, as she sat by the casement window sewing the ribbons on to the gown, Nick was near her, busily polishing the buttons on the earl's dress-coat.

They chatted happily. He was glad to be living in his home town again, and excited to see royalty and so many soldiers there. These things pleased Meg too – although she thought Newark a small town when compared to Nottingham.

She had the same thought that evening, when she went with some of the earl and countess's servants to Lord Deincourt's home. Compared with Pierrepont Hall, there was nothing remarkable about the old house, sited on the outskirts of the town. It was built on the site of an old friary. It was strange to think that the queen of England was dining here, and that she was a princess, born in a grand French palace, and now travelling across England, with a large army, bringing re-enforcements from France. Meg wondered whether she would have the chance to see this fabled lady, so famous for her vivacious ways, fine attire, and stunning jewellery.

Usually, on hot days, the cool of the evening is welcome, that tonight it was still airless, and flies were buzzing everywhere. 'They must have smelt the banquet', Meg thought. She was downstairs with the other servants, but she could hear the laughter coming from the room above. It sounded as if this queen was good company, but Meg had not been not one of those invited to serve at table, so she felt that she was missing out.

Her opportunity came after the banquet was over, when the countess sent a message that she needed a fan fetched from her carriage. Meg jumped to her feet before any other servant could respond. Running into the stable yard, she grasped the fan from the carriage seat and, after adjusting her own costume and hair, she walked up the stairs, head held high.

As she stood by the open door, Meg observed that the dinner guests had left the table and were mingling in small groups. There was a hum of subdued voices and the swish of satin, but everyone was facing the queen who sat in the centre. All eyes were on her, and Meg could see that she was revelling in the attention.

Queen Henrietta Maria was petite in stature, dressed immaculately in rich blue satin, trimmed with exquisite lace. Precious stones sparkled in her hair and around her long white neck. A small white spaniel nestled in her lap; one royal hand rested gently on its head, while the other was wafting away some huge buzzing flies with a magnificent embroidered fan.

Meg strained to hear what the queen was saying. The accent was so strong that she thought at first that she was speaking French. Then the queen made a small signal with her hand to indicate that Meg had leave to enter. So, she had been noticed! Meg curtseyed, and could not help blushing.

"Reinforcements! Bon! Just what we need!" laughed Queen Henrietta Maria. This remark was accompanied with a ripple of polite laughter. "Your Nottingham flies are verrie persistent. See, girl," she cried to Meg, "one iz flying over zere. Bat 'im quick with your fan! Bon, you 'ave 'im. And there is a big black one by Lady Leake. Get 'im too."

Meg obeyed, running towards the fly and chasing it across the room towards the window, where she squashed it on the pane with her mistress's fan.

"Bon girl," the Queen was clapping her hands and looking straight at her with squirrel-like eyes, as a row of dark ringlets danced on her brow. "You do better than all my courtiers and soldiers 'ere. These flies 'ave been a pest all evening. They are rebel flies, with no respect for the Royal Generalissimo."

Meg curtseyed again and left the room. Once downstairs, she went to wash the fan, which was now splattered with a squirt of blood and the remains of a fly. Nick appeared and worked the handle of the water pump outside.

"Did you see the queen?" he asked.

"Yes," said Meg. "She spoke to me. She's very light-hearted and she likes killing flies."

Once the fan was cleaned, Meg went back up the stairs and gave it to her mistress.

The queen saw her enter and smiled in her direction, although she was talking to Prince Rupert at the time.

As Meg left the room, she had to pass by the Earl of Kingston, who was listening to quiet words from Sir Richard Byron and she thought she heard, "If you were to attack Gainsborough, when I go for Nottingham, the rebels would not have enough troops in this region to send reinforcements. Think on that."

* * *

Six weeks days later

"Fire! Fire! Those devils have torched our thatch."

Nick rushed to escape. As he bolted through the front doorway, a rabble of angry faces booed, jeered and laughed at him fleeing the big house. He had no idea which way to go. He did not know Gainsborough. It was turmoil in the courtyard outside. Other servants were lost in the crowd. Some people were fighting and he didn't know friend from foe.

He pushed through a group gathered in the iron gateway, ran over the road and down a lane opposite. He had a glimpse of the river ahead and made towards it. Then he saw he had made a mistake. There were soldiers firing muskets at an armed royalist group, who were being driven into the water. There was no bridge and the road followed the water's edge, so he was trapped.

He turned right to get away for firing, and then saw a rough set of bullies running towards him along the cobbled pathway. There was no escape. He crouched against a doorway. Suddenly, it opened and a plump arm dragged him inside.

"You're safer indoors," a woman's voice said. "All hell's broken loose today."

Nick found himself looking at a middle-aged woman in an apron and mob cap.

"Stay here awhile, boy. Those soldiers are all wild animals whatever side they're on, an' there's local brutes tagging on who are no better. Are you a local lad? I don't know your face."

At first Nick didn't respond, Could her trust her? She seemed well meaning.

"No. I'm from Newark. I don't know Gainsborough."

"What are you doing here then?" she asked suspiciously.

"I came with the earl," he said nervously.

"You're one o' them Royalists, then. All these strangers comin' here with their quarrels, so that they can murder each other in a place where they're not known, and frighten honest working folk."

"I'm sorry. I didn't want to come here at all. I'm just a servant, not a soldier."

"I can see you're no soldier, but why did this blessed earl have to come 'ere at all, and take over one of the best houses in our town? I think 'e should go straight back to wherever 'e came from. We 'ad enough trouble with the siege and then wi' those Yorkshire men wi' the Duke of Newcastle, who said they'd come to save us an' roistered like wild pigs."

"I don't think the earl wanted to take sides at all, but he had no choice really when the queen came to Newark. He felt it was his duty to support her and keep Gainsborough free from the rebels. I'm in his service, so I had to come."

They eyed each other cautiously.

"Aye, that's the way it is wi' all the noble folk. They treat servants like dogs, and make them walk to heel. I know, 'aving been in service myself, and my daughter is still, poor bitch. Was

153

you workin' in that great house then? The one they've set fire to. We saw the blaze, me and Mistress Armitage."

"Yes, I've been there for eight days. Everything seemed quiet at first as far as I could see. The earl brought a big army with him to keep the peace and overthrow the siege. We didn't see much of him. He was out each day for long hours, sorting out the town defences, but yesterday this parliament man, Lord Willoughby, descended with a massive force. I've no idea what the situation is now. The guns have never stopped since cockcrow, and suddenly, this afternoon, a mob attacked our house chanting the earl's name, and they fired our thatch, so we all had to dash out and I don't know which way to turn."

"You was right to run away, boy, an' you'll stay away from that lot if you've sense in your head."

"But I can't desert my friends. I don't know whether they're dead or alive."

The woman looked out of the door. "Those bully boys have gone away," she said. "But they're still fighting each other like wildcats by the river. Best thing for you to do then, is slip out now and go the other way."

She stepped aside and indicated that it was time for Nick to leave so with a word of thanks he hurried out and quickly ran away from the river.

Not knowing the town, Nick kept to the quietest streets, and gradually made his way back towards the large house that had been commandeered for the Earl and his entourage. The thatch was still blazing, but the rioters had gone away, and there was a huddle of servants standing sadly in the courtyard.

Suddenly, there was a joyful shout "There he is!" and the crowd of servants ran over to surround him. "We thought you'd been lost in the fire," cried one. "Oh, Nick, God bless you, what a relief!"

In that moment Nick felt elated. They really cared. All of them. Then he looked around. "Is anyone missing?", he asked.

"No, we were all here, except you," said George Travers. Nick never forgot the relief of that moment.

* * *

As he gazed down from his hard seat aboard the military pinnace,

154

Nick watched the murky grey water reflecting his own mood of uncertainty. The River Trent looked sombre this grey afternoon. He heard the rhythmic stroke of the helmeted oarsmen, and noted the stony countenance of the parliamentary officer, who had taken the earl into captivity. Everything had changed so swiftly in the space of a day. He felt utterly bewildered.

Last night, the earl had been bought back to the big house, under parliamentary escort. The town had fallen, and he had been forced to surrender to Lord Willoughby. The earl had been wounded. Nick had to help Travers tend burns on his hands and a cut on his cheek. After such high hopes, it was all so humiliating. But the thing that grieved the earl most was to learn that his own son, William, had been one of the cavalry officers opposing him in battle.

Lord Willoughby had decided that the earl should be sent to the parliamentary stronghold in Hull. They had been hustled aboard this eight-oared boat. Travers and Nick had charge of the earl's travelling box. Everything else had to be left behind. Now they were all prisoners, being taken to one of the great parliamentary camps.

They were sailing downstream. Nick had no idea how long it would take to reach Hull. They were cold and dejected. Would they be put under house arrest or sent to prison? Might they even be hanged? He might never saw his family again? Was Newark safe? What was happening to Meg? Dozens of worry-worms were eating away his courage – and there were no answers to be had.

Nick and Travers sat huddled together on a hard bench, facing the sullen oarsmen. Nick found it best to avoid the faces; instead he stared at the swirling water and the river banks beyond. There was little to be seen except flat Lincolnshire fields, occasionally a windmill or a farm – mostly just grass and mud-banks.

Nick had not slept for two nights. He was exhausted. He must keep his eyes open: when they closed he saw terrible things. He forced himself to look at the fields. Monotonous fields and occasional trees, He started counting them. Then he saw some horsemen on the road: now they were trotting alongside the bank. It seemed as if they were trying to keep pace with the boat. They rode boldly and looked like gentlemen. One of them raised himself high in the saddle, shaking his fist at the parliamentary pinnace. They must be friends!

The officer in charge of the boat took no notice. Suddenly –
something else caught Nick's attention. Ahead he saw a bridge,
and beside this, a group of soldiers. These, without question, were
king's men – identifiable by their plumed hats. Nick's spirit rose.
If they were passing through Royalist country – might there be a
chance of rescue? He almost felt like shouting out that they were
prisoners. Dare he do it? Could they help?

A musket shot! Crack!

The oarsman facing him slumped forward with a thud,
whimpering as blood seeped from his arm. Travers seized Nick
and dragged him to a less exposed place on deck. They lay face
down, and waited. Screams and harsh voices bellowed order. The
pinnace pitched and rolled as soldiers and oarsmen collided with
one another in their confusion.

"Hold your fire!" It was the earl's voice. Nick raised his head
and saw his master leaping up to a vantage place in the prow.
"We're king's men and prisoners of the Roundheads," he shouted.

Too late! A deafening boom! – a spine-chilling howl as the
ball hit – the sound of shattering timbers and the stench of
burning flesh…The whole ship lurched and crashed down again,
deluging everyone. Nick gaped in horror as he saw the earl's
severed arm bobbing about in the bloodied water. A cannon ball
was rolling mercilessly on the deck, and the leaking body of the
earl lay in two halves before him.

The soldiers on the riverbank looked stunned by what they'd
done. The cannonball was clearly meant to hit the pinnace mid-
ships, but it had ripped the earl apart and a wisp of smoke was
rising from the mouth of a small mobile culverin sited by the
bridge.

Nick sat in tremulous shock! And, as he crouched there, he
heard Meg's voice telling him again what the earl had said nine
months ago: "Let a cannon ball divide me, if ever I take sword,
for king or parliament!"

* * *

Meg walked in solemn procession behind Lady Kingston. The
coffin was being carried by William and Francis. The countess
and Master Henry, followed. Nick was one of the onlookers as
the mourners made their slow progress to the Holme Pierrepont

churchyard. Nick was close enough to notice the tension between the brothers.

Henry was the Earl of Kingston now, and he lost no time in taking up ownership of Pierrepont Hall and in making his allegiance to the king clear to everyone. William had come from the parliamentary base in London and Francis from a troubled Nottingham. There had been little talk between them before the funeral and even less after it was over.

William had a brief meeting with the countess and then made a hurried departure. Henry went into his father's study and closed the door.

When Meg returned to her mistress's room the next day, there was a tender note pinned on her dressing table.

"This is a bad business, mother dear, but we must go our separate ways. I feel torn in two, like father. God help us all, F."

CHAPTER 7

THE SECRET LETTER

"The Earl of Kingston wants to see you," Grand-mamma burst upon Nick when he was busy in the counting house. He was taken aback. The earl was dead! Then he realised. Of course! She meant Mr. Henry, no longer Lord Newark, but the new earl.

"Is he here? I thought he was with the king in Oxford."

"He's just arrived and sent for you. He's in the governor's house."

Nick had been back working for his father for the past six months. In all that time, there had been no word from his former master. Why was he wanted now?

"You'd best hurry!"

He lost no time. The three-storey timbered house, commandeered for Sir Richard Byron was just over the road.

Mr. Henry was unusually genial. "This is the lad," he told Sir Richard. "I'm told that when you were working at Pierrepont Hall, you used to go bird's nesting over the water. You must know Colwick Woods and some of the tracks through Greendale and Thorneywood, mustn't you, boy?"

Nick hesitated. Surely, they weren't going to accuse him of poaching after all this time. "No sir, I only went bird watching, when you gave me leave. It wasn't nesting or trapping."

"No, of course not, but Travers says you used to know those paths, so perhaps you can be of service to Sir Richard here."

The governor looked up from the map he was studying. "This is the area, isn't it? The earl has brought some of his estate maps. I like exploring woodland paths nothing better than a walk through a forest, on a crisp winter day. The three of us will go there tomorrow. Be at the wharf at cockcrow, boy and you can show us the tracks. We'll take my boat upstream to Pierrepont, and then you can lead us on a ramble, eh lad. Do you know the path to St Ann's Well?"

"I've been there twice, sir. It's a strenuous walk uphill and

158

down dale from the river, but I enjoyed it last time I went." Nick was very puzzled.

"You shall go there again then, and take me with you!" Sir Richard clapped Nick on the shoulder, and he realized that the joviality must hide a secret.

* * *

Sir Richard and two soldiers joined Nick at the wharf in early morning light. A strong, north-easterly wind billowed the governor's cloak and the boatmen rigged a sail, which helped them to make good progress, passing the villages of Fiskerton and Gunthorpe as the morning wore on. The land to the right of the River Trent was mainly level grazing country, but on the left were red cliffs and clusters of trees.

Nick sat in the prow, while Sir Richard and the soldiers conversed in low tones.

Why were they so keen to come this way? What did it mean?

The wintry day closed in early, so they spent the night at Shelford Manor, held for the king by the Stanhope family. Nick had expected that they would sleep at Pierrepont Hall, but perhaps it was being watched by their enemies. Sir Richard and the soldiers had changed their clothing in the morning now and wore some inconspicuous country garments.

The smoke was rising from the chimneys at Pierrepont Hall, as they moored by a clump of willow trees opposite. Instructions were given to the head boatman to return to Shelford and come back to the same point to pick them up at sunset.

"And now, Master Nick, it's up to you," said Sir Richard in his cheery way, "Lead us on through the Greenwood Dale and over the brow to St. Ann's Well. The sun's up and we should enjoy a good day's walking in the woods."

But Nick did not enjoy it. He felt as if he had been tricked into something he had no desire to do, and when the hefty soldier with the axe began to chip the trees to way-mark the path, it seemed a desecration.

* * *

Meg was surprised when she was summoned abruptly to the

countess's boudoir one morning. Her mistress had kept herself apart ever since the earl's funeral, and most of the staff at Pierrepont Hall had seen little of her. There was an understandable rumour that she was suffering from depression; small wonder, the housemaids said, with her husband so brutally killed and her sons on opposite sides in the conflict. To make matters worse, she'd heard that a Royalist colonel was trying to seize some of Francis's property, because he had joined the parliamentary forces in Nottingham. It was all very troubling.

Meg tapped gently on the door and curtseyed as she entered. The countess was dressed in black from head to foot and looked at her with heavy, swollen eyes. Her face betrayed anguish, and yet there was a spirited ring in her voice as she asked, "Can I trust you, girl?"

"Of course you can ma'am!" Meg was shocked at the question.

"I believe I can, and God knows there are so few folk that I am certain of now. I am in deep trouble. I must get a letter to Mr. Francis but he's in the castle at Nottingham with that wretch, Hutchinson. He may be in peril and I don't mean from attack. I have no knowledge or truck with these military matters. It's our one time friend, Colonel Stanton, who's turned on us now. He's seized one of our houses and calls Francis traitor." She spoke in starts and Meg thought she might collapse in tears at any moment.

"Can I get you a drink, ma'am?"

"No, I'll be all right, once this matter's over. I recall that you used to go to Nottingham market, where your parents had a stall and I've been told that you have a young brother who works there sometimes too, but now I believe he's in that dreadful castle, with his master who pretends to be the governor of the place?"

Meg started. What might the countess say next?

"I haven't seen Tom for many a week."

"But perhaps you could. If I give you leave to help at your parents' stall next market day, and if I give you a sealed letter for Mr. Francis… could you ensure that it would reach his hands and no other?"

Meg felt flattered to be so trusted, but alarmed at the responsibility.

"I'd do all in my power, ma'am, but I can't promise that. Tom is constrained. He's honest, but he has his loyalties too. He'd only pass on the letter if he knew it wouldn't bring any harm on the parliament men."

"I can give you my word on that. The letter concerns our family matters only. I'll tell you plain. It concerns his wife. I've written asking her to intercede with Colonel Stanton about the goods he's seized. They're not his own things, they belonged to the earl...and I have a letter back from her saying she needs to hear from Francis on these matters. Stupid woman! Doesn't she know there can be no communication between Pierrepont Hall and the castle? What else can I do?"

The countess appeared to be about to break down. Meg was alarmed for her.

"Say no more, madam. If you wish it, I'll take the letter, and do as you say. I'll bring it back unopened, if Tom isn't able to come to the stall, or is unwilling to take it."

The countess opened a drawer in her bureau and gave a wax sealed parchment to Meg. On it was written in her own bold hand "To the Hon. Francis Pierrepont. private and confidential."

"When can you take it?"

"Wednesday is the weekday market. Tom usually manages to call there to get word from home."

"Wednesday – come to see me first thing." The countess replaced the letter in the drawer. "That will be all, Marriott."

Meg curtseyed and withdrew. Her legs trembled as she went back to the servants' hall, and she never breathed a word of what had passed.

* * *

Meg saw her parents that night and said she could run the market stall for them next Wednesday. Her father had been taking the cart there himself since Tom had been in the castle, but he had plenty of work on the farm and was only too pleased with this arrangement.

"Mind you look after yourself though, with all those soldiers in town. Don't linger. Come straight back here when the market closes."

Meg nodded, saying nothing further about the letter.

There was a red sky when Meg came to collect the cart on

Wednesday morning. Her mother had already loaded it. She drove to Nottingham in dull weather, in a biting wind. Her customers were anxiously laying in stores, almost as if they anticipated a siege.

Tom did not appear. Several soldiers from the castle came to the stall and she thought of asking after him, but decided against it.

Meg had sold her wares by mid-afternoon and decided to chance her luck. She'd go to the castle gatehouse, and ask if she could see Tom on family matters. Surely, the worst they could do was say no.

She had left the horse at the Angel Inn, so she went there first to tell the ostler to keep him a bit longer. Then she walked up Friar Lane, and was surprised to see that parliamentary soldiers were building barricades at the castle end of the street. A cart full of straw sacks stood by, and it was plain that they meant to close off all the lanes.

No one challenged her as she walked past the barricade and crossed the cobbled road alongside the castle walls. The drawbridge over the moat was down, and a sentry there asked her what she wanted.

"I wish to see my brother, Tom Marriott, on family business."

"Tom Marriott, who's he?"

"Servant to Colonel Hutchinson." Meg felt some pride in this.

"I dunno. You'll have to speak to the duty sergeant." He pointed to the guard room, and stepped aside to allow Meg to walk over the wooden bridge and under the frowning archway of the drum towered gatehouse.

The duty sergeant was a barrel of a man, with a mocking smile.

"This isn't regular, coming in to a castle, asking to see relatives. You're not goin' a step further until you've told me all your business." Meg felt he was making sport of her.

"Can I see a senior officer, please?"

"Can you what? Isn't a duty sergeant good enough for you, missy?"

"I don't mean any offence, but I'm not only sister to your governor's manservant, but I'm also maid to the Countess of Kingston, and I'll not be trifled with. Can I please see a senior officer?"

"Hoity toity, ma'am. So that's the way of it. Well then, we'll

162

see what the officer of the watch makes of you, Mistress Pertnose. It so happens that Captain Palmer is in the gatehouse now, and I think he'd be very pleased to quiz a maid with such dubious connections. Don't move an inch. Watch her, you."

He nodded to a spotty youth, who had been staring at her all the time. The sergeant crossed and disappeared into the opposite drum tower. Meg realised that she was handling this badly but, now she had to go through with it.

The sergeant reappeared and announced mockingly, "The duty officer will be pleased to grant you an audience, ma'am!" He indicated that she should go through the door into the officer's room.

Meg flounced past him and opened the door. The soles of two black booted feet faced her on a wooden table. Behind them were long legs, and beyond those a black coated officer lounged on a chair. On the table was an opened bottle of a wine.

"Come in, wench," he said curtly. "And shut the door behind you. There's a hellish cold wind blowing out there."

He looked at her curiously from head to toe. "Well, well, here's a turn of fortune. Who are you, girl, and what do you want?"

"My name is Meg Marriott, and I'm sister to Tom, Colonel Hutchinson's groom. I was sent with a family message for him and I'd like to see him now, if you please, but, if that's not possible, I'll leave." Her voice quavered.

"Oh, no you won't, miss. You can't go anywhere until you've given a proper account of yourself. You seem to be a go-between. One day you're living at Pierrepont Hall and serving a nest of vipers; the next you're coming to the castle and demanding to see a senior officer. What is this urgent family business?"

After a pause, Meg said. "I want to see my brother."

"What you want is of no concern to me. Answer my question – what's this urgent family business?"

Meg made a dash for it. She turned, seized the door handle and rushed out towards the drawbridge, where she ran into the arms of the sentry. She struggled and kicked him. He caught her shoe, and the threads holding the buckle broke. The sergeant and the spotty youth grabbed her from behind and she was hauled back in front of the fuming officer.

"You little hellcat," he shouted. "We'll soon cool you down. Take that bag off her that she's clutching so closely and lock her in the cell!"

The sergeant wrenched the bag from her hand and he and the youth thrust her into a small cell in the corner of the room. The iron cage door clanged to and was locked. Meg was distraught at losing the bag. She banged on the grill and shouted, "That's not your property!"

The officer laughed as he emptied the contents on to the table. There was the money from the market stall, her comb and kerchief and the letter.

"What's this?" he cried "'To the Hon. Francis Pierrepont. Private and Confidential.' I thought so, I've heard of letters passing between that fine gentleman and his Royalist mother. He's under suspicion already, now we'll see how the land lies."

"You can't open that letter. It's private – family matters."

The captain gave her a freezing look. "Can't I? I'm duty officer – in charge of the castle this night. The governor and his brother are dining in the town, and your precious Francis Pierrepont has seen fit to stay in Derby, ever since he was told to take that rebel Drury there. It's my responsibility to maintain security and that I'll do." Turning to the sergeant, he said in a lower tone. "We're expecting an attack from Newark in the next few days. I've suspected Pierrepont of double-dealing all along. This letter may give vital information."

He picked up a file and very gently broke the seal, spread out the letter and quietly read it.

"Well, well," he looked up. "This letter is private indeed. It will go to the governor's hands intact." He reached for a candle and gently repaired the damage.

"Does it say when the Newarkers are coming, Captain Palmer?" asked the sergeant.

"No. As missy there said, it is a family matter – but it's the Pierrepont family not a family of the clodhopping farming brood and no business of stable-boy brothers. Once the governor reads this, he'll know how things stand with his fellow colonel and with his own servants. Here's a letter entreating Pierrepont to write to that Royalist Stanhope, assuring him that he's still a loyal subject of King Charles."

The captain walked over to the prison bars.

"You lied about a letter for your brother. You were trying to sneak this missive to Francis Pierrepont. We'll see what the governor thinks of that in the morning and lodge her securely in the black hole. You and this lad with you can keep her guarded there until tomorrow. One of you must stay by the door all night. She'll be disciplined in the morning, when the governor reads this letter."

Meg was seized again by the two odious creatures. "'old her tight, Jed. She's a little vixen this one. If she struggles give 'er a smack with your club." said the sergeant. The spotty youth gripped her arm and together they dragged her across the lower bailey. "You'll be secure in the black hole," the sergeant sneered. "That's where the Scottish King David died long ago, but they say his bones are still there in the gloom."

Meg was propelled forwards, catching their bad breath, as she was pushed into a stone chamber and then down crumbling steps to an iron-studded door. Unlocking it, they thrust her through and banged it shut. She heard the key turn in the lock. Meg sank down in despair, crouching against the door. The footsteps died away, and she was left alone, in the darkness.

CHAPTER 8

THE CAVES OF CASTLE ROCK

Nick felt numb with cold, as he and the two soldiers climbed the path again through Colwick Woods and down through Greenwood Dale. This time they were guiding a silent army through the darkness, groping by lantern light to find the way-marks cut into the trees. Nick wished he was in his warm bed at home. It was a bitter winter night, but Mr. Henry was hard on his heels, so he had no escape.

They emerged out of the tree cover into a grassy area, where the path was more easily found by moonlight as it trailed through the meadowland. Then began the slow ascent into the shadows of the thorny wood. Nick felt a deep sense of resentment. He had been tricked into this – leading soldiers through his favourite haunts so that they could seize a town in darkness. Why hadn't they been open with him, instead of this stupid talk of going on a ramble? He'd known there was some other plan but what? Now he was pushed into violating an area he loved for its quietness and birdsong.

He'd heard the leaders talking. They'd decided on this approach because the river was watched and guarded. The assault on Nottingham was to be in three waves; the first was by these foot soldiers who were to seize the old town quietly by night; the second was by cavalry, who were bringing the horses by boat. This would alert the castle, and then when the fighting was at its height, another group would come over Trent Bridge disguised as market traders, and start to build a fort to protect the crossing. The timber was to be brought on barges.

The path through the woods brought them to the crest of a hill. They came this way to avoid the village of Sneinton and the outlying farms.

Now there was a rough descent. They had to walk carefully in the darkness. In a dell at the bottom, lay the keeper's cottage at St. Ann's Well. Nick's toes were dead with cold, as he gingerly led the way over frosty ground.

"Well met!" The words startled him coming out of pitch darkness, but suddenly Sir Richard Byron was beside them, whispering to the leaders. "A hundred cavalry are waiting upstream on the boats. All is well! Go on past the cottage, and from there you'll find it's a straight path between Hunger Hill on the right and Bluebell Hill on the left. Carry on till you come to the penny footbridge over the beck, and you're into the town. There's a woman guarding the footbridge. Take her from behind, and see she gives no shouts. Everyone must keep silence, or the whole device is ruined."

From now on, Nick was redundant, and he was heartily glad. Instead of having to lead, with the heavy breath of Mr. Henry on his tail, he was free to slip back into the shadows, following the foot soldiers at his own reluctant pace.

* * *

For a long time Meg lay locked in darkness and shivering in fear. It was dank and cold in the cave, and she was totally alone. Or was she? The sergeant had spoken of a Scottish king who had died in this place. Were his bones hidden somewhere in the blackness? She shuddered. Meg had never encountered a ghost. She had been very doubtful about them, but if ever there was a fearful place where they might linger, this was surely it!

After what seemed an eternity, she began to pull herself together. At least she was clear of her captors for a while, and for all she knew she might not be alone. There could be some other prisoners, further on. She was still lurking by the door. Slowly, she groped her way forward. "Is there anyone there?" At first she could only whisper the words, but then she repeated them more loudly. No reply. But how big was this cave? She had no means of knowing.

There was a clammy wall behind her. Meg stood up and began to feel her way along it. She spoke again – really loudly this time. Silence! She must be alone. The thought was reassuring and frightening at the same time. A slight clanking noise sounded by her foot. She froze in sudden fear. Silence. Gingerly, she moved a step forward. Horror! There it was again. Then she realised. It was probably her shoe buckle, broken lose when the soldiers seized her. She tried to feel it. Yes, it was flapping free. Reassurance flooded into her. She'd been losing her nerve. Slowly courage returned. She spoke again – really loudly, this time. Silence. She shouted. No reply. Yes, she must be alone.

What was to be done? She'd lost the letter. The countess would be furious with her. Her parents would be sick with worry when she didn't return home. She'd made a mess of everything.

No doubt, the officers would question her further in the morning. She'd probably have to appear before the governor, John Hutchinson. He was Tom's master. Could she turn that to advantage? Not really. What could she say? She really didn't know.

Could she escape? It didn't look possible. Could she try to get a message to Tom? She didn't want to even try it. He probably couldn't do anything, and she knew he'd crow about it, if he helped her. How humiliating! She'd rather work something out for herself. But ... what? She must explore further.

Meg edged further along the wall, feeling her way, tentatively. The ground began to slope downwards. It was pitch dark, so her steps had to be cautious.

Horror – something touched her hair! She ducked and raised her arm. Something soft brushed against it. She froze! Then she heard a familiar sound – the whir of tiny wings. She'd heard that noise in the old barn at home. It was a bat! She almost laughed with relief. She stopped moving and began to think again:

I only know of one way out – through the locked door. The sergeant and the spotty lad were told to guard it. Will I be brought some food and water? Possibly. Perhaps, if I stay near the door, I could make a dash for it? Not really. They'll catch me in the yard outside. I'd never get through the guardhouse. Might one of them help me escape? Certainly not the sergeant! But might that youth be persuaded? He seems obnoxious, but it's just possible. The sergeant called him Jed. I must remember that. How could I persuade him? I can't bribe him. They've taken all my money. Could I plead with him? No, that's repulsive. But I might be able to frighten him. How could I do that? I'm terrified myself. Might that help? Possibly. Fear can be infectious. Can I develop a plan?

* * *

It seemed as if hours had passed, but eventually Meg heard footsteps outside.

Then the key turned in the lock. A dim shaft of light appeared as the door creaked open. Meg darted a glance at the opposite wall. She saw the tiny bat stir, but it did not fly.

"'Ere's a jug of water and some broth. I'll put in by the door." The spotty youth was already about to close it.

"Jed – is that your name?"

"Yeah."

"Listen. I've something to tell you." Meg grasped his wrist urgently.

"What is it? I can't stop."

Whilst Meg kept hold of his wrist, he could not close and relock the door. She spoke in a hushed whisper, "It's the ghost!" Then in sudden alarm "Over here, quick. It's standing between you and the door!" Meg dragged Jed further into the cave towards the bat. She screamed. "There's something white above your head, squat down."

She knelt on the floor, pulling Jed down beside her with one hand and reaching out towards the bat with the other.

"What ghost?"

"I don't know. There's something here." She reached out again and disturbed the bat. Suddenly, Jed was cowering and covering his head.

"Something touched me, " he cried. "It touched my face."

They stood stock-still. Not daring to breathe.

"It could be the ghost of that Scottish king – the one whose bones are still lying here in the cave. But I suppose a lot of people have died in here over the years. I definitely heard footsteps in the darkness. They crossed over towards the door. When you opened it, I saw something in the half-light – white and gleaming. It could have been a skull. Didn't you see it?"

"No." But, Jed's hand was shaking. He was clearly terrified. She must play on this. It was her only hope.

"I heard a moaning noise too. It came from over there." Meg released his hand to indicate a dark area to their right. "What was that? Did you hear it?"

Jed wasn't sure, but was clearly imagining all sorts of horrors. "Don't move. There's something in front of you." They sat there in a terrified silence. Then she suddenly screamed, "It's getting closer.

It's moved between you and the door! Don't go near the door!"

In the darkness, Meg tore the loose buckle from her shoe and threw it against the opposite wall. It clattered to the ground. Jed screamed.

"What was that? Did you see?" he blubbered.

"It sounded like the clink of metal. Perhaps, it was a chain."

There was a long pause. Meg thought she'd chance her luck. "Are there some soldiers we could call down here from the yard outside?"

"No, it's the middle of the night. There's not many on guard. Most of them are down the town tonight. They've bribed that bastard, Captain Palmer. One of 'em's got a birthday."

"Where's the sergeant?"

"Havin' a nap in the guardroom. It's all deserted out there."

"We can't get any help from them, then." Meg tried to sound disappointed.

"I wouldn't go to them anyway," said Jed. "That sergeant's a brute."

"It must be grim for you, then."

"It's 'ell on earth, wi' all these jumped up corporals and sergeants, shoutin' and bawling at me. If I tried to escape, they catch me and flog me over a gun barrel. Palmer would just love to do that. 'Ere I am in this crumbling old ruin – at everyone's beck and call, an' they don't even give me any pay. An' now there's ghosts an' all!"

Seizing her opportunity, Meg took his trembling hand. "Sit down, Jed. I've been here in this cave much longer than you and I've got a bit more used to it. Do you know my brother, Tom Marriott?"

"Yes, I know 'im and I tried to let 'im know you wus 'ere, but no one seemed to know where 'e woz."

"It was good of you to try. I was wondering if we could get a message to him, but I can't see what he could do to help."

"I'm sorry if I was a bit rough, when we dragged you down 'ere. I didn't mean to be. It's that blasted sergeant and Captain 'Preacher' Palmer – right couple they are! Just my luck to be on guard duty wi' them two, when most of the lads are off down the town."

"Where are you from, Jed?"

"Shelford, that's where me ma lives anyway. Wish I was there now, not stuck in this dump, with a ghost by the door an' all."

"Perhaps you could make a break for it, if there's no one around outside. Is there any way out of the castle, except through the guardhouse?"

"Yes, there's a secret passage, through another cave. I know because I went there the other day with your brother when we 'ad to help build a gun emplacement on a ledge below the walls. They call it Mortimer's 'ole."

"Any chance of you escaping through it?"

"Reckon I could too, if it wasn't for the ghosts. Tonight 'ud be the best chance I'm likely to get. But I'd be scared to go down that stairway in the dark. I've 'ad enough of them caves."

"If I came with you, it might not be so bad."

"You? 'ow can yer? You're a prisoner!"

"I wouldn't be if I got out."

"But I'm you're gaoler. They'd flay me alive if I let you out."

"Oh, well. It was only a idea. Perhaps you prefer to stay here with the army brutes and the ghosts."

"No, I'd give my right arm to escape."

"And you said tonight's your best chance."

"Yes, but what if we get caught? An' anyway, we'd be on the wrong side of the moat."

"We have to make sure we don't get caught. You said most of the soldiers are sleeping out tonight. This is your best chance. Perhaps the only one you'll ever have. You know your way around, and with two of us, one can look each way. That moat isn't very wide to swim across."

"I can't swim!"

"I can. If you hold on to me, I'll get you over."

"Could you? Are you sure? I'd probably drown in that muddy water."

"No wouldn't. I can get you over. There's a big horse pond on our farm. I've been swimming there many a time, and I taught my little brothers to swim."

"I'm heavier than them, I bet."

"Not much. All you'd have to do is hold on. Two or three strokes and we'd be over."

"And then there's the bank on the other side. It's steep and slippery."

"We'll manage it together."

"I dunno." There was a long pause. "What if we gets caught?"

"I'll say I broke out and you were chasing me. You've got your club. If anyone comes, you can start hitting me with it, and I'll back any tale you tell."

That seemed to convince Jed. After a moment's further hesitation, he said "I'd run for it now– if it wasn't for the ghost by the door."

"It seems to have moved away now. Shall we make a break for it, while the going's good? I'll stay by you, Jed. It's not so scary, if there's two of us."

"Come on then," said Jed, scrambling up. "I'm goin' 'ome – back to Shelford. I'll never join another army as long as I live!"

"Quick, let's dash for it!"

They were through the door in a second. The crumbling steps beyond were lit by a shaft of moonlight, glinting through the grille in the door at the top.

Jed cautiously unlocked it, glanced around and then beckoned Meg through. He did not stop to lock the door, but hurried on. A few more paces and they were crossing the deserted middle bailey. Jed paused at the bottom of a flight of steps.

"I'll check if it's clear." There was no-one in sight. He beckoned her on. They ran across the upper bailey, and then suddenly hid in the shadow of an archway, as a sentry passed with a flint-lock musket.

When he had gone, Jed opened a great wooden door in the wall. They cringed as the hinges creaked. Beyond, was a stone-flagged chamber used as a food store. Another shaft of moonlight from an upper arrow slit provided the only light. Jed moved towards the centre, stooped, slipped his fingers in a crack and slowly raised the flagstone.

It was crow black below. "There's some iron rungs which form a ladder and brands on the wall as you go down," said Jed. "I've got a tinder box, so we can get some light." He hesitated all the same, clearly reluctant to plunge down the hole. Meg took the lead and clambered into the darkness. She felt for each rung and then tested it before giving it her whole weight.

When Jed followed her, he blocked the moonlight, and she groped gingerly in the darkness. "Where are those brands?" Jed found one, struck his flint and lit it. He held it over his head and the flame illuminated the shaft. Meg saw the rungs reaching down below her and carefully continued the sheer descent.

Eventually, she reached the bottom and found herself standing on the floor of a sloping cave. A tunnel yawned before her. She waited till Jed was down with his lighted brand, and now she let him lead the way. The passage was steep and twisty. At times they had to bend their heads, but slowly they made their way forwards, until at last they saw a starry night sky emerging before them, and the dank smell gave place to cold night air.

They emerged out of the cave on a rocky outcrop, near the bottom of the castle cliff. Jed hurriedly extinguished the light, and they edged forwards to find that the cliff-face continued down for a further twenty feet, falling sheer into the moat. Across the water, Meg could see the huddled roofs of houses and a church tower rising beyond, against the blue night sky. It was tantalisingly near but the moat and the steep banks separated them.

Meg led the way again. She found a fissure in the rock, and carefully climbed down, testing each ledge. Jed followed in her wake, really frightened now.

Soon Meg's feet were in the icy water. For a moment she paused, then carried on as the water reached up to her waist. Then she waited for Jed.

"Put your arm round my middle, grab my belt and hold on tight."

A moment later, she was struggling in the freezing moat, with the sudden dead weight of Jed pulling her down. She gasped and swallowed foul water. "Try to swim with your other arm," she urged and then struck out for the opposite bank. Half a dozen strokes were all that was needed. Then her free hand caught hold of tufts of grass, and she and Jed were clutching them for dear life.

They hung in the water panting for breath and then as soon as they had the strength, hauled themselves on to the bank to lie gasping in the slime, before tackling the final clamber up the muddy slope.

She turned to look at Jed. He was lying in the grass, shivering all over with cold or fright. "Are you all right?" she asked.

"I will be. I've got to get away from this place. Shelford's ten miles off, but my mum's got a sister 'ere in Nottingham. I'll go to 'er place now. Thanks." He scrambled to his feet, and disappeared into the darkness of the town.

Meg was soaking wet and shivering too and her hair was streaked with mud. Wherever could she go to? She had no idea.

CHAPTER 9

THE REFUGE

Where can I go?

This thought blanked everything out. Meg was wet through and shivering with cold. It was a bleak winter night and she was an escaped prisoner in a hostile town.

I must get as far away from the castle as possible, she thought. Can I go straight to the Angel Inn to collect the horse and cart? No, not in the middle of the night – people will question me. Someone might frog-march me back to the castle. Who can I trust? Dare I go to Mr Francis's house? No, he won't be there, and anyway he's one of the parliament men now. I can't just trust his servants.

Then Meg remembered Alice and Sam Drury. They'd always been friendly, and she'd rather confide in people of her own age. They were neither for king nor parliament. They took a neutral line. That was safest. She knew their parents' home, Vault Hall, where Tom had lodged when he went to school in Nottingham. But, could she get in at such an hour? She'd have to try. There was no option.

Houndsgate was deserted. She hurried along, and then climbed up the hill from Low to Middle Pavement. A dog barked, a beggar was huddled in a doorway, but no one was abroad to stare at her in her bedraggled state.

Vault Hall was dark and the doors were bolted but there was a light in the window over the archway, which joined the house and spanned Drury Hill. She banged on the door, and mercifully it was young Alice who put her head out in response.

Minutes later, the door was opened. Alice and Sam were the only ones awake. Apparently, they were keeping watch, because there was a rumour that there might be an attack from the Royalist forces at Newark. She learned that their father had been arrested by Colonel Hutchinson's men, and their mother was out with a women's street patrol. All this sounded very strange, but so too was the tale that Meg had to tell.

"You'll be safe here," Alice assured her. "You'd better come upstairs with me and get those wet things off. You can borrow some of my clothes and we'll find you somewhere to sleep till morning."

After all Meg had been through, it sounded too good to be true.

"I was locked in a prison in the castle. I had to swim the moat. I'd gone with a letter to Colonel Pierrepont from his mother, the countess, but the duty officer said he'd gone to Derby. Then he started insulting me and it ended up with him shutting me in a cell."

"He locked you in? How did you manage to escape?"

"I thought I'd never get out. One of the goalers helped me. He wanted to break free himself...he says he's finished with soldiering. He's tried both the armies and never got his pay from either side, so he's making for his mother's in Shelford."

Alice took it in her stride. "We'll do what we can for you," she said, "but we're very stretched just now. We've town watches posted at every gateway and there's a women's patrol in every ward. If the king's soldiers come, we've seven shelters for the families, one in each ward, including the caves beneath this house. We've laid in stores in case there's a long siege. It might be necessary to stay below for a week or more, so we have a woman in every street who's promised to knock up her neighbours if the Newarkers come."

"Who planned all this?"

"The women's watch. The men drew up rotas for manning the ditches. My mother told them this was all useless now that the castle has taken our cannons, so she arranged the shelters. She's organised food collections and she's going to meet the head woman in each of the town wards tonight to see how it's working out."

"Are you one of the watchers?"

"I'm the scribe. I keep the notes." Alice was proud of her responsibilities. "I've been involved ever since that captain arrested my father. I loathe that Palmer man. They say he's a preacher, but there's more hate than love in his heart."

"Palmer, that was his name!" Meg broke in. "That was the same man who locked me in the cell."

Meg started to explain, but suddenly, there was a loud wail from the street outside.

They jumped in surprise.

"That sounded like the signal," Alice said. They went to the window and peered out, but could see little in the darkness.

"The women were told to cry out if the enemy came and then to bang on every door."

"Is that someone by your doorstep?" Meg pointed down. They saw a shadowy figure move away. Something like a bundle of clothes was left behind.

"I'm going down." Alice led the way down the stairs. Cautiously, she drew the bolts and opened the door. The still figure of a woman lay spread on the cobbles.

"Mother!" Alice stooped beside her. Her mother's head fell foward as she tried to raise it, and a gush of blood streamed from a neck wound. Alice cradled her mother's head, as she tried to stanch the blood with a kerchief. "Get Sam!"

Meg ran back into the house, shouting for him. He came quickly. And they ran outside in time to hear Mistress Drury gasping, "Don't mind me, but quick, you must open the shelter… spread the word…the Newarkers … they've come!"

Meg felt a mixture of relief and terror.

"Mother, can you hear me?"

"She's passed out," Alice told Sam. "If I move, the blood will start again. I must hold her. You must raise the neighbours. We need their help to bind mother's neck and move her into the house. And we must tell them they can take refuge here. Meg, you can help too. Quick, but be quiet when you pass the word. We don't want the soldiers on us."

For a second Sam hesitated, appalled.

"Go on," Alice ordered. "Both of you. I'll cope with Mother. I must."

"Come." Sam seized Meg's arm and she followed him out into the street.

Sam started knocking on the doors. Meg watched what he was doing and then crossed the road and did the same. The message was simple. "The Newarkers are here!"

Some folk were ready to leave but others had either fled or were deep in slumber. Swiftly and silently, figures appeared, some muffled in greatcoats: some in night attire, others with babes in arms or leading aged parents. A line of refugees, clutching precious bundles, streamed up the hill to the safety of Vault Hall.

When Meg returned she found that neighbours were helping Alice. Mistress Drury had been carried in and laid on cushions. Her wound had been washed and dressed, whilst she was unconscious. Alice was at her side, still as a statue. She looked up:

"Meg, stay by mother," she commanded, "I must check the roster."

She went to a drawer, produced a scroll and unrolling it, began to check all the neighbours she had seen enter.

"Is Bessy Charlton here? Can you go and check, Susannah. See if she and her babe are in the cave, and while you're there ask if anyone has seen old Reuben Sandby. I didn't see him come. Meg, did you check the houses in Listergate?"

Meg marvelled at the way Alice had taken control.

"What about the castle. Has someone sent them word?" Sam asked as he came back in.

"Can't do that," was the terse reply of a grey-haired man in a striped nightshirt.

"Who says?"

"Alderman Toplady. 'E's guard commander tonight and no one crosses 'im."

"Guard commander! He's being held at gunpoint in the Guildhall, so I was told," said a sturdy matron. "Bound to a chair with ropes. He can't command a dog."

"Be that as it may," said the man in the nightshirt, "'e's our man in charge and one of the watch told me that 'e ordered 'em not to tell the castle if the Newarkers came. If we did that they said they'll fire all our thatches and set the town ablaze."

"God help us all," said a woman in widow's black.

"You'd best go down to the caves, the lot of you," said Alice. "Meg and Sam will keep watch up here, and I'll stay by mother. You'll find some ale down there to warm you, and there are skins and rugs on the floor." With muttered thanks, the neighbours moved towards the stone steps that led to the rock cellars below.

CHAPTER 10

WAR IN THE STREETS

Nick was very angry. Once the soldiers had found their way through the woods, he'd been forgotten. He had trudged reluctantly behind the troops, angry and humiliated. They entered the town quietly, with minimum opposition. Now it was daylight, and Nick felt like a prisoner, trapped with the Newark musketeers, who'd taken possession of houses facing the castle during the night.

He'd seen the people living there being ordered out and told to keep away. He'd been told by a sergeant to fettle the rough lead bullets, with a sharp iron bar. He could see that the shot had been crudely cast, and needed shaping before it would fit into the gun barrels. This task continued for two wearisome days. His head ached and he was desperately tired.

By mid-day, they needed a steady supply of bullets. They had smashed the window panes of the houses and were crouching beneath the empty frames firing at the castle battlements whenever they saw movement from the defending soldiers.

A line of marksmen were demanding Nick's services, and the task was never ending. The fuses were made from cord boiled in vinegar and the fumes made his eyes smart.

A man called Rogers seemed to have adopted Nick in a rough sort of way and joked with him as he took shots with his matchlock whenever he saw any movement on the castle gun platforms. It seemed to be a kind of game to him, he let out a yelp of delight whenever he scored a hit. Nick felt the pain each time. Yesterday, Nick had been alarmed to see the families tippled out of these houses and their windows smashed to make firing holes.

The musketeers were ruthless to their enemies, strong in loyalty to each other, but crude in their language. They called the wooden canisters swinging from their cartridge belts their twelve apostles. To Nick this was a form of sacrilege.

A church nearby had been commandeered by Sir Richard Byron as his headquarters, and a demi-culverin was firing from the tower. The women and children who had found sanctuary there had been turned out into the street, despite the protests of the vicar.

"Get ready to hold your fire when I command!" An officer had burst into the room.

Rogers turned to question the order. "There's no let up from the castle!"

"Flag of truce". The man moved quickly on to the next room, repeating the message. Rogers cursed a lost opportunity, but there was a stir of interest among the musketeers. Two of them left their positions by the window, and went to the outer door to see what was happening.

Nick followed. Looking over the rooftops, he saw a white flag, waving from the top of the church tower. Standing in the doorway, breathing the fresh morning air felt good, after so many hours cooped up in the smoky room.

Now that the firing had ceased, there was a chance for the fettlers to have a break. Nick and other boys ran down Castlegate. Someone would know how the battle stood.

A soldier was standing on the green, outside St Nicholas Church holding a white flag. A crowd of curious townsfolk gathered around, as Nick and the others joined them. One of the Newarkers spoke up: "What's this, then? Surely, you're never giving in?"

"It's a final ultimatum we're sending them," replied the soldier, "Surrender now, or face a long siege. We've got them caged like bears in a pit. Supplies can't get in, and they're bound to run out of gunpowder if they go on using it at this rate. We won't let up."

As the officer was speaking, Nick noticed one of the Royalist commanders, emerge from the church. He was wearing a plumed hat, rather than a steel helmet, and had discarded his armour breastplate for a formal buff coat. He carried neither tuck-sword nor rapier – just a pistol in a hip-holster. He spoke quietly to the flagman. When it became clear that the firing from the castle had stopped, he nodded to his companion who started walking slowly towards the castle. The officer walked a few paces behind him.

As they stepped forward, holding the white flag aloft, the crowd followed. Nick heard someone say "Sir Charles Lucas is going to give terms of surrender."

When they reached the top of Castlegate, the procession turned right along the castle walls and walked toward the gatehouse. At this point, the townsfolk were ordered to stand back. Nick heard Sir Charles shout from his position facing the drawbridge:

"I bring a letter from Sir Richard Byron for the governor!"

After a few tense moments, an officer was seen standing on the flat roof of one of the drum towers: "The drawbridge will be lowered. You must enter alone!"

Two armed soldiers escorted Sir Charles over the drawbridge, and through a small door in the great wooden gate, which was still firmly locked.

There was an anxious pause, which lasted several minutes.

The crowd cheered when he reappeared again. Nick and his companions were swept up in the flow of people, all eager to know the outcome. Sir Richard Byron waited for Sir Charles on the step of an inn opposite the church. Sir Charles looked grave as he spoke to him.

Boom! Suddenly, a massive explosion rent the air.

Nick threw himself to the ground. Huge blocks of stone crashed around him. Dust and debris clouded everything. He struggled to breathe. Would the pounding ever cease? A searing pain shot up his arm. He'd been hit by something. He lay very still, face down in the dust, his body flat on the cobbles. Waiting, waiting – until at last the area around him seemed less full of hysterical screaming and gunfire. There was moaning now, and pitiful cries of "Help me! Help me!"

Slowly, fearfully, Nick dared to open his eyes. He sat up. All around the dazed people lay the remnants of the church tower. Mercifully, he had been spared from serious injury, but two of his fingers had been crushed by falling debris.

Others were not so lucky. Some were screaming that they had lost legs or arms, and two dead bodies lay on the cobbles near him.

The tower had been destroyed by the largest cannon in the

castle, and there was little of it still standing. The flag that had signalled 'truce' now lay buried in the dirt and rubble. Colonel Hutchinson had answered his cousin, Sir Richard Byron, with a blood red flag – flying triumphantly from the top of the castle keep. Below it was a smoking cannon.

* * *

For the next few hours, Nick lived in a nightmare world. Devastation surrounded the area of the church, and many townspeople were in panic, yet others were spurred on to great acts of bravery. Nick saw some who seemed prepared to toil for hours to try to release buried people, despite the gunfire raining down on them. He staggered to his feet and struggled down the lane, away from the castle.

Opposite St. Peter's church an emergency centre had been set up by Parson Goodall, to care for the sick and homeless. A painted banner read 'Bring us your sick and wounded' and a team of volunteers was there to help all who needed it.

After waiting in a long queue, Nick eventually got his bloody fingers washed and bandaged. A woman helper fitted two wooden splints to hold the broken bones as straight as possible, and he was given a mug of ale, before he was discharged.

Nick limped back to his station in the house of the musketeers, but Rogers said he would be no use to them with a maimed hand. In any case, his place had now been filled by an enthusiastic ten-year-old. Thankfully, Nick went out to tramp the streets. His role as a reluctant boy soldier had been abruptly ended.

He felt like a lost soul, wandering through the old town. He went to the Earl of Kingston's town house in Stoney Street, but found it had been taken over by Royalist officers and he was sent away.

Everywhere he saw scenes of anguish or excess. Many of the king's foot soldiers seemed bent on pillage. Empty houses were being broken open, windows smashed and property stolen.

Some of the townsfolk were even joining in. Furniture was being carried from shattered houses by scavengers, and street urchins were fighting in the dust for souvenirs. Former neighbours were hurling insults at each other across the street, and a crazed, white-haired preacher seemed to have taken possession of the Malt Cross, and was screaming about the wrath of God, and shouting that the end was nigh.

Turning a corner into Goosegate, he found himself staring at a young girl, who looked about eight or nine-years-old carrying a young infant in her arms. She stared back at him, with pitiful wide eyes, and held out her hand, saying "Alms for the baby." Nick felt in his pocket and found a coin, which he gave the girl. She smiled and said "Thank you", but had no pocket to put it in, so she clutched it tight in her fist.

"What's your name?" asked Nick.

"Sarah", the girl said. "This is my brother Tim."

Nick was going to ask the child where she lived – but then he remembered that he'd seen her before. Yesterday morning, she'd been in one of the families thrown out of their homes opposite the castle, when the musketeers had arrived.

"I have a little brother called Tim too," he said, "He's much older than this little fellow, but he's safe with my father in Newark. I think I saw you yesterday
with your mother, where is she?"

The child began to whimper. "I don't know. I'm lost," she said "and I don't know where to find her."

"When did you last see her? Where were you then?" he asked.

"Last night," she said. "She found an empty house for us to sleep in. When I wakened this morning, she wasn't there. We waited and waited, and when she didn't come back, we went to look for her."

"Where was the house?"

"I don't know. There are so many streets."

"Have you had anything to eat today?"

"No, and Tim needs his milk", the child said.

At that the baby started to cry. "Come with me," Nick said. "I know where there is some milk, and more besides. Perhaps the people at the soup shelter can help to find your mother." Nick pointed the way and they set off together. The child slipped her fist trustingly in his hand, but she did not open her fingers, because they still grasped the small coin.

Nick was troubled to see that the girl had bare feet and only wore a thin garment, but she had a strength of character way beyond her years. They walked through the Market Square, and down a lane that led to St. Peter's Church where Nick handed the children over to the lady in charge of the soup kitchen. "You sit here by the warm fire, dearies," they were told. "Like as not, your mother will come here asking after you."

That evening, Nick realised that the girl had given him a good idea. After dark, when it began to sleet he took refuge on the floor of an empty house. His hand was aching, and the cold wind blew in through the broken windows. Feeling some guilt about the intrusion, he went upstairs and found a bed. He lay down beneath a coverlet and tried to sleep, but his painful arm would only allow him to lie on one side, and soon he got cramp, and found he was more comfortable sitting upright. He dozed, but hunger awoke him and as dawn broke, he stole forth again in search of food.

The baker's shop and the butcher's shambles were all shuttered, but he got a bowl of broth at Parson Goodall's shelter. When he asked after the two children, Nick learned that their mother had not appeared but that they had been taken to a safe house for the night and enquires were being made on their behalf.

After that he began to feel quite ill. He stumbled about in a weak and dazed condition, shivering with cold and scarcely noting where he was. Passing a house in Spaniel Row, he heard loud screaming, and turned to see a man being held down on a bench, while a barber surgeon was busy sawing off his shattered leg.

Nick nearly passed out, and when he had staggered clear of the place, he saw that all the lanes near the castle were blocked by cavalry and soldiers with long pikes, who looked as if they could be assembled for an assault on the fortress.

Nick turned the other way and found refuge again in Parson Goodall's soup kitchen. He sat in a corner to rest his arm, and soon slipped into a delirious half slumber. He could hear voices around him. A woman was saying that the mayor's wife was going to make a plea to the castle to stop the bombardment. A wounded Royalist was raging at the parliamentary forces who'd fired at the church tower while a white flag was flying, and another man quoted scripture and said that all these dire happenings were recorded centuries ago in the Book of Revelations. All these voices melted into confused dreams. He thought he was on a mission to end the fighting and a preacher was telling him that because of the sacrilege committed on both sides, there would be angels to support him.

CHAPTER 11

ESCAPE!

For four days, Meg was unable to leave the security of the Vault Hall, whilst lawless soldiers roamed the streets around and sporadic shooting could be heard outside. The refugees told them that the Newark foot soldiers were breaking into their empty homes and pocketing the plunder.

The hall was crowded with people who did not dare to go back home. All this while Elizabeth Drury was confined to her bed. Much of the time she slept, and when aroused, she seemed confused. It fell on Sam and Alice to run the household and Meg was a willing helper. She marvelled to see how adult Alice had become.

Close friends and neighbours were allowed use of the rooms in the hall. Some bedded down in the parlour, others were in the study, but most people had to be content with a place in the rock cellars below, where there was a labyrinth of underground caves. Those who had been turned out from the church refuges by the Royalists, also clamoured at the door, no-one was denied entry.

It was going dark on the third evening, when there was a loud ring of the front door bell. Meg went to open it and found a middle-aged woman on the step with two little waifs. A girl about eight was clutching a babe of about two years.

"I'm bringing Sarah and Tim here," the woman explained, "because they've lost their mother, and I'm told that this is the safest house in town. Can they come in?"

They both looked famished, cold and frightened. Meg opened her arms. "Of course they can."

"They've been with us at St. Peter's refuge," the woman said "and we haven't found mum yet. We're closing down, now it's getting dark. A few lost souls are sleeping on the church floor, but these two need special care. If anyone asks for them, we'll tell them that they're here."

"Of course," said Meg. "I'll take them straight to Alice. Thank you for caring."

Sarah and Tim spent that night sleeping beside Meg, but everyone was relieved when their mother appeared the next morning to collect them.

"I've been searching everywhere I could think of," she cried "and then, at last when I went to St. Peter's, they said that one of the helpers had brought two children here last night. Thank you so much. I can't thank you enough for looking after them!"

Meg and Alice were very concerned for the women with young children. They had done all they could to make them comfortable, rigging up curtains to provide screens, bringing down blankets and woollen shawls to protect them from the cold and damp. Porridge and hot broth bubbled incessantly in the kitchen above, and a team of young women took it in turns to serve it. Meg had even tried to devise some simple games to keep the young children amused, and to take their minds off the cramped conditions. She was touched by the simple prayers Alice said each night, before the families went to sleep.

Kneeling on the cave floor, she would close her eyes and pray for their protection through the night, using her own quiet words, in a way that was new to Meg, who had always heard parsons reading from prayer books. The families listened in silence – men, women and children – and appeared less afraid after the words of comfort.

By the fourth day, things were much quieter and Meg decided she must leave.

Meg: *The countess must be desperate to know what's happened to her letter. The horse and cart are still stabled at The Angel Inn and they have to be paid for. I haven't any money. Somehow, I've got to get them back to the farm. Mother and father will be very worried about me, and the countess will be furious when she finds out what's happened. But I must face up to all this. I can't just keep skulking here. War or no war, the situation's got to be faced. Elizabeth Drury seems to be recovering now, and there seems to be less fighting, so it's possible for me to leave.*

Alice was loath to see her go. "I'll miss you, Meg. You've been a tower of strength. Sam will go with you to the inn – and you must only leave with the cart if he's sure that you'll be safe."

Meg agreed willingly to this. She had become fond of Sam over the past days. She felt she could trust him. When he arrived at the door, a pistol tucked in his belt, she felt reassured.

The Low Pavement area looked deserted. They turned the corner and saw a sentry posted outside St. Peter's Church – this must mean that it had been taken over as a military base, despite the pleas of Parson Goodall. A few folks were hurrying along Wheelergate in the direction of the Great Market Square.

They followed, and found that prisoners had been tied back to back in the sheep pens and were being guarded by jeering soldiers, who fed them with scraps from their own leftovers, jestingly proffered on the end of their pikes.

Meg overheard an officer give an order for the prisoners to be marched to the fort. Sam was as puzzled as Meg: neither of them had ever heard of a fort in Nottingham.

They headed across to The Angel Inn to collect the horse and cart. A banner over the doorway proclaimed 'God Save the King', and the Royalist colours were draped over the mullioned windows. They could hear raucous singing and shouting from the stone-flagged bar.

A crowd of troopers sat around a fiddler, who was playing a merry jig. Others were jesting with the pot-girls handing out the tankards of ale. Squeezing through the crowd, they came to the stable-yard at the back and looked for the ostler.

A stable lad met them. "E's gone to save 'is 'ouse in St. James's Lane. There's a gang of troopers settin' fire to 'is thatch – all 'cos 'is daughter's pledged to a soldier in the castle, and Sir Richard Byron doesn't seem to care. 'E's in that very street."

The ostler returned, soon afterwards, drenched with sweat and as red with anger. "There's naught I can do!" he gasped. "They're burnin' my 'ouse down to the ground – all because my daughter slanged a long-haired pike-man, when he tried to sport with her. What's this world come to?" He sat down heavily on an upturned barrel, his head in his hands and wept.

Meg sat beside him until he had stopped shaking. When she looked up there was no sign of Sam.

"E's a brave 'un, is Sam. E's run off to the castle – going to shout them to train their fire on our street to clear it and stop the pillagin' – but then, I don't know what with shots from the castle and fire in the town, uz is caught both ways on!"

Meg led the ostler into the back kitchen and got him a mug of ale. All the time she could hear the harsh laughter and girls giggling from the tap room next door.

"The sooner I'm clear of this place the better," she said to the ostler.

No one stopped her as she went into the stables, found Charlie and her cart and fastened him back in familiar shafts.

Meg took the driver's seat, and grabbed the reins. Suddenly a corporal barred her way.

"And where do you be goin' me duck?" he asked, but he gave her no time to answer. Another soldier, who stood by him, holding a well carved wooden chair, placed the spoils of his looting on the cart, and said "Shelford, that's where she's going." They both laughed.

The corporal called to several others. "Here you are lads, a gift from heaven, a wench with a cart, our problem's solved."

Suddenly, the cart was piled high with furniture and pewter filched from some rich house, and the corporal clambered up to sit beside Meg, telling her that the cart had been requisitioned in the name of the king.

Protests were in vain, but Meg scowled disapproval.

"This isn't my cart. It belongs to Manor Farm by Owthorpe," she told them, "and I have to return it today."

"And so you shall, when you've delivered these chattels to Shelford Manor. 'Tis only a few miles out of your way."

"And who do these things belong to?"

"To the royal garrison at Shelford, now, and I'll come with you to take 'em there."

There was no more that Meg could do. She jerked the reins, giving Charlie the familiar click, and the cart rumbled out of the inn-yard. But the Market Square was a sudden battleground. Parliamentary cavalry from Derby had burst past the sentries at Castle Bar and were shooting wildly around them. People were rushing everywhere to take cover in the turmoil.

A gun cracked in front of them. Charlie shied and upset the heavily laden cart. Meg jumped down and tried to hold his head. The corporal pushed past her to see what was happening.

Could she escape, while all the fighting was going on around her?

There was no chance. The Roundheads were shooting at the soldiers holding the prisoners in the sheep pens. They shot back.

Others drew swords, but most fled in turmoil. Mayhem reigned.

The corporal edged the cart backwards away from the fray and then they were able to return into the yard. "There's a back entry. We'll go that way."

The soldiers replaced their fallen loot, and Meg climbed up again into the driving seat. The corporal sat beside her, with a pistol at the ready, and she had to follow his instructions, There was a narrow lane at the back which led into a long street. The turning to the left, which they wanted to take, was blocked off, so they had to turn right and drive towards the castle walls. They found themselves forced to go up the hill towards the gatehouse, where they could see some people gathered in a huddle. A Royalist commander mounted on horseback was given some instructions to a lady, who began to walk towards the drawbridge, holding a paper high above her head, so that everyone could see it.

The cart swung right, scattering people and causing a commotion.

Charlie took fright and bolted. The corporal tried to hold her back, but Meg called out to calm Charlie, who almost ran Sir Richard down. A moment later horse and cart were dashing back towards the Market Square, where chaos still ruled.

All Meg could think of was stopping Charlie from shying, while some of the furniture was falling from the cart. Meg tried to reassure the horse, and steered him away from the fighting, but she was fearful that they would crash into something.

The Royalists were trying to push the Roundheads back towards Chapel Bar, but they were fighting a losing battle. The word spread fast. "An army's here from Derby!" The open square was no place for battle. A cry went up "Go to the fort!"

The horse and cart careered out of the square, furniture being jogged and then tumbling as they drove up Middle Pavement and down the steep incline of Malin Hill whilst the soldiers in the cart clung on to everything they could. Meg was gently trying to slow the pace and reassure Charlie.

When they were crossing the boards of the Lean Bridge, Meg saw the wooden fort for the first time. The Royalists had built it hastily in the last three days to protect the town entrance to Trent Bridge. Gunfire rattled from the fort and puffs of smoke drifted across the mudflats, but a huge army could be seen approaching from the south bank of the river. A second look and she saw the orange sash of an outrider. These must be more parliament men.

Determined to beat them over the bridge crossing, the corporal seized the reins and whipped the horse into a canter. "Hold hard to the pewter!" he cried, as the horse plunged forward again.

Furiously, Meg punched him in the stomach. He toppled over backwards, falling on top of the other soldier. Seizing his seat again, Meg grabbed the reins and attempted to control the horse, but Charlie had panicked and there was no holding him. He rushed forward towards the bridge, scattering foot-soldiers on the narrow causeway. Fortunately the outriders could not reach the bridge before them.

As the cart dashed on to the long stone bridge, Meg could see the outriders approaching, banners flying in the wind. They were half way over at breakneck speed, she saw the leading rider, also reckless in his approach. She thought there might be a crash, but the other horse shied, as they rattled through to the dry land of the south bank.

Once over, they veered to the left to avoid the advancing parliamentary army and it took all Meg's coaxing to calm the horse down to a final panting halt. She turned to see that the foot soldier had fallen off into the mud. The angry corporal was checking his chattels, but she gave him the biggest tongue lashing of his life.

* * *

Nick was roused from his stupor by a woman shaking his arm. "Here, you're one of the Newarkers, aren't you? You'd best be gone. The parliament men have come from Leicester."

Nick tottered to his feet, and with a murmur of thanks staggered out into the street, still half asleep. He saw that the sentries had gone from outside St. Peter's, and sent a silent prayer as he hurried past. The road was alive with running people. Some were returning to their deserted homes, clutching babies, or carrying belongings. Royalist soldiers, with pikes and muskets, were hurrying out of town, and one woman was standing in the centre of the street, calling for her lost children.

In a daze, Nick made his way eastwards, following the road

by which they'd entered. He looked in vain for familiar faces. People all ignored him. Firing echoed from somewhere behind them, but everyone was concerned to escape and no one heeded him. In Swine Green a dead man lay on the cobbles, and people stepped over him in their hurry.

At the corner of Goosegate, Nick turned into Beck Lane, where the steep little road ran down to the rivulet. The penny footbridge had been replaced by a drawbridge, but the sentries were gone. He ran over the wooden boards to the open fields beyond. It was such a relief to be out of the town, but now he faced the long trek through the woods. How would he ever make it to Newark?

The road led up a rising valley, bordered by clumps of trees and occasional outcrops of red rock. This was the lane to St. Ann's Well, a pleasant walk on a summer's day, but a bleak place in this hostile winter. The black trees were silhouettes against a menacing sky. Snow began to fall as Nick passed the deep track known as Robin Hood's Chase.

The people on this path were all Newark soldiers fleeing the town on horseback or on foot. None of the cavalry gave him a glance, and soon they were lost in the trees ahead. The foot soldiers overtook him too, and soon Nick was shivering with cold and fatigue.

Five days ago, he had been treated with respect as he led the way to Nottingham. Now he realised that the same people were leaving him behind.

The snow was staying on the ground, and the flakes were getting bigger. As Nick climbed painfully towards the head of the valley, an early darkness was closing in. His feet were wet and his fingers numb with cold. How could he find his way back through the woods in the dark? When they had come, they had followed the way-marks cut into the trees, but he had no lantern. He could trace the path in the snow as far as St. Ann's Well, but beyond that it would be very difficult.

The cold pierced him. He was chilled to the bone and his hand was still throbbing. He was hungry and thirsty, and now there was no one to be seen. It was better when there was someone in sight, but now all the fleeing soldiers had passed him and the snow was turning to blizzard. If only he could reach St. Ann's Well, he could get a drink. That thought spurred him on. It was said that the well contained healing waters.

There was a track of frozen blood on the snow now. One of the soldiers must have had a foot wound. Perhaps it had opened up with the walking. He followed the trail up the path.

Eventually, Nick saw a huddle of buildings at the edge of the looming dark woods. He had nearly made it to the well. He would be there in a few minutes... only another twenty painful paces.

Nick stooped to scoop the water from the stone basin in which it always flowed sparkling and crystal clear, but the basin was sealed with a thick rim of ice. He tried to break it, but he only hurt his fingers more. He swayed for a moment, holding on to the basin, and then pulling himself together, staggered over to the cottage door.

No sooner had he knocked than he felt his knees give way and, when the door was opened, his unconscious body slumped forward to fall over the threshold.

CHAPTER 12

ST. ANN'S WELL

When Meg returned to Pierrepont Hall after all her adventures, she found things in turmoil. Despite the loyalty of her younger sons to parliament, the countess feared an attack on Pierrepont Hall in revenge for the raid on Nottingham. Meg's absence had added to the lady's displeasure, and when she learned that the letter had been read by others, Meg was dismissed from the room with a flick of the hand.

Meg learned from the other servants that the countess had resolved to return to Newark, where she had Royalist friends. Meg was relegated to mundane tasks, and replaced as one of my lady's personal attendants by a new girl.

"I will stay with Lord and Lady Deincourt, at the Friary", the countess announced, "and taking Leticia to lodge with me there. Some of the other servants must find lodgings in the town."

Meg was told that she was to go and work as a seamstress on her lady's dresses. Meg was quietly pleased with this. If she had been one of those left at the hall, she would be detailed to do heavy cleaning, but if she was to go to Newark, she knew that she would be welcome helping to look after the children at the mayor's house.

Meg and Bartlett set off for Newark in one of the smaller Pierrepont coaches, crammed full with my ladies finest costumes.

Dorothy and the younger children dashed down the stairs and through the shop, when they saw the coach arrive.

"Oh, Meg. It's only you. We saw the coach draw up, through the upstairs window and thought it must be someone grand," said Ned thoughtlessly.

"Meg Meg, we're so glad you're here. You'll brighten things up. Life's so dull here with grand-mamma these days," shouted Will. He suddenly went quiet, when he saw the old lady scowling at him through the shop doorway.

"Have you heard anything about Nick?" Dorothy was quite

tearful. "We've been told nothing since he went to Nottingham with the soldiers. Now they've returned and there's no sign of him. Father's making all sorts of enquiries, but nobody knows what's happened."

Not knowing how to reply, Meg simply hugged Dorothy and whispered "I haven't heard anything, but I'm sure he'll be all right." But she felt a stab of uncertainty even as she spoke.

* * *

Nick was living in a world of nightmares, not knowing where he was, but slowly he became aware that he was in a bed, being cared for by kindly folk. From time to time, he was roused and encouraged to sup some broth from a steaming bowl. He became dimly conscious of a middle-aged woman, her face lined with care, and of a white-haired man who sometimes sat silently at his bedside.

A pattern of light danced on the ceiling over his bed. Later he saw a shelf with earthenware pots on it. Sometimes, he heard a dog bark in a room beyond. He ceased to worry about where he was. He felt safe.

One day, he roused more fully and tried to sit up. His arm was hurting. He realised that he'd been lying on it and that had probably given him the nightmare about having it twisted by taunting soldiers. Slowly, his memories began to return. He had been walking through a blizzard along a country lane. Soldiers had overtaken him and he had been left on his own.

"Where am I?" He must have spoken his thoughts out loud, for a man's voice replied "You're safe at St. Ann's Well mi duck. No one will trouble you here."

"Who are you?" Nick tried to focus on the figure sitting still in a chair by the hearth, where a fire was blazing.

"I'm the keeper, name of Zachary, an' you're welcome to stay as long as you please, lad. I can see you've been in the wars. God help you."

On the third day, he was able to converse with the man and his wife. He learned that the keeper's cottage was the only inhabited building left at the site of the well. The inn had been deserted for several years, and the pleasure gardens and the bowling green had been neglected since the outbreak of the war.

"Just bide ye here with us, and stop your worrying," said the woman. "The good Lord brought you to our door and here you'll stay until you're strong again. This is a place of healing. St. Ann's Well's been a sacred spot long before the gentry found it out and turned it into a place of revelry. You can rest easy here. On the crest of the hill over yonder, there be a turf maze. It was cut by holy men in the ancient times and their spirits still protect us here."

The keeper smiled. "Martha's family have lived in this place long years, and she has learned their wisdom in the healing arts. It's our pleasure to have you share our board and, if there's less for three of us than there would be for two, t'will serve to remind us of the hermits who lived here in years gone by and ministered to the sick and the pilgrim folk."

Each day, Martha unwound the bandages she had put on Nick's wounded hand, washed it and dressed it again. "I washed it first in wine and vinegar," she told him. "Now I'm using fried parsley in butter for the bruising, and carrot leaf and honey for the wound. See, how it heals."

* * *

A week later, Nick was clear in his mind again, and he thanked the good folk who were looking after him, and explained that his father was the Mayor of Newark and he must let him know where he was. "He'll come and collect me. My brothers and sisters won't know whether I'm dead or alive. They will be desperate to know if I'm still alive."

"We must give you quill and ink and you can write your father a letter. We'll give it to the carrier when the snows allow him to get this way again. He will deliver it as soon as he has business in Newark."

Nick struggled to write the letter with his left hand, because he could not hold the quill with his sore right one. He made several attempts, but eventually he was satisfied that he had done his best.

Zachary and Martha marveled over it. Neither of them had learned the skills of writing.

The carrier promised he would take it to the mayor when next he was in Newark, but he was not sure when that could be. Nick had to be patient.

The next day, there was a wintry sun and the snows began to melt. Nick felt it would do him good to smell fresh air and, well wrapped, he went out with Zachary for the first time.

The keeper led him gently along winding paths, where he had brushed away the snow. Crumbling summer-houses, and wooden benches nestled in hedgerows on either side. There were splintering oak tables, where the gentry would have rested tankards when the inn was open and shady bowers where lovers might recline. At the heart of the garden stood the deserted tavern, now shuttered and barred.

"When was all this built?" Nick asked, wondering at the elaborate lay-out.

"About a hundred years ago, I think," said Zachary. "But our home is much older. If you look at the rough stones on the east wall, you'll see part of the old chapel of St. Ann. The monks lived as hermits and they sanctified this place. But the healing well goes back to pagan times. Some still call it Robin Hood's Well, for people came here to turn bad luck into good and others came seeking love charms. But I like it best as it is now, restored to nature. In the spring, the woodlarks come and on a summer eve, you can hear the blackbirds and sometimes after dark even the nightingale sing."

So saying, Zachary led the way back into the warmth of the house.

Later that day, Nick watched while the keeper bent at his potter's wheel, gently shaping damp clay into plates and drinking vessels.

"I sell my pots through the carrier and he takes them to markets in Nottingham, Newark and Mansfield," he explained. "Sometimes I do special ones like this vase with a pattern of snowdrops. Some of them are done to order, but there's times when I am loath to part with them. Like my children they are when you shape and paint them. They can be molded to shape whilst they're supple, and if they are marred they can be put right if you catch them in time. If not, you have to melt them down and start again. But once they're fired in the oven – they're set good and strong, be they fine or flawed. There's a lesson for life in that, I reckon."

The next day, Nick chopped wood whilst Zachary fired his pots in the kiln. They had to wait for two hours after the oven door was closed, but at one point, Zachary opened it and gestured to Nick to look inside. The heat hit his face as he peered through the opening to see a line of pots framed against the intense red haze, and a phrase came to mind "Tested by fire!" Perhaps in the last few weeks he had been tested too. Was he emerging fine or flawed?

That night, Nick dreamed that he was home with his family in Newark, when disaster suddenly struck the house. Everything was ablaze and he was struggling to escape with several of the young children. The dream was very real and he woke in a sweat of fear. Had something really happened? Had his family been killed? Or was this a memory of Gainsborough and Nottingham, or a more recent echo of watching the pots in the kiln. Whatever had triggered it, he could almost smell the charred wood and the fumes. He didn't regain his composure all day and was almost afraid to sleep that night.

There was a loud knock at the door the next afternoon. Zachary opened it, and to his huge relief Nick heard his father's excited voice as the words stumbled out. "Excuse me, sir, My name is Clay. Do I have I have the pleasure of speaking to Mr Zachary, the keeper?"

Nick rushed to the door, "Nicholas, my boy! My boy!" Hercules was quite overcome. "How wonderful! We were all so worried, so worried!" he blew his nose on a large blue kerchief. "We were distraught when the soldiers came back from Nottingham and you weren't with them. None of them knew where you were. I spoke my mind to the earl, that I did! I told him straight that you were in his charge, and he should have taken better care of you. He looked rather shame-faced, and said there was a big explosion when a church tower fell and he hadn't seen you since. And I had to tell the girls and grand-mamma and they were all in tears! Then we got your letter this very morning and we were all so relieved, so relieved. The children would not let me wait another day. They all wanted to come too, but of course that would have been foolish and I knew that grand-mamma would not allow it. No indeed! And now, Mr Zachary, what do I owe you for my son's keep?"

"You owe me nothing. Mr Clay. 'Tis my bounden duty to take in a waif who falls at my doorstep. Who could do less?"

"Our reward is to see you with him again, sir!" Martha had joined them at the door.

"This is very fine and noble of you," said Hercules. "But you've been put to considerable expense. Nick has been here over two weeks, I understand."

"If they won't take money, father, perhaps we could buy some of Zachary's pots. He's a master craftsman, and I'd like a reminder."

Well before sundown, and warmed by ale, Nick clambered on to the family wagonette, carrying several clay pots for the children, and Hercules had offered to display them in his shop, and try to get further orders. "I will send the money to you, fever near. Who knows, we may get you some orders from gentry folk in Newark."

Zachary and Martha stood in the doorway and waved them goodbye.

Hercules smiled at his son. "Good Christian folk those – an answer to my prayers."

"And how are things in Newark, now?"

"Quite well, but people are getting fearful. There's talk of the Roundheads from Nottingham coming back to get their revenge. Your Uncle Edward is very busy preparing for the defence of the town, but our family is well and hearty."

"Oh Father, I'm so relieved. I must tell you why. The night before last, I had a dreadful dream and it was so vivid. I dreamed that our home was ablaze with fire, and we couldn't get out! I was terrified that it might be true."

"On fire!" Hercules was alarmed. "You dreamed this two nights ago! Why, so did I – that very night. Pray God – this is not an omen! Tell me about it!"

Nick told his dream as best he could remember it and then added I thought that it might just have been memories of the wars I have seen, and of watching the clay being shaped in the fire."

They gazed at one another solemnly.

"You may be right. The bible tells us that we are all pieces of clay, and so we are named, you and I." Then Hercules told his dream.

"It may be a message. I don't know. I really don't know. But please, Nicholas – not a word to the children. This shall be our shared secret. We must not worry them. If either of us ever have such a dream again, we will confide in each other and make a decision, but meanwhile, we must say prayers for our home and our family – but not a word. You understand – not a word!"

It was a shaken pair that arrived back in Stodman Street, to be received by a crowd of excited children.

CHAPTER 13

THE WARNING DREAM

Meg was with the children when Nick arrived back home. It was getting dark and he was wrapped in a great travelling rug. Once in the house, she saw that he was very pale-faced and weary and his cheeks were hollow, but his eyes smiled at them all. Thank goodness that he had no worse wounds.

Everyone wanted to hear his story, but Grand-mamma was having none of it and wisely bundled them off to bed saying there would be plenty of time in the morning.

Over the next few days, Dorothy and Meg cosseted him back to better health.Nick was soon able to go out again to explore the changing town. Many new fortifications and gun emplacements were being constructed, as the tide had now changed and it was Newark's turn to expect a reprisal raid from Nottingham. To make matters worse, there were also rumours of another much larger force approaching under the parliamentary commander, Sir John Meldrum.

John Twentyman, the innkeeper, was forced to provide quarters for several high ranking Royalist officers, whilst Nick's other uncle, Edward, as captain of militia was organizing the local volunteers.

"We'll be ready for them this time," he assured Nick. "I've had a large earthwork built beside my house, near the old dovecote. It's big enough for us to mount a cannon. They call it the King's Sconce. We'll hold them at bay now, never fear. They won't be storming Baldertongate, like they did last time." But Nick, having seen combat at first hand was not so sure.

At the height of these uncertainties, Grand-mamma Twentyman was taken ill.

Meg knew that she had a weak heart but had no idea how

serious it was. The house went very quiet and the children began to feel sorry they had been a trial to her. She was in bed for a week and then one morning, when Dorothy went in to bring her some breakfast, she found the old lady could not be roused.

Hercules sent for the doctor, but she had died by the time he arrived.

It was clear that the war and the responsibilities of looking after the children had been too great a strain. No wonder her temper had been so short.

Changes were afoot at Lord Deincourt's house too. Henry had gone to join the king and the countess had received a smuggled letter from Francis to warn her that there was a plan to completely encircle Newark and organize a siege. She shared this information with Lord Deincourt. The countess decided she would be safer now at Pierrepont Hall, and her retinue of servants were sent messages to return there within two days. Everyone in Newark was preparing either for battle or a siege.

Meg was in a dilemma. The countess had seldom sent for her since the affair of the lost letter and had been testy with her throughout. Meg had become a valuable member of the Clay household, and was especially valued since the death of the old lady. Hercules had just allowed her to move into the grandmother's old room and she had set about adapting it to suit her tastes. She was touched by this kindness as she'd never had a room of her own before. Meg decided to pluck up courage and ask the countess if she could remain in Newark for a week or two.

Timorously, she broached the subject. "I don't want to inconvenience you in any way, ma'am, but I wondered if I could stay on with the mayor's family for a few weeks. Now that the grandmother has died, there's a lot to be done, and it's difficult for the children…"

The countess cut her short. "Go then, Marriott. I have no use for you now, being very well served by Letitia."

After four years service, Meg felt this was insulting. She curtsied and left the room, tears of anger blurring her eyes.

Meg had brought all the dresses she'd trimmed in a box, which she'd struggled to carry through the streets. Twice on the way, she'd needed to sit down on it, to rest her aching arms.

"All the dresses are in there," she briskly told Letitia, who smiled at her with triumph in her eyes. *I never could abide that girl*, Meg thought, as she walked out of the Friary. She did not see her former mistress again and never went back to Pierrepont Hall, Meg knew that she was wanted by the Clay family. She was fond of all of them, even bumbling Hercules, who had a kind heart lost somewhere behind his grand name and pompous bearing.

He's a gentleman I can talk to, she thought. It even puts me at ease when he stumbles over words. I'm not afraid of those Roundheads camped outside the town. I'm probably safer here behind these defences than I would be at Pierrepont Hall, as it's so near to Nottingham.

Two days after the countess left Newark, with all her retainers and all her dresses, the parliamentary forces arrived and encircled the town.

"We've Hutchinson's soldiers to the west of us and Meldrum's men all around. east and west. But fear not, children," Hercules told the family. "The good Lord is with us. King Charles is our anointed ruler and right will prevail!"

The next few days were fairly quiet. The enemy were consolidating their positions, and the Newark people braced themselves for an onslaught. The besiegers imposed a blockade on anything coming or going beyond the town defence walls. Hercules went over to the governor's house each morning to confer with Sir Richard about anything that concerned the townspeople, and he had meetings with the councillors to discuss what could be shared with the townspeople. Food supplies were a first priority. Being a market town, there were reasonable stocks, but the enemy would not allow any new produce to be brought in from the countryside.

The parliamentary troops made no attempt to enter the town, but the atmosphere was tense and the people were determined to stand together and see it through.

A bombardment began from Beacon Hill. A cannonball landed in the market place and scattered stallholders and shoppers alike. Fortunately, it did no damage, but the next one smashed through the thatched roof of a cottage near the governor's house, killing a woman who was baking bread. A roar of anger swept through the town. Nobody knew whose home might be hit or which innocent person might fall victim. The next day more men enlisted as soldiers in the defence force, and Edward Twentyman had a hard time providing them all with weapons and training.

Hercules looked soberly at his young family at breakfast next morning. He said his usual grace before they ate, and then he added these frightening words:

"Preserve us Lord from the perils and snares of the evil ones who surround this faithful town and press so hard upon us with cannon and with flame."

Then he spoke quietly to the children. "Last night I was troubled by a dream." Nick caught his eye and a flash of understanding passed between them.

"There is no cause for panic. The Lord can speak to us in this way. It's a helpful sign, but I dreamed that this house was on fire. I fear it was a warning to us that this could happen. We all know now that the cannon on Beacon Hill can reach into the town centre, and the governor's house opposite must be a target. So, I am going to talk to Uncle John and see if he can accommodate us at the Saracen's Head. If he agrees, I want you each to pack some clothes and Dorothy and Meg can prepare a bag with food and chattels, just in case we need to move there quickly."

Glances were exchanged, but no one spoke as Hercules nodded to the older girls to pass the porridge bowl and the water jug along the table.

It was Ned who broke the silence. "I hate those men from Nottingham!"

"Nothing is gained by hating anyone." Hercules was quiet and firm. "The rebel soldiers are victims themselves, deluded and debased. We must pray that they will be guided to open their eyes and change their ways."

The cannon struck again at noon and twice in the afternoon. A drover was killed with his two young children.

11 March 1644

At night there was a full moon. Nick lay sleepless in the big bed he shared with Will and Ned. Will was warming his cold feet on one of his legs and Nick was staring at the oak rafters. Were they safe here? He could not forget the dream he'd had in the keeper's cottage. It was all so vivid. And his father had the same dream too. Why? What did it mean? How could he sleep in this room with that on his mind? He listened intently. All he could hear was the breathing of his brothers and the footsteps of the night watchman in the street outside. He didn't dare go to sleep in case the dream returned.

Suddenly, the chamber door flew open. "Get up, all of you. We're going to your uncle's now!" His father stood pale-faced in the doorway, fully dressed and illuminated by the lighted candlestick in his shaking hand.

Nick was up in an instant and pulling on his clothes. "Was it the dream again?" he asked, but his father had gone to knock on the door of the girl's room.

"Wake up. We've got to leave, now!" Nick shook his younger brothers, dragging the bedclothes from them. They protested, trying to pull them back again.

Then Meg appeared. "Come on," she demanded. "No arguments. You must come at once!"

Reluctantly, they scrambled into their clothes and seized ready packed bags, not understanding the need for this urgency.

Hercules, clad in greatcoat and muffler, stood at the bottom of the stairs waiting for them all to gather, beside him was the young maid-servant Nell. When they were all ready, he opened the outer door, and waited until they had all filed through. Then he followed them out, locked the big shop door and led his family from the house.

The street was deserted, except for the watchman. Meg held the hand of the youngest girl, Bessie. As far as the children were concerned, there seemed to be no reason for this sudden desertion of a warm home on this cold winter night, but they had never seen their father so determined. Only Nick understood.

The mayor nodded to the soldier, who was guarding the governor's house and led his family through the market square to the sleeping Saracen's Head. He banged on the locked door and shouted loudly, "Open up, John. We're here!"

An upper window opened and the plump head of the inn-keeper appeared. "This is an emergency, John. We're all here!"

"I'll come!" he groaned, in a tone suggesting that his brother-in-law had lost his wits. Minutes later, the bolts were thrust back and the family admitted to the stone flagged bar parlour. "What's the emergency?" he asked. "I said you could come in an emergency, but I've no spare beds. You know that, with all these Royalist officers billeted here."

"I've had the dream again. It was so vivid."

"A dream. You've had a dream and you drag the children out of their beds at this hour!" His usually jovial face was perplexed and angry, "and where am I supposed to bed you all?"

"The floor is good enough…" Hercules was cut short. An enormous crash shook the inn, followed by the sound of falling timbers and the shout of "Fire!"

"Mercy on us!" Both men ran back into the street. The others followed. Nick had a vision of his dream flashing before his eyes. Down the pavement they ran, back to the corner of Stodman Street – where the frantic watchman was shouting for water. A cannon ball had splintered a main king-post holding the roof of their home, and the whole thatch had collapsed.

"It's the mayor's house," shouted a voice. "There's a young family in there!"

"No, thank the Lord," cried Hercules. "We're all safe!"

But, as they spoke, another post collapsed, bringing down roof timbers and Meg saw her room disappear into an inferno, as the orange flames began to lick the outer walls.

CHAPTER 14

DELIVERANCE AT NEWARK

Meg found that she was much more at ease than she had expected to be in St. Mary's Church. She disliked stark Puritan preaching houses, and this had inclined her to say that she would not join them when Hercules announced that the family were all going to give thanks for their deliverance. Afterwards she regretted her hasty response and, now she was here, the stained glass windows and the heady smell of incense touched a gentle chord in her. Lit by soft candle light, the crowded parish church had become a sanctuary for the townsfolk.

As she stooped down to kneel in the pew behind the mayor's family, Nick turned to give her a quick smile. He had seen her come in. Then she realised that the middle-aged woman beside her was praying passionately, her cheeks wet with tears. Perhaps she'd lost someone last night? There was no way of telling. Meg felt she was intruding, but it would not help to move to another place. She started to whisper the familiar prayers herself. Perhaps the woman would draw some comfort from this.

Then she glanced up and saw that Parson Trueman was moving quietly along the pews, offering consolation where he could. He stopped by the mayor's pew and in a moment, Hercules was on his feet talking earnestly to him. Meg realised that he was explaining about his dream and the way that they had all been spared. Hercules was quite overcome and she saw the parson smile and nod at each of the six children in turn. "We do not understand these things," he said. "The Lord works in mysterious ways!" He blessed them all with the sign of the cross, and then moved to speak to the woman beside Meg, who was looking at him with sorrowful eyes, saying quietly "And what is your sorrow, sister?"

It was a while before the woman found her voice. Then she

whispered "It's my Dan. 'E were too young to die. They say it was falling masonry – after that cannon-fire. 'E went to 'elp the others, Father Trueman. It's not right, 'E were a good lad." The parson put an arm round her shoulders and whispered a prayer and words of comfort. Meg noted that he spent as long with the poor as with the gentry and was glad to see it. It reminded her of the way Alice had behaved in Nottingham.

They were startled by the opening of the heavy wooden door. Sir Richard Byron entered with Edward Twentyman and a dark gentleman she did not recognise. The three men went towards the Clay family, and again Hercules jumped to his feet and would have recounted his story, but Sir Richard spoke first, introducing the sallow stranger, in hushed tones:

"I want to introduce Sir Bernard de Gomme," he whispered. "He's a Dutch engineer, who's helping Prince Rupert with his armaments." They shook hands gingerly. "He was with him yesterday. He's ridden here overnight and managed to slip through the enemy cordon." He paused and lowered his voice. "He brings great news. The prince and his army are coming! They will attack our enemies today."

Parson Trueman looked puzzled. "I thought the prince was in Chester?"

"He was two days ago – since then he's hastened here. He's a fast rider and so are his men!"

The governor held up his hand for silence. "All of us must keep this news to ourselves. The enemy must not know of it." He glanced anxiously at those around him. For a second, his eyes rested uneasily on Nick and Meg, who were both within earshot. He turned to the parson. "Keep the people here solidly at their prayers. Sir Bernard and I must scan the field, and the tower is our best look out. Come with us, mayor, and bring that sharp-eyed son of yours!"

Hercules put his arm round Nick, and whispered to the others. "To your prayers, all of you. Beseech the Lord for the safety of Newark."

Meg saw the four men go to the tower door. Nick followed them through. Why can't I go with Nick, she thought? Why is it all the men and boys who have exciting things to do? She was stiff from kneeling on the hard wooden board, and not all her prayers were for the town.

Hercules struggled to keep up the pace on the spiral steps. The nimble soldiers led the way, and Nick was delayed by his panting father. In the bell-ringers' loft, the three men paused to let the stragglers catch up. Nick entered the large, round room where a circle of ropes disappeared through holes in the timbered ceiling. He had never been in a belfry before and was impressed.

The way up from here was more perilous. A wooden ladder reached up through the yawning trap door above their heads. "Up there!" Hercules mopped his brow. "It's good that we said our prayers, son."

Sir Richard led the way. The mayor was slow to follow, and Nick was glad. His head was aching and the shock of last night had left him feeling weak.

On the landing above, he stood in awe of the ring of huge wrought iron bells. They ranged in size, but the largest one was big enough to hide in. His thoughts were cut short by his Uncle Edward's comment, "See that hole – a cannonball made that last week!"

Nick almost lost his footing on the narrow platform, as he peered through the gap about the size of a man's hand, with its glimpse of red rooftops below. It made him dizzy. Turning back, he saw heavy boots disappearing through the trap door. The three leaders had gone ahead. Hercules indicated that he would follow, when he had got his breath back. Nick took the hint and started to climb up the rickety ladder, which was shaking with the weight of the men above him.

The ladder led to another platform above the bells, and then on again to a narrow doorway, through which he could see the sky. His uncle hovered about the door. "Crouch down, Nick, below the parapet," he urged. "We can be seen here by the enemy."

Nick ducked, as his father emerged from the doorway, wiping his perspiring forehead, with a large white kerchief. "Down, Hercules," his uncle whispered and the bulky Mayor squatted hastily on the stone flags.

Nick peered carefully between the battlements. He could see a huddle of roofs and chimneys far below. The Market Place was alive with tiny people and, beyond he gazed in horror at the blackened shell of his former home in Stodman Street.

Then, he looked angrily at the enemy lines across the river. It could be seen clearly from here – a sizable redoubt, built for defence but now captured and held for Parliament, built on the large flat island where the Trent divided and rejoined its tributary upstream.

"These walls and ditches of yours are no good for defence. You need sconces to protect this town." The Dutchman addressed Sir Richard. "If I were in charge, I would build two huge earth mounds, one there on the north where you have those guns by the old hospital and one on the other side. Let's look at possibilities." The two men crawled across the roof to peer with spyglasses out of the other range of battlements.

"See, that's your site. It would protect the Nottingham road. If the castle and Beacon Hill are well fortified too, this town could hold out for a year."

"I've got a large defence mound already on my land," said Edward, sounding a little crestfallen.

"But it's no way big enough," Sir Bernard was dismissive. "It needs to be six times the size. I've planned defences in the low countries, and I've seen how successful they can be."

The governor seized his arm. "We value your advice, and we'll take it. We'll make Newark a town the king can be proud of. I'll have a hundred people build one on your land, Twentyman, and we'll call it the King's Sconce, and you and your men will defend it. The south one will be the Queen's Sconce, because that's where she rode out. We'll make the name of Newark ring through the land."

"Perhaps they won't be needed, governor. See there on Beacon Hill." Edward pointed east. A posse of cavalry were galloping towards it, with the royal standard proudly flying above them. Another troop were riding to join them from Balderton, and the rebels, who still held the hilltop, were clearly taken by surprise. They fired, and two horses fell, but within minutes they were fleeing towards the town, and the king's standard was being waved from the crest.

"It's Rupert, by God," Sir Richard was elated. The field before the hill became a battleground, as the cavalry rushed into the midst of the fleeing foot-soldiers, hacking to left and right, mercilessly. Terrified sheep ran in all directions to escape the violence and cries of the wounded carried on the wind.

There was cheering from the town defenders, but they withheld their fire, for fear of hitting the relief force.

"Wonderful!" Sir Richard was elated. "Rupert's driving forward. Come, Twentyman, we must join our forces." The commanders plunged back down the tower steps, leaving Hercules and Nick to follow at their own pace.

The fighting continued all day, but it was soon clear the Royalists had the upper hand.

Sir Richard attacked the enemy at Muskham Bridge to create a diversion, and early next morning he led a Newark force on to the island to try to seize the parliamentary base there.

The noise of gunfire kept the family indoors till noon, when Hercules came home with wonderful news that a white flag had been seen over the rebel garrison. He led the children back to the church again to pray for victory, but Meg, feeling jealous that Nick had seen so much more than she had, dared him to go up the tower again with her, to view the field.

Nick hesitated, but Meg was impatient, and when Hercules was deep in prayer, she slipped away. The door was unlocked, for others had the same idea. Nick followed her up the stairs, worried that this would annoy his father, and worse, that there was danger the younger ones would try to follow, but mercifully they were in the same pew as Hercules, had their eyes closed, and did not notice.

"We shouldn't be here," Nick told her, but Meg was ahead of him and did not trouble to reply.

Once on the roof, they saw that a small crowd had gathered there and the scene was far too exciting to spend time arguing. Royalist troops were pouring on to the island, and they could see a white flag flying from the Roundhead fort. Prince Rupert had cleared the fields below Beacon Hill and his men were now on the island, too.

"That'll put paid to the rebels!" Meg was full of triumph.

Suddenly there was a tremendous clatter. The whole tower shook! They jumped and held one another in panic. Had a cannonball struck the church? Then they heard the deafening sound of the bells. The people of Newark were ringing for their victory.

* * *

There was a great feast in the Town Hall this evening. Prince Rupert was the guest of honour. Meg and Nick sat together near the mayoral table, where Sir Richard presided as host, and the king and queen were toasted.

The prince lolled back in a wide-armed chair. His white dog, Boy, was in attendance, resting his head on polished black boots.

The mayor stood up to give his thanks. He looked round the room, resting his eyes briefly on all present.

"Dear friends," he began, "we are gathered to thank our saviour. My family and I have special cause – and also to honour you, the people of Newark, who rallied in your darkest hour and never lost hope. But especially we thank Prince Rupert, who rescued us from direst peril. I truly believe that Newark is the most loyal town in England, and you, sir, are the most loyal prance."

Meg noticed the slip, and so did Nick, but the prince was too courteous to mind and perhaps too flushed with wine.

The mayor was applauded loudly. As he sat down, there was something in his expression that Meg would long remember. She had often thought of him as rather pompous, but tonight she was aware of a shy man deeply touched by sadness, hiding behind the public face.

CHAPTER 15

QUARREL ROYAL

A knock brought Ned hurrying to the door of the room he now shared with his father, Nick, and Will. It was a relief to escape from the cramped garret at the overcrowded Saracen's Head.

"An urgent message for Master Nick. He's wanted at the governor's house!"

Nick was taken aback. He'd not been there since that day when Mr. Henry summoned him to reveal the woodland path. That was two years ago and he thought that Henry Pierrepont had been away ever since on the king's business. What could Sir Richard want with him?

Putting on his coat, Nick hurried through the busy market place. These days it was usually thronged with rich gentlemen, soldiers and servants, and had been ever since the loss at Naseby.

But it was not Sir Richard who wanted him. Henry Pierrepont had returned from Oxford, his faced lined with care and his manner brusque as ever.

"Ah, Clay. Glad you're still around. You were useful to us over the Nottingham raid and now you will be again. You've a good hand, I recall, and there are urgent letters to be copied. Travers is at work on them now in the next room. He'll show you what to do, and another thing, the king dines here tonight and we need more servers at table. You know the drill, so be back here in good time." He dismissed Nick with a point to an inner door.

Travers was already busy with his quill. A pile of parchment lay on the table.

"Ah, another scribe – not before time. This letter needs copying thirty times and addressing to that list of people. Not seen you for a few years, have I? You've been in Newark I suppose. I've travelled all over with the earl – Oxford mostly, then, yesterday, we came here as part of the royal escort."

"I'd no idea the king was here." Nick picked up a quill and sat down to his copying task.

"Came yesterday, in haste. We were set to go to Chester, but things went wrong, as usual. He had to make for the nearest safe place. The rebels are everywhere now. The king's a sick man – deeply troubled he is by the fall of Bristol!"

"Bristol, but Rupert's there!"

"Was. He capitulated – and the king will never forgive him for it. He calls him traitor!"

"Rupert – never!"

"Well that's what many of us feel, but the king had put all hope in him. This was too much! Now we've lost the west country, and they talk of a Scots invasion, so we must muster every loyal man in Britain. That's our task. You'd better start writing before it's too late."

Nick laboured all day over the papers. Although he did not understand some of the references, it was clear that these were pleading letters to gentry urging them to support the king at this time of dire peril. Travers told him that twenty or so scribes were busy copying the pleas to noblemen and squires across the land.

"I fear many will find deaf ears," he said, "even supposing the letters get past enemy lines."

As the light declined, in the late afternoon, Nick was relieved of the task, given a coin for his trouble, and allowed to run back to his family for hurried food, before returning for his evening duties.

Meg and Dorothy and Nell had prepared a simple meal as best they could, in a corner of the great kitchen downstairs, where cooks and maids scurried to feed the important guests at the inn. Their own supper was lukewarm by the time it had been carried up three flights of stairs to the girls' attic chamber, which boasted a table. Here the family huddled twice a day to eat. The young servant girl, Nell, was like another family member now. Being an orphan, the family had all but adopted her.

Hercules said grace and praised the cooks. Then Nick told them his news.

"I've already been told the king was here," the Mayor said, "but kept my counsel. Times are perilous...perilous. It's an honour for you, Nicholas, to be employed this way. I know you'll do your very best."

Later that evening, Nick served the wines at the royal table, where Sir Richard's steward carved the venison and acted as headwaiter. Two prim maids assisted. The king cut a sad figure, his beard prematurely grey and his eyes downcast. It was Henry Pierrepont and Lord Deincourt, sitting on either side of him, who did most of the talking.

Half way through the meal, Nick was sent down to the cellars to fetch more wine. He was returning through the yard, with the bottle, when three horsemen clattered in, thrusting past the guardsman posted by the arch-way. Nick recognized the leading rider immediately. It was Prince Rupert, his face clouded with anger.

Jumping down from his horse, he demanded sharply of Nick if the king was here. Before he could reply, the officer on guard was trying to bar the way.

"I'm very sorry, sir, but the king has given express orders…"

"Damn his orders. I'm here on his business and I will see him!"

Brushing past, the prince marched through the side door into the parlour.

Disconcerted, Nick followed with the wine. The dining room was beyond another guarded door, but one glance from Rupert and the soldier let him pass. Through the opening, Nick had a clear view of the king rising, his face creased in anger.

"Rupert, I forbade you to come here!"

"Needs must, your Majesty. I am no traitor, as you called me in your letter. I sought no parley with the Scots. You wrong me, sir! It broke my heart to surrender Bristol, but it was necessary. Your people would have been massacred and to no purpose! And now, since you have seen fit to relieve me of my command, I ask for military justice – no more, no less – a court martial, if you please, your Majesty, where I may state my case to brother officers and be shot if they so decide!"

The king was thunderstruck. He swayed, as if he might fall, and Mr. Henry rose to offer him his arm. Then, with sudden resolution, he steadied himself, and said with quiet, grave authority, "Since you have chosen to force your way in here, I will speak with you, alone. Sir Richard, please escort us to your study."

After they had left, Nick cautiously crept into the room and handed the wine to the steward. Mr. Henry and Lord Deincourt looked at each other with dismay and then sat down in gloomy silence.

Later that night, Nick told his father what had happened. Hercules shook his head. "So sad...so sad. Rupert is a gallant prince and faithful, I am sure. Our good king must have misjudged him, I fear. Keep this to yourself, Nicholas. Not a word to anyone!"

Two days later though, it was Hercules who saw the end of the matter. Walking past the governor's house, he saw the prince ride out through the gateway, with two companions. Later, in hushed tones, he described it to Nick.

"I bowed to him, and he acknowledged me. He had the grace to do that, although his face was grimly set: so different from when he last was here. And then, I looked at the upper window, Nicholas, and I could swear I saw the king watching him go, and there was sorrow writ large upon his face. Do not speak of this, son. These are high things, and no concern of ours."

The next day, King Charles left Newark and a week later a Scots army arrived in the area, commanded by Lord Leven, and Newark was besieged once again.

CHAPTER 16

RING O' ROSES

November, 1645

Since there were few shop duties now and the war pressed hard, Hercules was fully occupied with Town Hall duties. Nick was pleased to be able to help him there as an unpaid clerk and general messenger. He found it a relief to escape from the overcrowded rooms at The Saracen's Head and it gave him a thorough understanding of the growing problems of the besieged town.

One day, Uncle Edward looked in and Nick found himself listening spellbound to the talk between the two men. His father held up a diamond-shaped piece of silver metal.

"Look at that, Edward," he said. "That's our new coinage, minted in Newark. It can be exchanged anywhere here during the siege. The governor set up a mint in the castle this morning. This token can be exchanged for goods anywhere in this town."

Edward studied it carefully. "But nowhere outside it," he commented.

"No, I'll grant you that," said the mayor. "But it serves its purpose locally. We need to be able to barter and trade here inside Newark, but there are no coins coming in from outside."

"Of course not," said Uncle Edward. "In the past, we've managed to drive off Hutchinson and his Nottingham men to the west, Ballard and the Lincoln men from the east, but now we have General Poyntz and the Leicester men to the south, and, worst of all, this damned great Scottish army bedding themselves down on the island to the north. They've got us in a stranglehold, Supplies can't get through and our trade can't get out."

"I know it well," said Hercules. "What worries me most are the low stocks of food. We've no contact with the farms because of this blockade. I fear pestilence."

"We're doing all we can. 'Tis eighteen months since that Dutchman told us to build the earthworks, and by heavens he was right. I'm holding the King's Sconce successfully against those damned Scots, with our local militia, and we'd never have survived in the old ditches. My greatest worry's been getting all the bullets we needed, but now you and the governor have given the order to seize bedsteads, we should have enough metal for melting."

Nick nodded in agreement, but his father said, "I did not like doing it, though. Sick folk need a comfortable bed, Edward, not a mattress on the floor. You're doing wonders with your militia, but it's the townsfolk I fear for, penned in as they are. We can't get the food in from the farms, so the butchers are starting to slaughter horses and dogs for meat now. It's all affecting the health and spirits of the town."

He shook his head, sadly. Edward handed the newly minted coin back to the mayor, who gazed at it for a moment in silence.

* * *

Meg recognized the signs. Dorothy had been suffering a raging fever for two days. Even though, she'd been dosed with brandy, treacle and mint, nothing stopped the sweating and shivering. With the outbreak of the circular red rash, the doctor was confirming her worst fear.

"The plague," he whispered quietly, so as not to alarm the children peeping round the door. "There's no doubt. I saw another case this morning in Appletongate. I must report it."

Meg looked at Nick. They both knew that there was no cure or hope in this besieged town, where enemies now crowded around on every side. For some time, no one spoke, as the doctor dipped into his bag and produced a nosegay to hold to his own face. Then Dorothy began to cough again.

"I'll go and fetch father. If he's not at the Town Hall, he'll be at the King's Sconce with Uncle Edward. You see to Barbara, Meg, and keep the children out."

He left. Meg looked into Dorothy's anxious eyes. "It's all right. I won't leave you. Don't you be too concerned for me. I'm used to sickness. I'll wash everything, and we'll keep the children in the other room."

The doctor reached into his bag again and handed Meg a small green bottle.

"This contains bay salt mixed with meal and egg yoke. You can make some up yourself when that's done. Apply it to the sores when they appear. And you must steep walnuts in white wine. Give her a spoonful, morning, noon and night. You may add comfits, but stir them well until dissolved. I have other patients to go to now." With that, he was gone.

When he went through the door, the younger children tried to enter. Meg shooed them out again.

"How is she?"

"What did the doctor say?"

"Has she got the plague?"

"She's very ill and must not be disturbed. You must all keep away. It's very catching? Nick's gone for your father. I've got to take care of Dorothy, so you must all be very good. Keep quiet in the other room. When your father comes, he will explain things to you."

Nick's mind was in a whirlwind as he ran out of the inn and across to the Town Hall. The doctor's voice kept saying: "It's the plague. There's no doubt."

Then, his own thoughts crowded in: *It's a death sentence...I can't bear it...but I must for the children's sake! We're all in danger! Father's just signed an order saying those with the plague must be isolated! Will Dorothy have to go to Millgate with all those dying people? How can we get the herbs she needs when we can't get into the fields because of this siege?*

Nick wiped his tear-filled eyes as he went into the Town Hall. The mayor was not there. "He's gone to the King's Sconce."

He ran down Northgate, towards the Goat Bridge Port, He must get permission to go through the defence gate. He spoke to the sentry, who told him to go over the see the duty officer, who had gone to inspect the cleaning of the master cannon, 'Sweet Lips'. Fortunately, the officer knew that Nick was the mayor's son, and seeing the urgency in his eyes, he gave permission and the guard duly unlocked the picket door in the great gate.

Nick stepped through it: out of the fetid air of the trapped town. It was months since he had been outside the town walls, and now here at last was greenery and the scent of grass and wild thyme. The lane was familiar, but not the huge earth mound with ditch and bastions or the defensive rows of spiked poles protecting it from attack by cavalry. The sheer size of the sconce awed him.

Another guard challenged him. "If you have business in the sconce, you'll have to go inside under military escort," he was told. Two soldiers took him up across the wooden bridge over the stream to a closed gate bedded in the side of the great sconce wall. A sentry unlocked the door and Nick saw that inside the ground fell away.

Soldiers were cleaning cannons and mortars and, beyond them, a fort had been built embracing the walls of the old hospital called Exeter House. In its shadow, lay two smaller buildings. One of them was Uncle Edward's cottage, looking strangely out of place in these unlikely surroundings.

Confused by these great changes, Nick had to force himself to focus on his task. "Where is the mayor?" He asked the sentry.

"He went into Exeter Fort to see Captain Twentyman."

Nick broke into a run downhill. His escorts shouted after him and a guard at the door of Exeter Fort, levelled his musket and challenged him.

"I've news for the mayor," he shouted.

The man lowered his gun. "I know you," he said, "The lad with the drum."

Nick explained, and he was allowed to enter the hall, where his uncle was sitting talking earnestly to a huddled figure with his back towards him.

Nick stammered out the dreadful message. "It's Dorothy. She has the plague. Where's father?"

The huddled figure turned and, with horror, Nick saw the empty, frightened face of his father. He was sitting shivering in the chair, uncomprehending.

Uncle Edward gently put his arm round Nick and said, "Your father's ill, Nick. He's been visiting sick families ever since he gave out the order about the isolation. Now he's paying the penalty for his zeal. He came to tell me that he felt he was going downhill. It suddenly overcame him this morning. He can't continue as mayor. I'll lend you a horse and you can lead him gently back. Put him to bed and send for the doctor. He needs rest."

"But we've got the plague, uncle. Dorothy's down with it."

"God help us all!" Edward crossed himself.

Nick looked at his father. There were beads of perspiration on his face.

Hercules struggled to rise, and then he leaned heavily on Nick's shoulder. Nick started to lead him out, then paused to speak to his uncle.

"But we're staying at The Saracen's Head. They can't let us stay there, can they?"

Uncle Edward was troubled. "You must speak to my brother about that," he sighed. "I'm still fighting a war!"

Hercules heard none of this. Clearly in a daze, he could not follow what was being said. Nick realized he was trying to speak as they left the room. With tremendous effort he managed to say, "I'm sorry to be such a trouble, son. I…I think I'll feel better when I'm back at work in my shop."

Gently, Nick helped his father leave the sconce on a borrowed horse.

"Don't bring him in." John Twentyman cried, blocking the door to The Saracen's Head. His face was creased with worry, but he was resolute. "I've already moved Dorothy to the outhouse at the back. I can see your poor father has plague too. Take him there, please. This house is full of guests. I'm sorry, Nick, it's his own order. 'Those with plague must be separated!' Most are being taken to the back end of Millgate. I'll do better than that for your family, though and I'm taking a dangerous risk!"

"But what about the children?"

"I'm letting the others stay here for the time being, with Meg. We'll check for signs each day. If necessary, they'll have to be moved in with Dorothy and your father."

"But they can't sleep in an empty stable!"

"I've scoured the place and put clean straw bedding and blankets there. Even our guests sleep on these now that the soldiers have taken our bedsteads. We'll send food over every day."

Hercules struggled to say, "A stable was good enough for our Lord." Nick looked at his worn face. "If Dorothy and father are to sleep there, I will too. Someone must see to them."

"I was hoping you'd say that. You're a good lad, Nick."

"And by the way – we borrowed this horse from Uncle Edward."

"I'll see it's returned."

John Twentyman patted Nick on the shoulder, and stood by the doorway watching, as Nick led the horse across the yard and helped his father climb down.

He saw them disappear through the outhouse door.

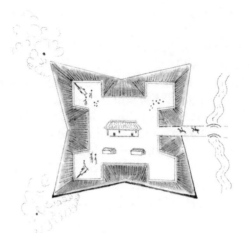

CHAPTER 17

TESTED BY FIRE

What on earth am I doing here?

That question again. Meg asked herself this several times a day. *I came to Newark to serve the countess, and it's all sickness and danger.* Young Will was her right hand assistant now. When a cry for help from came from Tim, Ned, or little Bessie the question in her head melted into nonsense. Meg was needed, more than she ever had been in her whole life.

Nick looked hollow-eyed and sad, when he called to them each day. They all ran to the garret window to wave to him, but he never came inside, for fear of spreading the disease. Meg left the food for three and the medicines for Dorothy and Hercules outside the outhouse door, but she was under strict instructions not to go over the threshold. The town watch had painted the black cross on it to warn everyone to keep away, and Meg knew they were carrying out the mayor's own order.

She and the four young children were now living in a single attic room. The other room had been scrubbed and now housed servants again. Meg felt she and the youngsters were in a twilight world. Uncle John supplied food to the family each day, but no-one had the courage to visit them in case there was infection, so they lived like prisoners.

The cannon fire was merciless. Every day, there was damage

done to someone's home. The children were terrified. Might the inn be hit? Meg tried to reassure them, and Bessie, would climb on her straw mattress and cuddle up close, if they were resting.

Bessie's twin, Tim, was the next to sicken. A day later, the ring of roses appeared on his chest.

He understood that there was nothing that could be done to help him, and elected to go across the yard to join with the others in the stable. "Anyway", he said "I won't be on my own, will I? I'll be joining the rest of the family."

His twin, Bessie, sobbed her heart out. Fifteen-year-old Will and eleven-year-old Ned put on brave faces for the sake of the little ones.

* * *

A week later, early one morning, Meg was aroused by a clod of earth hitting the window. She hurried to look out, and there standing in the breaking light was Nick.

"It's over!" That's all he said, choking on the words.

"What do you mean?"

"They've all gone, first Dorothy, then father. They both died in their sleep, and Tim went early this morning. He told me, he wanted to go with them." He looked at the ground.

Meg gazed at him. Her eyes welled with tears.

"Oh, Nick, I'm so very sorry." She could not say any more.

"They went together, and they're at peace now I trust, after all that suffering."

"How about you? Come in, Nick."

"No, I mustn't. Uncle's orders and I wouldn't anyway, just in case…you tell the children. I should be the one to do it, but I can't, I could be infected. Could you tell Uncle John to go to the Town Hall to report the deaths and then they'll send the men with the cart to take them to the plague pit. I'll be scouring out the stable for the rest of they day and after that I'll see the doctor and perhaps he'll say I'm clear. If so, I can come in then. Oh Meg! Why must everything be so terrible?"

"That's war, Nick. That's war…"

* * *

221

Parson Trueman would like to have held a special service for the mayor, but he could not, as there were so many victims these days. He was holding weekly funeral services and reading out the list of those who'd died – the names of those in combat first and then the plague victims. "Hercules Clay, our former mayor, and his daughter Dorothy, aged seventeen, and his son Timothy aged 8." These names headed the second list.

The new mayor sat on the front row on one side of the aisle. The Clay family were on the other front row, all wearing light masks covering their mouths and nostrils; Meg had Bessie beside her with Nick, Will and Ned. Behind them was the Twentyman family.

As they came out, Nick spoke to the doctor, who always came to the weekly services.

"Do you think it's safe now for me to join the rest of the family?"

The doctor looked gravely at his sallow face. "Not just yet. Wait a week, and then I'll come to see you."

They trooped back across the market place to the Saracen's Head in silence. Nick paused in the inn-yard, and said to Meg. "There's a letter father told me about, before he was ill. He wanted me to get it from his wooden chest, if anything happened to him. You know the old iron bound oak chest. He said it was laid on top of all his clothes and marked 'Nicholas or William – To be opened in the event of my death.' Will you bring it to me. please?"

Later, Nick opened the parchment and read the letter, with blurred eyes:

My dear son,

I am penning this the day after I have signed the fatal order for the plague victims to be isolated. It is a cruel thing I had to do, but necessary for the town.

My heart goes out to those people. For all I know, I could become one of them myself!

Ever since we were all spared by my warning dream, I have felt a conviction that you and the children, or at least most of you, will be saved from these terrible events. If I should fall, either through enemy fire or the plague or any other way, look after the little ones. Meg will help you. She is a brave girl, in whom I have come to have faith. Your Uncle Edward has my will. When it is disclosed you will find I have provided for you all. I have also remembered the townsfolk through an annual payment to be made to the poor by the vicar of Newark, as a mark of thanksgiving for the warning dream.

Let Christ be your guide, God bless you and all my little ones, till we meet again
in His presence,
   Your loving father,
   Hercules Clay

* * *

Meg sat down wearily on a stool by Nick's straw mattress and despaired of the crudity of their life in this out-house. Nick was ill now, shivering and delirious. Could he too be sickening for the plague? It was now three days since they had all had to move into the outhouse, because of little Bessie's illness. She had refused to eat after her twin had died, and the roses had appeared the day after the funeral. Nick had carried the little bundle to the man with the cart the following day and Bessie's body had gone to the plaque pit. Every day a new communal grave was quickly filled with earth and another hole dug for tomorrow.

Nick was clearly struggling. He had been weak ever since his ill fated visit to Nottingham, and now he obviously felt the family responsibilities weighing him down too.

Her eyes strayed to the old drum that Will had insisted on bringing to the outhouse. How stupid! It seemed like a mockery.

Meg: *Suppose I were to fall ill, What would happen to Nick, Will and Ned? Thank God, none of them have the plague symptoms, but they're pale and sickly – small wonder in these conditions. I must keep going for their sakes!*
My back and arms are aching. Is this a bad sign? No, it's only natural after the scrubbing and lifting I've had to do – chopping wood – building the fire, cooking the meals, but if I lost Nick? I couldn't bear it. Should I go back to him and wipe the perspiration again from his forehead? He's sleeping. It might wake him. I'm not sure.

Nick was in another world. He was sitting with Zachary by the kiln. The door had been opened and the heat hit them as they watched three glowing pots being fired. They were coming alive in that dark red furnace. He looked at Zachary and his smile showed satisfaction. He looked back at the furnace and then alarmingly, felt himself being propelled towards it and he could feel the the sweat on his brow.

Then it all changed, he was struggling to climb the top of the sconce... there were enemies down below shouting abuse at him...he must get to the crest...he could escape from them on the other side...but he wasn't sure if he could do it...he had to for the children's sake...a hand reached down and he seized it. He was helped up the last few yards – and suddenly he was there!

He was standing on the top of the sconce, and he had a sense of peace, freedom and release. The enemies had disappeared and he was looking down on Newark, with its red rooftops and the tower of the church, and there were sheep grazing in the green fields beyond. He wasn't panting for breath any longer. The sweating was easing. There was something cool on his brow, a cloth – gently soothing. And then he saw Meg's face, bending over him.

"Your eyes are brighter, now," she said. "That's better."

He felt a great tiredness, and he closed his eyes again, and slipped into a dreamless natural sleep.

Meg had hope in her heart again.

CHAPTER 18

NEWARK MARCHES OUT

8th May, 1646

"It's good to be in the sun again."

Nick was sitting beside Meg and Nell on the bench in the yard at The Saracen's Head.

"If only Ned were feeling better he could join us here, but I think he's very tired today," said Meg. "He's sleeping again now."

"We're all so worried, that's the trouble," said Nick, "he didn't sleep at all last night, but he's all right really, I'm sure. There are no marks on him, so I'll ask Uncle John in a few days if we can all go back inside. He said that we could when he was sure we were all clear."

Meg was doubtful, but she said nothing. Probably, Nick had not heard the latest stories of how the plague was spreading again in the town. How could he have done? He had not gone out beyond the yard yet. He was so out of touch.

Then, she saw Uncle Edward coming towards them. He kept his distance, but smiled sadly.

"Good to see you up again, Nick. I've brought you a little treat. He produced a dead rabbit from a bag he was carrying. "I found him in the field by the sconce. I guess it's a while since you've eaten good meat. All we can usually get these days is horse flesh and dog."

Meg took the rabbit gratefully. It was good of Uncle Edward. No doubt his own family would have relished the fare.

"I come with news. Our troubles may be ending at last. Sir Richard came to see me this morning to say that he has been officially informed that, after everything we've been through, the king's struck a deal with the Scots and ordered us to surrender. Sir Richard's resigned as governor."

It was hard to believe it could be true, but Meg was so exhausted, that all she felt was relief – an end to the fighting, hope for the sick family. Nick looked dazed.

Edward Twentyman seemed to accept it with a soldier's resignation. "At least we'll be spared slaughter. The Earl of Kingston's back and he's brought the news to the governor. Apparently, the king has been exchanging messages with Lord Leven for some days. I'm told he's come from Oxford to the Scottish camp on the island, and is there now."

"But what does this mean for the king?" Nick was incredulous.

"I'm not sure. I think the idea is that he can stay as king, if he agrees to all their terms. I don't know what terms, but when the king asks us to stand down, we've no alternative. At least they've agreed our militia can march out proudly, without harassment. And the sconce is still intact. It was never assaulted, that's something."

"But it all seems such a waste," said Nick. "All those people who've died…"

"Newark has shown her mettle. We were determined to fight to the last man, if that's what the king demanded. No other town can claim that in the length of the land, unless it's Oxford. I'd have stayed in the sconce until we were murdered there, but that's not called for now. I won't say I'm sad about it, but I'm certainly a wiser man."

Nick felt weak again. "Excuse me uncle," he said. "I feel I must lie down for a bit."

Meg took his arm. "Don't worry," she said, "It 's a shock for him after all he's seen and been through. He'll be all right, and thank you again for the rabbit. I'll skin it and cook it tonight."

* * *

Nick was sleeping peacefully now. A few hours had passed since Uncle Edward had brought the startling news. All Newark was stunned by it.

Meg only felt relief and she needed some time by herself to think things through. She had skinned the rabbit and now she was sitting on the bench in the yard again, but this time by herself. Weariness made her shut her eyes.

Someone spoke.

"The earl is asking for the drum."

Meg started and glanced up. Sir Richard Byron was looking down on her. How changed he was. Gone was the old bravado. His clothes were dusty, the buttons unpolished, the boots down-at-heel. A resigned sadness had replaced his eternal optimism.

Was this really the man she had admired? The one who had led his men at Standard Hill and the attack on Nottingham, and had been Governor of Newark until yesterday?

"I believe you have a drum here…"

"What drum?"

"The one that young Nicholas Clay used – the day the first siege began. I was told it was here. The Earl of Kingston says it was used by young Nicholas to rally the people – so perhaps he can use it again to drum us out with pride. It'll be a tribute to our late mayor too. How is Nicholas, by the way?"

"He's very sick. The war and the worry have wasted him."

"Oh – I'm so sorry, my dear…" Sir Richard looked embarrassed.

Still, Meg did not move. There was a time when she would have been all curtseys and blushes in Sir Richard's presence. Now she looked at him as if he were an equal. He did not seem to mind. What he was asking had not registered with her.

"He wouldn't be well enough." Meg took the initiative to speak for him. Perhaps he would be tempted, and he was still so weak and resting on his bed. He need never know she had prevented it. But she'd been overheard – Will's voice broke in. "Here it is, sir. Can I beat it – on Nick's behalf? I'm the age now that he was all those years ago."

He stood in the stable doorway, the drum strapped to his belt, with the faded sash across his chest.

"Are you really? Do you want to, Will?"

"Of course, sir – if he can't do it. Nick would want me to."

"Then you shall! As we began, so shall we finish. You can go before them all, and beat out the retreat!"

* * *

Nick heard about this a few minutes later. He was woken from his sleep by the noise of Will practicing on the drum. When Meg explained, he had no strong feelings. He was still weary and he was grateful for her response.

"I'd have hated to do it, if Will wants to, let him, as far as I'm concerned," he said. "I feel I was used by Mr. Henry and by the governor and I owe them nothing. But I'm glad of this tribute for the town. Uncle Edward, our soldiers and the people deserve no less."

Ned was keen to see the march and Nick said he'd accompany him. As Nell was sickly, Meg said she would stay behind with her. So, a little while later, the boys walked over to the castle, where the soldiers were assembling, Will wore the sash and strap over his shoulder, and the old drum on his hip.

"As Edward Twentyman's troop has held the King's Sconce so stoutly, they will have the honour of leading the parade," said Sir Richard, who was now spruced up for the occasion. "Will, you must go first to beat the retreat."

His uncle came up to school him in what was required.

Other troops were to follow: those who had held the Queen's Sconce, were also to be led by a drummer, and then the rest of the Newark militia, who had manned the castle ramparts and the other defence lines surrounding the town. Soldiers from other places who had come in recent months were to follow. The officers and gentry were to march behind, led by Earl Henry on horseback, with Lord Deincourt and Sir Richard riding side by side at the end, indicating that the leaders of the town forces were the last to capitulate. Altogether about 1,550 men were involved.

The young brothers joined a line of spectators outside the castle entrance, whilst others gathered by cross roads and on the lane down to the shattered wall of bridge over the River Trent.

A shout of command brought everyone to attention, and then the march past started. Nick heard the rattle of the drum from inside the castle yard and then they saw the small figure of Will marching through the castle archway. He was closely followed by Edward Twentyman and his faithful militia, their heads held high. They lined up and stood to attention on the banks of the river. Slowly, the ranks increased in number, and when Lord Deincourt and Sir Richard finally emerged to take their places, there was a loud hurrah and a burst of clapping for the bravery of them all.

Meg was glad of the quietness. The inn-yard was deserted. Everyone had gone to see the march past.

Nell, the twelve-year old orphan sat looking at her, listless and hollow-eyed. She'd joined the family as a servant, after her mother had died.

"What'll happen to us all, now we've surrendered?" The child sounded terrified.

"Don't say surrendered, Nell. We've made a settlement and the fighting's over. That's good. There'll be no more cannon fire, and we'll be able to go out in the fields again. We can collect the morning milk from the farms and bring in fresh vegetables. That'll help build you up. Nick's looking stronger already."

"Will we be able to leave this place?"

"I'm sure we will, soon."

There was a loud knock on the door. "I won't be a moment, Nell." Meg moved over and lifted the latch.

Outside, standing on the threshold she saw a youth, a little younger than herself, worried and travel stained.

He gazed at her, relief written large on his face. His eyes lit up.

"Meg," he said.

"Tom" she replied. The years melted as brother and sister studied each other again.

"Oh, Meg," he said, "I'm so glad to find you at last. I've been searching everywhere. Father wrote telling me you were in Newark, and when I got here, I heard the Clay family was ridden with plague. I've been looking everywhere. This town's blighted. I've come to take you home again."

He was so animated and she wanted to leap at the suggestion, but how could she?

"I can't leave the children."

"Then bring them, for heaven's sake. I've got a horse. We can be there by nightfall."

Could this be possible?

* * *

Some hours later, Tom and Meg were trudging south along the

road from Newark. Tom was leading his horse, riding on its back were Ned and the orphan, Nell who had nowhere else to go. Nick and Will walked beside them.

"We won't go to the farmhouse in case Ned or Nell is sickening," Meg was resolute.

"You must ride ahead on the horse when we approach to warn mother and father, so they can decide what's best. I think we could live in one of the outlying barns until all's well. Nick and I will stay there with the boys and Nell to see them through. The fresh country air will help."

There was hope in her voice and selfless determination. Tom noted the change in her.

"It won't be very comfortable in a barn."

"It'll be a refuge; that's all that matters," said Nick gratefully.

"It wasn't comfortable in the stable behind The Saracen's Head, but we survived," Meg added. "Three of the children didn't. They were taken to the pit on the death cart. It came round every day and the man used to shout 'Bring out your dead!' After those horrors, a safe barn will be a blessing."

Meg's words were cut short by confusion over a delay on the road. The stream of Newark refugees was held up by an approaching coach. Walkers had to step into the ditches to let the horses go by. It seemed an insult. Here were gentry riding against the tide, but there was nothing the walkers could do except grumble and stand aside to be splashed with mud. Tom was angry, and was about to shout a complaint, but then he saw Meg's face light up with pleasure.

"It's Bartlett," Meg cried. This meant nothing to Tom, until he saw the Pierrepont Coat of Arms blazoned on the carriage door. The coach stopped, and there was Francis Pierrepont gazing at them through the carriage window. He opened the doors to speak to the youngsters, concern in his eyes.

"Tom Marriott, the last time I saw you was at the siege in Nottingham, and Meg, I heard you'd left my mother's service and were helping the mayor's family in Newark. Are these waifs his children?"

"You remember Nick. He was at Pierrepont Hall too. They are the only ones left. The mayor and the others died in the plague," Meg explained, "Of course, I remember you too, Nick. I'm very sorry to hear about your tragedy."

"We're trying to get to Manor Farm. We've walked all the way from Newark, but I don't think we'll make it before dark."

"I doubt you will. Isn't it better to stay in Newark tonight, and set out early in the morning."

"Oh, Mr. Francis, there's no going back. The whole town's ridden with the plague."

"Oh, I'm sorry. I'd no idea." Francis Pierrepont gazed closely at the pale, exhausted younger children huddled and shivering in cloaks on the horse, then at Nick, Will, Meg and Tom in turn. He looked up at the darkening sky, and stood thoughtfully in the mire, whilst refugees pushed past them.

"Here, Bartlett," he called "lift those little mites into the coach, and you get in with them, Nick. You look half starved. Meg and I will sit with the coachman, and Tom, you can ride the horse. We'll be at your father's farm before sundown."

Bartlett did as he was bid and the cumbersome coach was turned round in the lane, causing another hold up. When all were settled, off they went – on the road south. Meg thanked Mr. Francis profusely. This kindness was so unexpected, a complete breaking of traditions between masters and servants.

"I wasn't looking forward to those victory celebrations at Newark," Francis Pierrepont smiled. "I've seen too many broken heads and broken hearts. Perhaps taking you young folk to Manor Farm is just about the best thing I've done in this dreadful war. Now it's about to end and the hardest task of all lies ahead – building the peace. Pray God we are equal to it." Then he noticed that Tom was riding on ahead. He turned the corner at the end of the lane and was hidden from view.

The coach arrived in the gloaming. Farmer Marriott, who'd been told by Tom that they were coming, walked down the lane to greet them with a big horn lantern, and when they reached the farm-yard, they were welcomed with hot gruel and warm bread loaves baked fresh in the oven.

Meg saw the familiar old farmhouse table with huge relief. The anguish was ending. She'd been nourished in this kitchen as a child. Now she was home again; but transformed by her experiences into a strong woman.

AUTHOR'S NOTE

These stories are fictional, but they are based on real events which took place during the first English Civil War. The incidents are largely seen through the eyes of children caught up in the conflict.

The first draft of this story was written about thirty years ago, after I had participated in a local studies course on the subject. I was living in Nottingham then and working for the County Council. In the contemporary accounts we studied I found several things of particular interest: the fierce rivalry between the county town and Newark, squabbles between the Nottingham aldermen and the parliamentary soldiers who hastily took occupation of the crumbling castle, references to a strong group of women who opposed the war altogether, and brief glimpses of children who had no voice. There was a novel waiting to be written. The big problem was that there were scores of characters who flitted briefly through the numerous changing scenes.

My draft remained just that for years. It was not until I had retired from my work in the Education Department at County Hall that I found the time for developing it. I started writing but the book became long and cumbersome. It was shelved. Some years later, I resolved to invite the children to take centre stage and as it unfolded, it became two separate tales of a brother and sister, who left the family farmstead when they went to work in grand houses. Tom became a stable lad, working for a young squire who later became the parliamentary governor of Nottingham Castle. His sister, Meg, became a maidservant at

Pierrepont Hall. These alert young people had eyes open to what was brewing all around them.

Most of the adult characters melted into walk-on parts – some disappeared altogether – but more youngsters came on stage: Nick, the trainee footman who caught Meg's eye; Sam, Tom's old school friend, and his sister, Alice, who was developing a new role for a girl in fast-changing times. Then there was Jed who took the proffered shilling, dressed up as a soldier, and served with both armies but never got paid. Now, I was seeing the adults through youthful eyes. Some of them remained strong people but others became ridiculous.

Fortress Nottingham

I owe a great debt to Lucy Hutchinson, who wrote a memoir of what she claimed had happened. It is a rambling account; full of praise and admiration for her husband, John, and blame for all that went wrong on those around her. She never mentions her servants, but there may well have been a stable-lad at Owthorpe Manor and, if so, John could have taken him with the horses that he had moved to the castle. Could this be the person who was secretly dispatched to bring help from Derby, after the Newark men captured Nottingham by night?

The Nottingham Records tell us that Alderman Drury was seized for trying to stop the cannons being moved into the castle. His name was given later to Drury Hill, because he owned the big house on the corner. I have developed the Drury family to suit my story, making the father a master tanner, like many of the councillors, and giving him the tannery in the caves below. In my story, he represents that group of sturdy burghers who defied Colonel Hutchinson at the Guild Hall meeting. Elizabeth and Alice represent the staunch group of women who opposed the fighting and tried to stop the war. Sam becomes the anonymous boy who Lucy tells us called over the castle walls to advise the gunners where best to train their fire.

There were really three separate attacks on Nottingham by the Newarkers. I have merged them into one big one, taking details from each of them to build the story. Laurence Collin, the master gunner, had a son who endowed the Collin's almshouses. I have used this fact to develop "leveller" tendencies in him. He stands for all those Roundheads who dreamed of a new Jerusalem. Chirpy Dr. Huntington Plumtree was no Roundhead, but he had similar ideas, and improved his ancestor's endowment of the Plumtree Hospital. Traces of all these people can still be found in Nottingham today.

There are several references to the boy who was caught by Hutchinson's soldiers in Shelford Church and how he was bullied into giving useful information to the enemy. Jed stands for the legion of youths who have suffered, down the ages, in the hands of brutish soldiers.

Readers may be interested to know that Nottingham Castle Museum and the caves below are open to the public, as are the tannery caves at Drury Hill. Pierrepont Hall is a private residence, but opens for visits occasionally.

Besieged

This story opens with a dispute within the Pierrepont family, which is well recorded in *Brothers at War* by Robin Brackenbury and elsewhere. Lucy Hutchinson describes the fatal words "When I am forced to take up arms with the King against Parliament, or Parliament against the King – let a cannon ball divide me." She also described the fateful death of the Earl of Kingston.

Meg and Nick are servants in the household of this family, at their beck and call so to speak. Lucy Hutchinson records that a maidservant was sent to Nottingham Castle with a letter for Francis Pierrepont from the Countess. The letter was intercepted. We do not know what happened to the maid, but Meg's adventures at the castle are based on this fact. Nick is an imaginary character, but we do know that Sir Richard somehow managed to find a woodland track which enabled him to take Nottingham by surprise.

There were four military governors of Newark during the war, and many leaders of militia. For clarity I have let Sir Richard hold that post throughout, and brought Henry Pierrepont to Newark more frequently than would have been likely.

It is true that a drummer boy alerted the people of Newark to an imminent attack from rebel forces. The lad was the nephew of Edward Twentyman, as in this story, but I have also made him son of the Mayor of Newark in order to reduce the number of families. Hercules Clay was only mayor for his fateful year, but I have given him a longer term too for simplicity's sake. I hope I will be forgiven for adding a little humour to the character of Hercules. It seemed that the sombre tale needed a bit of lightening, and the rather pompous style of his letters suggests the possibility of a shy man hiding somewhere inside him. I felt it right to alter the names of his children, as I have changed some of the things that occurred to them, in order to illustrate the sufferings of the ordinary people of Newark during the third siege, when plague attacked the town. Keen historians will find numerous deviations, but I hope the main thrust of the story carries conviction.

Readers may like to know that a Civil War Museum is opening in Newark in spring 2015 and a Civil War trail round the town can be followed with the help of an explanatory leaflet. The inn at Southwell where King Charles met the Scots' army leaders is still open for customers, under the sign of "The Saracen's Head".

I owe a debt of gratitude to several people for help with this book. Lin-Marie Milner-Brown supported me by typing, sharing ideas and providing illustrations; Tim Warner of the Nottinghamshire Library Services helped with information and encouragement and my wife, Jenny, assisted with her careful proof reading and helpful suggestions, including the title, *Uncivil War*.

ACKNOWLEDGEMENTS

The Memoirs of Colonel Hutchinson by his widow, Lucy
Edited by Julius Hutchinson 1906

The Records of the Borough of Nottingham 1625-1702,
Nottingham Corporation

The Annals of Nottingham by Thomas Bailey
Simpson, Marshall & Co

Nottingham Castle, a castle full royal by Christopher Drage
Marshall& Co

The History of Newark by Cornelius Brown

Brothers at War by Robin Brackenbury

A Cavalier Stronghold – a Romance of Belvoir by Mrs Chaworth Musters
James Bell. Published 1890

Civil War and Siege Works in Newark by Tim Warner